MARTIAN MAYHEM

"An Earthman who happens to be handy with a blaster. I can't use you."

"Not even," David's voice fell to a whisper, "if I tell you that I'm interested in food poisoning?"

Hennes's face didn't change; his eyes didn't flicker. "Working on a Mars farm isn't easy."

"I'm not the easy type," said David.

The other looked over his rangy frame again. "We'll sit in front," he said. "You and your friend may sit in back, Earthman."

Bigman moved into the rear and David followed him. Someone was behind him. David half turned as Bigman called suddenly, "Watch out!"

It was the second of Hennes's henchmen who was now crouching in the car door, his pasty bearded face snarling and taut. David moved quickly, but it was far too late. His last sight was that of the gleaming muzzle of a weapon. . . .

Also by Isaac Asimov:

DAVID STARR, SPACE RANGER

LUCKY STARR AND THE PIRATES OF THE ASTEROIDS

ISAAC ASIMOV
writing as Paul French

BANTAM BOOKS

NEW YORK · TORONTO · LONDON · SYDNEY · AUCKLAND

This edition contains the complete text
of the original hardcover edition.
NOT ONE WORD HAS BEEN OMITTED.

LUCKY STARR, BOOK 1

A Bantam Spectra Book / by arrangement with Doubleday

PUBLISHING HISTORY

David Starr, Space Ranger copyright © 1952 by Doubleday
Lucky Starr and the Pirates of the Asteroids
copyright © 1953 by Doubleday
Bantam edition / April 1993

ISBN 0-553-29166-1

Published simultaneously in the United States and Canada

Bantam Books are published by Bantam Books, a division of Bantam
Doubleday Dell Publishing Group, Inc. Its trademark, consisting of the
words "Bantam Books" and the portrayal of a rooster, is Registered in
U.S. Patent and Trademark Office and in other countries. Marca
Registrada. Bantam Books, 666 Fifth Avenue, New York, New York
10103.

PRINTED IN THE UNITED STATES OF AMERICA

RAD   0 9 8 7 6 5 4 3 2 1

David Starr, Space Ranger

CONTENTS

Preface

B ack in the 1950s, I wrote a series of six derring-do novels about David "Lucky" Starr and his battles against malefactors within the Solar System. Each of the six took place in a different region of the system, and in each case I made use of the astronomical facts—as they were then known.

DAVID STARR: SPACE RANGER was written in 1951 and at that time, there was still a faint possibility that there were canals on Mars, as had first been reported three-quarters of a century earlier. There was, therefore, a faint possibility that intelligent life existed there, or had existed at one time.

Since then, though, we have sent probes past Mars and around it to take photographs of its surface, and map the entire planet. In 1976, we even landed small laboratories on the Martian surface to test its soil.

There are no canals. There are instead, craters, giant volcanoes and enormous canyons. The atmosphere is only 1 percent as dense as Earth's and is almost entirely carbon dioxide. There is no clear sign of any life at all upon

Mars, and the possibility of advanced life upon it, now or ever, seems nil.

If I had written the book today, I would have had to adjust the plot to take all this into account.

I hope my Gentle Readers enjoy the book anyway, as an adventure story, but please don't forget that the advance of science can outdate even the most conscientious science-fiction writer and that my astronomical descriptions are no longer accurate in all respects.

ISAAC ASIMOV

1

The Plum from Mars

David Starr was staring right at the man, so he saw it happen. He saw him die.

David had been waiting patiently for Dr. Henree and, in the meanwhile, enjoying the atmosphere of International City's newest restaurant. This was to be his first real celebration now that he had obtained his degree and qualified for full membership in the Council of Science.

He did not mind waiting. The Café Supreme still glistened from the freshly applied chromosilicone paints. The subdued light that spread evenly over the entire dining room had no visible source. At the wall end of David's table was the small, self-glowing cube which contained a tiny three-dimensional replica of the band whose music filled in a soft background. The leader's baton was a half-inch flash of motion and of course the table top itself was of the Sanito type, the ultimate in force-field modernity and, except for the deliberate flicker, quite invisible.

David's calm brown eyes swept the other tables, half-hidden in their alcoves, not out of boredom, but because people interested him more than any of the scientific gadgetry that the Café Supreme could gather. Tri-television and force-fields were wonders ten years before, yet were already accepted by all. People, on the other hand, did not change, but even now, ten thousand years after the pyramids were built and five thousand years after the first atom bomb had exploded, they were still the insoluble mystery and the unfaded wonder.

There was a young girl in a pretty gown laughing gently with the man who sat opposite her; a middle-aged man, in uncomfortable holiday clothing, punching the menu combination on the mechanical waiter while his wife and two children watched gravely; two businessmen talking animatedly over their dessert.

And it was as David's glance flicked over the businessmen that it happened. One of them, face congesting with blood, moved convulsively and attempted to rise. The other, crying out, stretched out an arm in a vague gesture of help, but the first had already collapsed in his seat and was beginning to slide under the table.

David had risen to his feet at the first sign of disturbance and now his long legs ate the distance between the tables in three quick strides. He was in the booth and, at a touch of his finger on the electronic contact near the tri-television cube, a violet curtain with fluorescent designs swept across the open end of the alcove. It would attract no attention. Many diners preferred to take advantage of that sort of privacy.

The sick man's companion only now found his voice. He said, "Manning is ill. It's some sort of seizure. Are you a doctor?"

David's voice was calm and level. It carried assurance. He said, "Now sit quietly and make no noise. We will have the manager here and what can be done will be done."

He had his hands on the sick man, lifting him as though he were a rag doll, although the man was heavy-set. He pushed the table as far to one side as possible, his fingers separated uncannily by an inch of force-field as he gripped it. He laid the man on the seat, loosening the Magno-seams of his blouse, and began applying artificial respiration.

David had no illusion as to the possibility of recovery. He knew the symptoms: the sudden flushing, the loss of voice and breath, the few minutes' fight for life, and then, the end.

The curtain brushed aside. With admirable dispatch the manager had answered the emergency signal which David had tapped even before he had left his own table. The manager was a short, plump man, dressed in black, tightly fitting clothing of conservative cut. His face was disturbed.

"Did someone in this wing——" He seemed to shrink in upon himself as his eyes took in the sight.

The surviving diner was speaking with hysterical rapidity. "We were having dinner when my friend had this seizure. As for this other man, I don't know who he is."

David abandoned his futile attempts at revival. He brushed his thick brown hair off his forehead. He said, "You are the manager?"

"I am Oliver Gaspere, manager of the Café Supreme," said the plump man bewilderedly. "The emergency call from Table 87 sounds and when I come, it is empty. I am told a young man has just run into the booth of Table 94, and I follow and find this." He turned. "I shall call the house doctor."

David said, "One moment. There is no use in that. This man is dead."

"What!" cried the other diner. He lunged forward, crying, "Manning!"

David Starr pulled him back, pinning him against the

unseeable table top. "Easy, man. You cannot help him and this is no time for noise."

"No, no," Gaspere agreed rapidly. "We must not upset the other diners. But see here, sir, a doctor must still examine this poor man to decide the cause of death. I can allow no irregularities in my restaurant."

"I am sorry, Mr. Gaspere, but I forbid the examination of this man by anyone at the moment."

"What are you talking about? If this man dies of a heart attack——"

"Please. Let us have co-operation and not useless discussion. What is your name, sir?"

The living diner said dully, "Eugene Forester."

"Well, then, Mr. Forester, I want to know exactly what you and your companion ate just now."

"Sir!" The little manager stared at David, with eyes swelling out of their sockets. "Are you suggesting that something in the food caused this?"

"I'm not making suggestions. I'm asking questions."

"You have no right to ask questions. Who are you? You are nobody. I demand that a doctor examine this poor man."

"Mr. Gaspere, this is Council of Science business."

David bared the inner surface of his wrist, curling the flexible Metallite sleeve above it. For a moment it was merely exposed skin, and then an oval spot darkened and turned black. Within it little yellow grains of light danced and flickered in the familiar patterns of the Big Dipper and of Orion.

The manager's lips trembled. The Council of Science was not an official government agency, but its members were nearly above the government.

He said, "I am sorry, sir."

"No apologies are necessary. Now, Mr. Forester, will you answer my first question?"

Forester muttered, "We had the special dinner number three."

"Both of you?"

"That's right."

David said, "Were there no substitutions on either part?" He had studied the menu at his own table. The Café Supreme featured extraterrestrial delicacies, but the special dinner number three was one of the more ordinary meals native to Earth: vegetable soup, veal chops, baked potato, peas, ice cream, and coffee.

"Yes, there *was* a substitution." Forester's brows drew together. "Manning ordered stewed marplums for dessert."

"And you didn't?"

"No."

"And where are the marplums now?" David had eaten them himself. They were plums grown in the vast Martian greenhouses, juicy and pitless, with a faint cinnamon flavor superimposed on their fruitiness.

Forester said, "He ate them. What do you suppose?"

"How soon before he collapsed?"

"About five minutes, I think. We hadn't even finished our coffee." The man was turning sickly pale. "Were they poisoned?"

David did not answer. He turned to the manager. "What about the marplums?"

"There was nothing wrong with them. Nothing." Gaspere seized the curtains of the alcove and shook them in his passion, but did not forget to speak in the softest of whispers. "They were a fresh shipment from Mars, government tested and approved. We have served hundreds of portions in the last three nights alone. Nothing like this has happened till now."

"Just the same you had better give orders to eliminate marplums from the list of desserts until we can inspect them again. And now, in case it wasn't the marplums at all, please bring me a carton of some sort and we will transfer what is left of the dinner for study."

"Immediately. Immediately."

"And of course speak to no one of this."

The manager returned in a few moments, smearing his brow with a feathery handkerchief. He said, "I cannot understand it. I really cannot."

David stowed the used plastic dishes, with scraps of food still adhering to them, in the carton, added what was left of the toasted rolls, recapped the waxed cups in which the coffee had been served, and put them aside. Gaspere left off rubbing his hands frantically to reach a finger toward the contact at the edge of the table.

David's hand moved quickly, and the manager was startled to find his wrist imprisoned.

"But, sir, the crumbs!"

"I'll take those too." He used his penknife to collect each scrap, its sharp steel sliding easily along the nothingness of the force-field. David himself doubted the worth of force-field table tops. Their sheer transparency was anything but conducive to relaxation. The sight of dishes and cutlery resting on nothing could not help but leave diners tense, so that the field had to be put deliberately out of phase to induce continual interference sparkles that gave rise to an illusion of substance.

In restaurants they were popular since at the conclusion of a meal it was necessary only to extend the force-field a fraction of an inch to destroy whatever adhering crumbs and drops remained. It was only when David had concluded his collection that he allowed Gaspere to perform the extension, removing the safety catch first by a touch of the finger and then permitting Gaspere to use his special key. A new, absolutely clean surface was instantly presented.

"And now, just a moment." David glanced at the metal face of his wrist watch, then flicked a corner of the curtain aside.

He said softly, "Dr. Henree!"

The lanky middle-aged man who was sitting on what had been David's seat fifteen minutes earlier stiffened and looked about him with surprise.

David was smiling. "Here I am!" He put a finger to his lips.

Dr. Henree rose. His clothes hung loosely upon him and his thinning gray hair was combed carefully over a bald spot. He said, "My dear David, are you here already? I had thought you were late. But is anything wrong?"

David's smile had been short-lived. He said, "It's another one."

Dr. Henree stepped within the curtain, looked at the dead man, and muttered, "Dear me."

"That's one way of putting it," said David.

"I think," said Dr. Henree, removing his glasses and playing the mild force-beam of his pencil-cleaner over the lenses before replacing them, "I think we had better close down the restaurant."

Gaspere opened and closed his mouth soundlessly, like a fish. Finally he said in a strangled gasp, "Close the restaurant! It has been open only a week. It will be ruin. Absolute ruin!"

"Oh, but only for an hour or so. We will have to remove the body and inspect your kitchens. Surely you want us to remove the stigma of food poisoning if we can, and surely it would be even less convenient for you to have us make arrangements for this in the presence of the diners."

"Very well then. I will see that the restaurant is made available to you, but I must have an hour's grace to allow present diners to finish their meals. I hope there will be no publicity."

"None, I assure you." Dr. Henree's lined face was a mask of worry. "David, will you call Council Hall and ask to speak to Conway? We have a procedure for such cases. He will know what to do."

"Must I stay?" put in Forester suddenly. "I feel sick."

"Who is this, David?" asked Dr. Henree.

"The dead man's dinner companion. His name is Forester."

"Oh. Then I am afraid, Mr. Forester, you will have to be sick here."

The restaurant was cold and repulsive in its emptiness. Silent operatives had come and gone. Efficiently they had gone through the kitchens atom by atom. Now only Dr. Henree and David Starr remained. They sat in an empty alcove. There were no lights, and the tri-televisions on each table were simply dead cubes of glass.

Dr. Henree shook his head. "We will learn nothing. I am sure of that from experience. I am sorry, David. This is not the proper celebration we had planned."

"Plenty of time for celebration later. You mentioned in your letters these cases of food poisoning, so I was prepared. Still, I wasn't aware of this intense secrecy which seems necessary. I might have been more discreet if I had known."

"No. It is no use. We cannot hide this trouble forever. Little by little there are tiny leaks. People see other people die while eating and then hear of still other cases. Always while they're eating. It is bad and will grow worse. Well, we will talk more of this tomorrow when you talk to Conway himself."

"Wait!" David looked deep into the older man's eyes. "There is something that worries you more than the death of a man or the death of a thousand. Something I don't know. What is it?"

Dr. Henree sighed. "I'm afraid, David, that Earth is in great danger. Most of the Council does not believe it and Conway is only half-convinced, but I am certain that this supposed food poisoning is a clever and brutal attempt at seizing control of Earth's economic life and government. And so far, David, there is no hint as to who is behind the threat and exactly how it is being accomplished. The Council of Science is entirely helpless!"

2

The Breadbasket in the Sky

Hector Conway, Chief Counselor of Science, stood at his window in the topmost suite of Science Tower, the slender structure which dominated the northern suburbs of International City. The city was beginning to sparkle in the early twilight. Soon it would turn to streaks of white along the elevated pedestrian promenades. The buildings would light up in jeweled patterns as the windows came to life. Almost centered in his window were the distant domes of the Halls of Congress, with the Executive Mansion snuggled between.

He was alone in his office, and the automatic lock was adjusted to Dr. Henree's fingerprints only. He could feel some of his depression lifting. David Starr was on his way, suddenly and magically grown up, ready to receive his first assignment as a member of the Council. He felt almost as though his son were about to visit him. In a way, that was how it was. David Starr *was* his son: his and Augustus Henree's.

There had been three of them at first, himself and Gus Henree and Lawrence Starr. How he remembered Lawrence Starr! They had all three gone through school together, qualified for the Council together, done their first investigations together; and then Lawrence Starr had been promoted. It was to be expected; he was by far the most brilliant of the three.

So he had received a semi-permanent station on Venus, and that was the first time the three had not tackled a proposition together. He had gone with his wife and child. The wife was Barbara. Lovely Barbara Starr! Neither Henree nor himself had ever married, and for neither were there any girls to compete with Barbara in memory. When David was born, it was Uncle Gus and Uncle Hector, until he sometimes got confused and called his father Uncle Lawrence.

And then on the trip to Venus there was the pirate attack. It had been a total massacre. Pirate ships took virtually no prisoners in space, and more than a hundred human beings were dead before two hours had passed. Among them were Lawrence and Barbara.

Conway could remember the day, the exact minute, when the news had reached Science Tower. Patrol ships had shot out into space, tracing the pirates; they attacked the asteroid lairs in a fury that was completely unprecedented. Whether they caught the particular villains who had gutted the Venus-bound ship none could ever say, but the pirate power had been broken from that year on.

And the patrol ships found something else: a tiny lifeboat winding a precarious orbit between Venus and Earth, radiating its coldly automatic radio calls for help. Only a child was inside. A frightened, lonely four-year-old, who did not speak for hours except to say stoutly, "Mother said I wasn't to cry."

It was David Starr. His story, seen through childish eyes, was garbled, but interpretation was only too easy. Conway could still see what those last minutes within the gutted ship must have been like: Lawrence Starr, dying in the control room, with the outlaws forcing their way in; Barbara, a blast gun in her hand, desperately thrusting David into the lifeboat, trying to set the controls as best she could, rocketing it into space. And then?

She had a gun in her hand. As long as she could, she must have used it against the enemy, and when that could be no longer, against herself.

Conway ached to think of it. Ached, and once again wished they had allowed him to accompany the patrol ships so that with his own hands he might have helped to turn the asteroid caves into flaming oceans of atomic destruction. But members of the Council of Science, they said, were too valuable to risk in police actions, so he stayed home and read the news bulletins as they rolled out on the ticker tape of his telenews projector.

Between them he and Augustus Henree had adopted David Starr, bent their lives to erase those last horrible memories of space. They were both mother and father to him; they personally supervised his tutoring; they trained him with one thought in mind: to make him what Lawrence Starr had once been.

He had exceeded their expectations. In height he was Lawrence, reaching six feet, rangy and hard, with the cool nerves and quick muscles of an athlete and the sharp, clear brain of a first-class scientist. And beyond that there was something about his brown hair with the suggestion of a wave in it, in his level, wide-set brown eyes, in the trace of a cleft in his chin which vanished when he smiled, that was reminiscent of Barbara.

He had raced through his Academy days leaving a trail of sparks and the dead ash of previous records both on the playing fields and in the classrooms.

Conway had been perturbed. "It's not natural, Gus. He's outdoing his father."

And Henree, who didn't believe in unnecessary speech, had puffed at his pipe and smiled proudly.

"I hate to say this," Conway had continued, "because you'll laugh at me, but there's something not quite normal in it. Remember that the child was stranded in space for two days with just a thin lifeboat hull between himself and solar radiation. He was only seventy million miles from the sun during a period of sunspot maximum."

"All you're saying," said Henree, "is that David should have been burnt to death."

"Well, I don't know," mumbled Conway. "The effect of radiation on living tissue, on *human* living tissue, has its mysteries."

"Well, naturally. It's not a field in which experimentation is very feasible."

David had finished college with the highest average on record. He had managed to do original work in biophysics on the graduate level. He was the youngest man ever to be accorded full membership in the Council of Science.

To Conway there had been a loss in all this. Four years earlier he had been elected Chief Counselor. It was an honor he would have given his life for, yet he knew that had Lawrence Starr lived, the election would have gone in a worthier direction.

And he had lost all but occasional contact with young David Starr, for to be Chief Counselor meant that one had no life other than the beetling problems of all the Galaxy. Even at graduation exercises he had seen David only from a distance. In the last four years he might have spoken to him four times.

So his heart beat high when he heard the door open. He turned, walking rapidly to meet them as they walked in.

"Gus, old man." He held out his hand, wrung the other's. "And David boy!"

An hour passed. It was true night before they could stop speaking of themselves and turn to the universe.

It was David who broke out. He said, "I saw my first poisoning today, Uncle Hector. I knew enough to prevent panic. I wish I knew enough to prevent poisoning."

Conway said soberly, "No one knows that much. I suppose, Gus, it was a Martian product again."

"No way of telling, Hector. But a marplum was involved."

"Suppose," said David Starr, "you let me know anything I'm allowed to know about this."

"It's remarkably simple," said Conway. "Horribly simple. In the last four months something like two hundred people have died immediately after eating some Marsgrown product. It's no known poison, the symptoms are those of no known disease. There is a rapid and complete paralysis of the nerves controlling the diaphragm and the muscles of the chest. It amounts to a paralysis of the lungs, which is fatal in five minutes.

"It goes deeper than that too. In the few cases where we've caught the victims in time, we've tried artificial respiration, as you did, and even iron lungs. They still died in five minutes. The heart is affected as well. Autopsies show us nothing except nerve degeneration that must have been unbelievably rapid."

"What about the food that poisoned them?" asked David.

"Dead end," said Conway. "There is always time for the poisoned item or portion to be completely consumed. Other specimens of the same sort at the table or in the kitchen are harmless. We've fed them to animals and even to human volunteers. The stomach contents of the dead men have yielded uncertain results."

"Then how do you know it's food poisoning at all?"

"Because the coincidence of death after eating a Martian product time after time, without known exception, is more than coincidence."

David said thoughtfully, "And it isn't contagious, obviously."

"No. Thank the stars for that. Even so, it's bad enough. So far we've kept this as quiet as we can, with full co-operation from the Planetary Police. Two hundred deaths in four months over the population of all Earth is still a manageable phenomenon, but the rate may increase. And if the people of Earth become aware that any mouthful of Martian food might be their last, the consequences could be horrible. Even though we were to point out that the death rate is only fifty per month out of a population of five billion, each person would think himself certain to be one of those fifty."

"Yes," said David, "and that would mean that the market for Martian food imports would fall through the floor. It would be too bad for the Martian Farming Syndicates."

"That!" Conway shrugged his shoulders, thrusting aside the problem of the Farming Syndicates as something of no moment. "Do you see nothing else?"

"I see that Earth's own agriculture can't support five billion people."

"That's it exactly. We can't do without food from the colonial planets. There would be starvation on Earth in six weeks. Yet if the people are afraid of Martian food, there will be no preventing that, and I don't know how long it can be staved off. Each new death is a new crisis. Will this be the one that the telenews will get hold of? Will the truth come out now? And there's Gus's theory on top of everything."

Dr. Henree sat back, tamping tobacco gently into his pipe. "I feel sure, David, that this epidemic of food poisoning is not a natural phenomenon. It is too widespread. It strikes one day in Bengal, the next day in New York, the day after in Zanzibar. There must be intelligence behind it."

"I tell you—" began Conway.

"Let him go on, Uncle Hector," urged David.

"If any group were seeking to control Earth, what better move could they make than to strike at our weakest point, our food supply? Earth is the most populous planet in all the Galaxy. It should be, since it is mankind's original home. But that very fact makes us the weakest world, in a sense, since we're not self-supporting. Our breadbasket is in the sky: on Mars; on Ganymede; on Europa. If you cut the imports in any manner, either by pirate action or by the much more subtle system being used now, we are quickly helpless. That is all."

"But," said David, "if that were the case, wouldn't the responsible group communicate with the government, if only to give an ultimatum?"

"It would seem so, but they may be waiting their time; waiting for ripeness. Or they may be dealing with the farmers of Mars directly. The colonists have minds of their own, mistrust Earth, and, in fact, if they see their livelihood threatened, may throw in with these criminals altogether. Maybe even," he puffed strenuously, "they themselves are—— But I'll make no accusations."

"And my part," said David. "What is it you would have me do?"

"Let me tell him," said Conway. "David, we want you to go to Central Laboratories on the Moon. You will be part of the research team investigating the problem. At this moment they are receiving samples of every shipment of food leaving Mars. We are bound to come across some poisoned item. Half of all items are fed to rats; the remaining portions of any fatal pieces are analyzed by all the means at our disposal."

"I see. And if Uncle Gus is right, I suppose you have another team on Mars?"

"Very experienced men. But meanwhile, will you be ready to leave for the Moon tomorrow night?"

"Certainly. But if that's the case, may I leave now to get ready?"

"Of course."

"And would there be any objection to my using my own ship?"

"Not at all."

The two scientists, alone in the room, stared down at the fairy-tale lights of the city for a long time before either spoke.

Finally Conway said, "How like Lawrence he is! But he's still so young. It will be dangerous."

Henree said, "You really think it will work?"

"Certainly!" Conway laughed. "You heard his last question about Mars. He has no intention of going to the Moon. I know him that well. And it's the best way to protect him. The official records will say he is going to the Moon; the men at Central Laboratories are instructed to report his arrival. When he does reach Mars, there will be no reason for your conspirators, if they exist, to take him for a member of the Council, and of course he will maintain an incognito because he will be busy fooling us, he thinks."

Conway added, "He's brilliant. He may be able to do something the rest of us could not do. Fortunately, he's still young and can be maneuvered. In a few years that will be impossible. He would see through us."

Conway's communicator tinkled gently. He flipped it open. "What is it?"

"Personal communication for you, sir."

"For me? Transmit it." He looked wildly at Henree. "It can't be from the conspirators you babble about."

"Open it and see," suggested Henree.

Conway sliced the envelope open. For a moment he stared. Then he laughed a bit wildly, tossed the open sheet to Henree, and slumped back in his chair.

Henree picked it up. There were only two scrawled lines which read, "Have it your way! Mars it is." It was signed, "David."

Henree roared with laughter. "You maneuvered him all right."

And Conway could not help but join.

❸

Men for the Farms of Mars

To a native Earthman, Earth meant Earth. It was just the third planet from that sun which was known to the inhabitants of the Galaxy as Sol. In official geography, however, Earth was more: it included all the bodies of the Solar System. Mars was as much Earth as Earth itself was, and the men and women who lived on Mars were as much Earthmen as though they lived on the home planet. Legally, at any rate. They voted for representatives in the All-Earth Congress and for Planetary President.

But that was as far as it went. The Earthmen of Mars considered themselves quite a separate and better breed, and the newcomer had a long way to go to be accepted by the Martian farmboy as anything more than a casual tourist of not much account.

David Starr found that out almost at once when he entered the Farm Employment Building. A little man was at his heels as he walked in. A really little man. He was about five feet two and his nose would have rubbed against David's breastbone if they had stood face to face. He had pale red hair brushed straight back, a wide mouth, and the typical open-collar, double-breasted overall and hip-high, brightly colored boots of the Martian farmboy.

As David headed for the window over which glowed the legend, "Farm Employment," footsteps rattled about him, and a tenor voice cried out, "Hold on. Decelerate your footsteps, fella."

The little man was facing him.

David said, "Is there anything I can do for you?"

The little man carefully inspected him, section by section, then put out one arm and leaned negligently against the Earthman's waistline. "When did you descend the old gangplank?"

"What gangplank?"

"Pretty voluminous for an Earthie at that. Did you get cramped out there?"

"I'm from Earth, yes."

The little man brought his hands down one after the other so that they slapped sharply against his boots. It was the farmboy gesture of self-assertion.

"In that case," he said, "suppose you assume a waiting position and let a native attend to his business."

David said, "As you please."

"And if you have any objection to taking your turn, you can take it up with me when we're through or any time thereafter at your convenience. My name is Bigman. I'm John Bigman Jones, but you can ask for me anywhere in town by the name of Bigman." He paused, then added, "That, Earthie, is my cognomen. Any complaints about it?"

And David said gravely, "None at all."

Bigman said, "Right!" and left for the desk, while David, breaking into a smile as soon as the other's back was safely turned, sat down to wait.

He had been on Mars for less than twelve hours, just long enough to register his ship under an assumed name in the large sub-surface garages outside the city, take a room for the night at one of the hotels, and spend a few hours of the morning walking through the domed city.

There were only three of these cities on Mars, and their fewness was to be expected in view of the expense required to maintain the tremendous domes and to supply the torrents of power necessary to provide the temperature and gravity of Earth. This, Wingrad City, named after Robert Clark Wingrad, the first man to reach Mars, was the largest.

It was not very different from a city on Earth; it was almost a piece of Earth cut out and put on a different planet; it was as though the men on Mars, thirty-five million miles away at the very nearest, had to hide that fact from themselves somehow. In the center of town, where the ellipsoidal dome was a quarter of a mile high, there were even twenty-story buildings.

There was only one thing missing. There was no sun and no blue sky. The dome itself was translucent, and when the sun shone on it, light was uniformly spread over all its ten square miles. The light intensity at any region of the dome was small so that the "sky" to a man in the city was a pale, pale yellow. The total effect, however, was about equivalent to that of a cloudy day on Earth.

When night came, the dome faded and disappeared into starless black. But then the street lights went on, and Wingrad City seemed more than ever like Earth. Within the buildings artificial light was used day and night.

David Starr looked up at the sudden sound of loud voices.

Bigman was still at the desk, shouting, "I tell you this is a case of blacklist. You've got me blacklisted, by Jupiter."

The man behind the desk seemed flustered. He had

fluffy sideburns with which his fingers kept playing. He said, "We have no blacklists, Mr. Jones——"

"My name is Bigman. What's the matter? Are you afraid to exhibit friendship? You called me Bigman the first few days."

"We have no blacklists, Bigman. Farmhands just aren't in demand."

"What are you talking about? Tim Jenkins got placed day before yesterday in two minutes."

"Jenkins had experience as a rocket man."

"I can handle a rocket as well as Tim any day."

"Well, you're down here as a seeder."

"And I'm a good one. Don't they need seeders?"

"Look, Bigman," said the man behind the desk, "I have your name on the roster. That's all I can do. I'll let you know if anything turns up." He turned a concentrated attention on the record book before him, following up entries with elaborate unconcern.

Bigman turned, then shouted over his shoulder, "All right, but I'm sitting right here, and the next labor requisition you get, I'm being sent out. If they don't want me, I want to hear them say so to me. To me, do you understand? To me, J. Bigman J., personally."

The man behind the desk said nothing. Bigman took a seat, muttering. David Starr rose and approached the desk. No other farmboy had entered to dispute his place in line.

He said, "I'd like a job."

The man looked up, pulled an employment blank and hand printer toward himself. "What kind?"

"Any kind of farm work available."

The man put down his hand printer. "Are you Mars-bred?"

"No, sir. I'm from Earth."

"Sorry. Nothing open."

David said, "Well, look here. I can work, and I need work. Great Galaxy, is there a law against Earthmen working?"

"No, but there isn't much you can do on a farm without experience."

"I still need a job."

"There are lots of jobs *in* town. Next window over."

"I can't use a job in town."

The man behind the desk looked speculatively at David, and David had no trouble in reading the glance. Men traveled to Mars for many reasons, and one of them was that Earth had become too uncomfortable. When a search call went out for a fugitive, the cities of Mars were combed thoroughly (after all, they were part of Earth), but no one ever found a hunted man on the Mars farms. To the Farming Syndicates, the best farmboy was one who had no other place he dared go. They protected such and took care not to lose them to the Earth authorities they half-resented and more than half-despised.

"Name?" said the clerk, eyes back on the form.

"Dick Williams," said David, giving the name under which he had garaged his ship.

The clerk did not ask for identification. "Where can I get in touch with you?"

"Landis Hotel, Room 212."

"Any low-gravity experience at all?"

The questioning went on and on; most of the blanks had to be left empty. The clerk sighed, put the blank into the slot which automatically microfilmed it, filed it, and thus added it to the permanent records of the office.

He said, "I'll let you know." But he didn't sound hopeful.

David turned away. He had not expected much to come of this, but at least he had established himself as a

somewhat legitimate seeker after a farming job. The next
step——

He whirled. Three men were entering the employment office and the little fellow, Bigman, had hopped angrily out of his seat. He was facing them now, arms
carried loosely away from his hips although he had no
weapons that David could see.

The three who entered stopped, and then one of the
two who brought up the rear laughed and said, "Looks as
if we have Bigman, the mighty midget, here. Maybe he's
looking for a job, boss." The speaker was broad across the
shoulders and his nose was flattened against his face. He
had a chewed-to-death, unlit cigar of green Martian tobacco in his mouth and he needed a shave badly.

"Quiet, Griswold," said the man in front. He was
pudgy, not too tall, and the soft skin on his cheeks and on
the back of his neck was sleek and smooth. His overall
was typical Mars, of course, but it was of much finer material than that of any of the other farmboys in the room.
His hip-high boots were spiraled in pink and rose.

In all his later travels on Mars, David Starr never saw
two pairs of boots of identical design, never saw boots that
were other than garish. It was *the* mark of individuality
among the farmboys.

Bigman was approaching the three, his little chest
swelling and his face twisted with anger. He said, "I want
my papers out of you, Hennes. I've got a right to them."

The pudgy man in front was Hennes. He said quietly,
"You're not worth any papers, Bigman."

"I can't get another job without decent papers. I
worked for you for two years and did my part."

"You did a blasted lot more than your part. Out of my
way." He tramped past Bigman, approached the desk, and
said, "I need an experienced seeder—a good one. I want

one tall enough to see in order to replace a little boy I had to get rid of."

Bigman felt that. "By Space," he yelled, "you're right I did more than my part. I was on duty when I wasn't supposed to be, you mean. I was on duty long enough to see you go driving wheels-over-sand into the desert at midnight. Only the next morning you knew nothing about it, except that I got heaved for referring to it, and without reference papers——"

Hennes looked over his shoulder, annoyed. "Griswold," he said, "throw that fool out."

Bigman did not retreat, although Griswold would have made two of him. He said in his high voice, "All right. One at a time."

But David Starr moved now, his smooth stride deceptively slow.

Griswold said, "You're in my way, friend. I've got some trash to throw out."

From behind David, Bigman cried out, "It's all right, Earthie. Let him at me."

David ignored that. He said to Griswold, "This seems to be a public place, friend. We've all got the right to be here."

Griswold said, "Let's not argue, friend." He put a hand roughly on David's shoulder as though to thrust him to one side.

But David's left hand shot up to catch the wrist of Griswold's outstretched arm, and his right hand straight-armed the other's shoulder. Griswold went whirling backward, slamming hard against the plastic partition that divided the room in two.

"I'd *rather* argue, friend," said David.

The clerk had come to his feet with a yell. Other desk workers swarmed to the openings in the partition, but made no move to interfere. Bigman was laughing and clapping David on the back. "Pretty good for a fellow from Earth."

For the moment Hennes seemed frozen. The remaining farmboy, short and bearded, with the pasty face of one who had spent too much time under the small sun of Mars and not enough under the artificial sun lamps of the city, had allowed his mouth to drop ridiculously open.

Griswold recovered his breath slowly. He shook his head. His cigar, which had dropped to the ground, he kicked aside. Then he looked up, his eyes popping with fury. He pushed himself away from the wall and there was a momentary glint of steel that was swallowed up in his hand.

But David stepped to one side and brought up his arm. The small, crooked cylinder that ordinarily rested snugly between his upper arm and body shot down the length of his sleeve and into his gripping palm.

Hennes cried out, "Watch your step, Griswold. He's got a blaster."

"Drop your blade," said David.

Griswold swore wildly, but metal clattered against the floor. Bigman darted forward and picked up the blade, chortling at the stubbled one's discomfiture.

David held out his hand for it and spared it a quick glance. "Nice, innocent baby for a farmboy to have," he said. "What's the law in Mars against carrying a force-blade?"

He knew it as the most vicious weapon in the Galaxy. Outwardly, it was merely a short shaft of stainless steel that was a little thicker than the haft of a knife but which could still be held nicely in the palm. Within it was a tiny motor that could generate an invisible nine-inch-long, razor-thin force-field that could cut through anything composed of ordinary matter. Armor was of no use against it, and since it could slice through bone as easily as through flesh, its stab was almost invariably fatal.

Hennes stepped between them. He said, "Where's your license for a blaster, Earthie? Put it away and we'll call it quits. Get back there, Griswold."

"Hold on," said, David, as Hennes turned away. "You're looking for a man, aren't you?"

Hennes turned back, his eyebrows lifting in amusement. "I'm looking for a man. Yes."

"All right. I'm looking for a job."

"I'm looking for an experienced seeder. Do you qualify?"

"Well, no."

"Have you ever harvested? Can you handle a sand-car? In short, you're just, if I may judge from your costume"—and he stepped back as though to get a better over-all view—"an Earthman who happens to be handy with a blaster. I can't use you."

"Not even," David's voice fell to a whisper, "if I tell you that I'm interested in food poisoning?"

Hennes's face didn't change; his eyes didn't flicker. He said, "I don't see your point."

"Think harder, then." He was smiling thinly, and there was little humor in that smile.

Hennes said, "Working on a Mars farm isn't easy."

"I'm not the easy type," said David.

The other looked over his rangy frame again. "Well, maybe you're not. All right, we'll lodge and feed you, start you with three changes of clothing and a pair of boots. Fifty dollars the first year, payable at the end of the year. If you don't work out the year, the fifty is forfeited."

"Fair enough. What type of work?"

"The only kind you can do. General helper at the chowhouse. If you learn, you'll move up; if not, that's where you spend the year."

"Done. What about Bigman?"

Bigman, who had been staring from one to the other, squawked, "No, sir. I don't work for that sand-bug, and I wouldn't advise you to, either."

David said over his shoulder. "How about a short stretch in return for papers of reference?"

"Well," said Bigman, "a month, maybe."

Hennes said, "Is he a friend of yours?"

David nodded. "I won't come without him."

"I'll take him too, then. One month, and he's to keep his mouth shut. No pay, except his papers. Let's get out of here. My sand-car's outside."

The five left, David and Bigman bringing up the rear.

Bigman said, "I owe you a favor, friend. You may collect at will."

The sand-car was open just then, but David could see the slots into which panels could slide in order that it might be enclosed against the drifting dust storms of Mars. The wheels were broad to minimize the tendency to sink when crossing the soft drifts. The area of glass was reduced to a minimum and, where it existed, merged into the surrounding metal as though they had been welded together.

The streets were moderately crowded, but no one paid any attention to the very common sight of sand-cars and farmboys.

Hennes said, "We'll sit in front. You and your friend may sit in back, Earthman."

He had moved into the driver's seat as he spoke. The controls were in the middle of the front partition, with the windshield centered above. Griswold took the seat at Hennes's right.

Bigman moved into the rear and David followed him. Someone was behind him. David half turned as Bigman called suddenly, "Watch out!"

It was the second of Hennes's henchmen who was now crouching in the car door, his pasty bearded face snarling and taut. David moved quickly, but it was far too late.

His last sight was that of the gleaming muzzle of a weapon in the henchman's hand, and then he was conscious of a soft purring noise. There was scarcely any sensation to it, and a distant, distant voice said, "All right, Zukis. Get in back and keep watch," in words that seemed to come from the end of a long tunnel. There was a last momentary feeling of motion forward, and then there was complete nothingness.

David Starr slumped forward in his seat, and the last signs of life about him vanished.

4

Alien Life

Ragged patches of light floated past David Starr. Slowly he became aware of a tremendous tingling all about him and a separate pressure on his back. The back pressure resolved itself into the fact that he was lying face up on a hard mattress. The tingling he knew to be the aftermath of a stun-gun, a weapon whose radiation worked upon the nerve centers at the base of the brain.

Before light became coherent, before he was thoroughly aware of his surroundings, he felt his shoulders being shaken and the distant sting of sharp slaps on his cheeks. The light washed into his open eyes and he brought his tingling arm up to ward off the next slap.

It was Bigman leaning over him, his little rabbity face with its round snub nose nearly touching his. He said, "By Ganymede, I thought they finished you for good."

David brought himself up to an aching elbow. He said, "It almost feels as if they did. Where are we?"

"In the farm lockup. It's no use trying to get out, either. The door's locked; the windows are barred." He looked depressed.

David felt under his arms. They had removed his

blasters. Naturally! So much was to be expected. He said, "Did they stun you too, Bigman?"

Bigman shook his head. "Zukis horizontaled me with the gun butt." He fingered a region of his skull with gingerly distaste. Then he swelled, "But I nearly broke his arm first."

There was the sound of footsteps outside the door. David sat up and waited. Hennes entered, and with him there came an older man, with a long, tired-looking face set off by faded blue eyes under bushy gray eyebrows that seemed fixed in a permanent furrow. He was dressed in city costume, which was much like that of Earth. He even lacked the Martian hip boots.

Hennes spoke to Bigman first. "Get out to the chowhouse and the first time you sneeze without permission you'll be broken in two."

Bigman scowled, waved to David with an "I'll be seeing you, Earthman," and swaggered out with a clattering of boots.

Hennes watched him leave and locked the door behind him. He turned to the man with the gray eyebrows. "This is the one, Mr. Makian. He calls himself Williams."

"You took a chance stunning him, Hennes. If you had killed him, a valuable lead might have gone with the canal-dust."

Hennes shrugged. "He was armed. We could take no chances. In any case, he's here, sir."

They were discussing him, David thought, as though he weren't there or were just another inanimate part of the bed.

Makian turned to him, his eyes hard. "You, there, I own this ranch. Over a hundred miles in any direction is all Makian. I say who is to be free and who is to be in prison; who works and who starves; even who lives and who dies. Do you understand me?"

"Yes," said David.

"Then answer frankly, and you'll have nothing to fear. Try to hide anything and we'll have it out of you one way or another. We may have to kill you. Do you still understand me?"

"Perfectly."

"Is your name Williams?"

"It's the only name I will give on Mars."

"Fair enough. What do you know about food poisoning?"

David swung his feet off the bed. He said, "Look, my sister died over an afternoon snack of bread and jam. She was twelve years old, and lay there dead with the jam still on her face. We called the doctor. He said it was food poisoning and told us not to eat anything in the house till he came back with certain analytical equipment. He never came back.

"Somebody else came instead. Someone with a great deal of authority. He had plain-clothes men to escort him. He had us describe all that had happened. He said to us, 'It was a heart attack.' We told him that was ridiculous because my sister had nothing wrong with her heart, but he wouldn't listen to us. He told us that if we spread ridiculous stories about food poisoning, we would get in trouble. Then he took the jar of jam with him. He was even angry with us for having wiped the jam from my sister's lips.

"I tried to get in touch with our doctor, but his nurse would never admit he was in. I broke into his office and found him there, but all he would say was that he had made a mistaken diagnosis. He seemed afraid to talk about it. I went to the police, but they wouldn't listen.

"The jar of jam the men took away was the only thing in the house my sister ate that day that the rest of the family hadn't eaten as well. That jar was freshly opened and it was imported from Mars. We're old-fashioned people and like the old food. That was the only Mars product in the house. I tried to find out through the newspapers whether there had been any other cases of food poisoning. It all seemed so suspicious to me. I even went to International City. I quit my job and decided that in one way or another I would find out what had killed my sister and try to nail anyone that might be responsible. Everywhere I hit a blank, and then there came policemen with a warrant for my arrest.

"I was almost expecting that, and got out a step ahead of them. I came to Mars for two reasons. First, it was the only way to keep out of jail (though it doesn't seem so now, does it?), and second, because of one thing I *did* find out. There were two or three suspicious deaths in the restaurants of International City and in each case they were at restaurants which featured Martian cuisines. So I decided the answer was on Mars."

Makian was running a thick thumb down the long line of his chin. He said, "The yarn hangs together, Hennes. What do you think?"

"I say, get names and dates, and check the story. We don't know who this man is."

Makian sounded almost querulous. "You know we can't do that, Hennes. I don't want to do anything that would spread news of all this mess. It would break the entire Syndicate." He turned to David. "I'm going to send Benson to speak to you; he's our agronomist." Then, again to Hennes, "You stay here till Benson comes."

It was about half an hour before Benson came. During that interval David leaned carelessly back on the cot paying no attention to Hennes, who, for his part, played the same sort of game.

Then the door opened and a voice said, "I'm Benson."

It was a gentle, hesitant voice and it belonged to a round-faced individual of about forty, with thinning sandy hair and rimless eyeglasses. His small mouth spread itself in a smile.

Benson went on, "And you, I suppose, are Williams?"

"That's right," said David Starr.

Benson looked carefully at the young Earthman, as though he were analyzing him by eye. He said, "Are you disposed to violence?"

"I'm unarmed," David pointed out, "and surrounded by a farm full of men quite ready to kill me if I step out of line."

"Quite right. Would you leave us, Hennes?"

Hennes jumped to his feet in protest. "That's not safe, Benson."

"Please, Hennes." Benson's mild eyes peered over his spectacles.

Hennes growled, clapped one hand against a boot in disgruntlement, and walked out the door. Benson locked it behind him.

"You see, Williams," he said apologetically, "in the last half-year I've grown to be an important man here. Even Hennes listens to me. I'm still not used to it." He smiled again. "Tell me. Mr. Makian says you actually witnessed a death by this strange food poisoning."

"My sister's."

"Oh!" Benson flushed. "I'm dreadfully sorry. I know it must be a painful subject to you, but might I have the details? It's very important."

David repeated the story he had earlier told Makian.

Benson said, "And it happened as quickly as that."

"It could only have been five to ten minutes after she had eaten."

"Terrible. Terrible. You have no idea how distressing all this is." He was rubbing his hands together nervously.

"In any case, Williams, I'd like to fill in the story for you. You've guessed most of it, anyway, and, somehow, I feel responsible to you for what happened to your sister. All of us here on Mars are responsible until such time as we clear up the mystery. You see, this has been going on for months now, these poisonings. Not many, but enough to have us at our wit's end.

"We've traced back the poisoned foodstuffs and we are certain they come from no one farm. But one thing did turn up: all the poisoned food is shipped out of Wingrad City; the other two cities on Mars are clean so far. That would seem to indicate that the source of infection is within the city, and Hennes has been working on the assumption. He has taken to riding to the city, nights, on detective expeditions of his own, but he has turned up nothing."

"I see. That explains Bigman's remarks," said David.

"Eh?" Benson's face twisted in puzzlement, then cleared. "Oh, you mean the little fellow who goes about shouting all the time. Yes, he caught Hennes leaving once, and Hennes had him thrown out. Hennes is a most impulsive man. In any case, I think Hennes is wrong. Naturally all the poison would travel through Wingrad City. It is the shipping point for the entire hemisphere.

"Now Mr. Makian himself believes the infection to be deliberately spread through human agency. At least he and several others of the Syndicate have received messages offering to buy their farms for a ridiculously small sum. There is no mention of the poisoning and no evidence whatsoever of any connection between the offers to buy and this horrible business."

David was listening intently. He said, "And who makes these offers to buy?"

"Why, how should we know? I have seen the letters and they only say that if the offers are accepted, the Syndicate is to broadcast a coded message over a particular sub-etheric waveband. The price offer, the letters say, will decrease by 10 per cent each month."

"And the letters can't be traced?"

"I'm afraid not. They pass through the ordinary mails with an 'Asteroid' postmark. How can one search the Asteroids?"

"Have the Planetary Police been informed?"

Benson laughed softly. "Do you think Mr. Makian, or any of the Syndicate for that matter, would call in the police for a thing like this? This is a declaration of personal war to them. You don't properly appreciate the Martian mentality, Mr. Williams. You don't run to the law when you're in trouble unless you're willing to confess it's something you can't handle yourself. No farmboy is ever willing to do that. I've suggested that the information be submitted to the Council of Science, but Mr. Makian wouldn't even do that. He said the Council was working on the poisoning without success, and if that were the kind of darned fools they were, he would do without them. And that's where I come in."

"You're working on the poisoning too?"

"That's right. I'm the agronomist here."

"That's the title Mr. Makian gave you."

"Uh-huh. Strictly speaking, an agronomist is a person who specializes in scientific agriculture. I've been trained in principles of fertility maintenance, crop rotation, and matters of that sort. I've always specialized in Martian problems. There aren't many of us and so one can get a rather good position, even though the farmboys sometimes lose patience with us and think we're just college idiots without practical experience. Anyway, I've had additional training as well in botany and bacteriology, so I've been put in charge by Mr. Makian of the entire research program on Mars with respect to the poisoning. The other members of the Syndicate are co-operating."

"And what have you found out, Mr. Benson?"

"Actually as little as the Council of Science, which is not surprising considering how little I have in the way of equipment and help in comparison with them. But I have developed certain theories. The poisoning is too rapid for anything but a bacterial toxin. At least if we consider the nerve degeneration that takes place and the other symptoms. I suspect Martian bacteria."

"What!"

"There *is* Martian life, you know. When Earthmen first arrived, Mars was covered with simple forms of life. There were giant algae whose blue-green color was seen telescopically even before space-travel was invented. There were bacteria-like forms that lived on the algae and even little insect-like creatures that were free-moving, yet manufactured their own food like plants."

"Do they still exist?"

"Why, certainly. We clear them off the land completely before converting areas to our own farms and introduce our own strains of bacteria, the ones that are necessary to plant growth. Out in the uncultivated areas, however, Martian life still flourishes."

"But how can they be affecting our plants, then?"

"That's a good question. You see, Martian farms are not like the Earth farm lands you're used to. On Mars, the farms are not open to sun and air. The sun on Mars doesn't give enough heat for Earth plants and there is no rain. But there is good, fertile soil and there is quite enough carbon dioxide which the plants live on primarily. So crops on Mars are grown under vast sheets of glass. They are seeded, cared for, and harvested by nearly automatic machinery so that our farmboys are machinists more than anything else. The farms are artificially watered by a system of planet-wide piping that carries back to the polar icecaps.

"I tell you this so you will realize that it would be difficult to infect plants ordinarily. The fields are closed and guarded from all directions except from beneath."

"What does that mean?" asked David.

"It means that underneath are the famous Martian caverns and within them there may be intelligent Martians."

"You mean Martian *men?*"

"Not men. But organisms as intelligent as man. I have reason to believe that there *are* Martian intelligences that are probably anxious to drive us intruding Earthmen from the face of their planet!"

5

Dinnertime

"What reason?" demanded David.

Benson looked embarrassed. He moved one hand slowly over his head, smoothing the sparse strands of light hair that did not manage to hide the pink streaks of hairless skull that lay between. He said, "None that I could convince the Council of Science with. None that I could even present to Mr. Makian. But I believe I'm right."

"Is it anything you would care to talk about?"

"Well, I don't know. Frankly, it's been a long time since I've spoken to anyone but farmboys. You're a college man obviously. What did you major in?"

"History," said David promptly. "My thesis concerned the international politics of the early atomic age."

"Oh." Benson looked disappointed. "Any courses in science at all?"

"I had a couple in chemistry; one in zoology."

"I see. It occurred to me that I might be able to convince Mr. Makian to let you help me in my laboratory. It wouldn't be much of a job, especially since you have no scientific training, but it would be better than what Hennes will have you doing."

"Thank you, Mr. Benson. But about the Martians?"

"Oh yes. It's simple enough. You may not know it but there are extensive caves under the Martian surface, perhaps several miles under. So much is known from earthquake data, or, rather, Marsquake data. Some investigators claim they are merely the result of natural water action in the days when Mars still had oceans, but then radiation has been picked up that has its source beneath the soil and which can't have a human source but must have some intelligent source. The signals are too orderly to be anything else.

"It makes sense, really, if you stop to think about it. In the youth of the planet there was sufficient water and oxygen to support life, but with a gravity only two fifths that of Earth, both substances leaked slowly away into space. If there were intelligent Martians, they must have been able to foresee that. They might have built huge caverns well underneath their soil, into which they could retire with enough water and air to continue indefinitely, if they kept their population stable. Now suppose these Martians found that their planet's surface was harboring intelligent life once more—life from another planet. Suppose they resented it or feared our eventual interference with them. What we call food poisoning might be bacteriological warfare."

David said thoughtfully, "Yes, I see your point."

"But would the Syndicate? Or the Council of Science? Well, never mind. I'll have you working for me soon, and perhaps we'll be able to convince them yet."

He smiled and held out a soft hand which was swallowed up in David Starr's large one.

"I think they'll be letting you out now," Benson said.

They did let him out, and for the first time David had the chance to observe the heart of a Martian farm. It was domed, of course, as the city had been. David had been sure of that from the instant he had regained consciousness. You couldn't expect to be breathing free air and living under Earth-strength gravity unless you were within a powered dome.

Naturally the dome was much smaller than that of a city. At its highest it was only about one hundred feet, its translucent structure visible in all its details, strings of white fluorescent lights outdoing the translucent glimmer of the sunlight. The whole structure covered about half a square mile.

After the first evening, however, David had little time to extend his observations. The farm dome seemed full of men and they all had to be fed three times a day. In the evenings particularly, with the day's work done, there seemed no end to them. Stolidly he would stand behind the chow table while farmboys with plastic platters moved past him. The platters, David found out eventually, were manufactured especially for Martian farm use. Under the heat of human hands they could be molded and closed about the food at such times as it was necessary to carry meals out to the desert. Molded so, they kept the sand out and the heat in. Within the farm dome they could be flattened out again and used in the usual way.

The farmboys paid David little attention. Only Bigman, whose lithe frame slipped among the tables replacing sauce bottles and spice containers, waved to him. It was a terrible drop in social position for the little fellow, but he was philosophical about it.

"It's only for a month," he had explained one time in the kitchen, when they were preparing the day's stew and the head cook had left on his own business for a few minutes, "and most of the fellows know the score and are making it easy for me. Of course there's Griswold, Zukis, and that bunch: the rats that try to get somewhere by

licking Hennes's boots. But what in Space do I care? It's
only a few weeks."

Another time he said, "Don't let it bother you about
the boys not cottoning to you. They know you're an
Earthman, see, and they don't know you're pretty good
for an Earthman, like I do. Hennes is always poking about
after me, or else Griswold is, to make sure I don't talk to
them, or else they would have heard the facts from me.
But they'll get wise."

But the process was taking time. For David, it remained the same: a farmboy and his platter; a dollop of
mashed potatoes, a ladle of peas, and a small steak (animal
food was much scarcer on Mars than plant food, since
meat had to be imported from Earth). The farmboy then
helped himself to a sliver of cake and a cup of coffee.
Then another farmboy with another platter; another dollop of mashed potatoes, another ladle of peas, and so on.
To them, it seemed, David Starr was just an Earthman
with a ladle in one hand and a large-tined fork in the
other. He wasn't even a face; just a ladle and a fork.

The cook stuck his head through the door, his little
eyes peering piggily over the sagging pouches beneath.
"Hey, Williams. Rattle your legs and get some food into
the special mess."

Makian, Benson, Hennes, and any others who were
considered especially worthy in point of view of position
or of length of service dined in a room by themselves.
They sat at tables and had the food brought to them.
David had been through this before. He prepared special
platters and brought them into the room on a wheeled
service table.

He threaded his way quietly through the tables, beginning with the one at which Makian, Hennes, and two
others sat. At Benson's table he lingered. Benson accepted
his platter with a smile and a "How are you?" and pro-

ceeded to eat with relish. David, with an air of conscientiousness, brushed at invisible crumbs. His mouth managed to get itself close to Benson's ears and his lips scarcely moved as he said, "Anyone ever get poisoned here at the farm?"

Benson started at the sudden sound of words and looked quickly at David. As quickly he looked away, tried to appear indifferent. He shook his head in a sharp negative.

"The vegetables are Martian, aren't they?" murmured David.

A new voice sounded in the room. It was a rough yell from the other end of the room.

"By Space, you long Earth jackass, get a move on!"

It was Griswold, his face still stubbled. He must shave sometimes, David thought, since the stubble never grew longer, but no one ever seemed to see it shorter, either.

Griswold was at the last table to be visited. He was still mumbling, his anger boiling over.

His lips drew back. "Bring over that platter, dish-jockey. Faster. Faster."

David did so, but without hurry, and Griswold's hand, with the fork in it, jabbed quickly. David moved more quickly, and the fork clanged sharply against the hard plastic of the tray.

Balancing the tray in one hand, David caught Griswold's fist with the other. His grip grew tight. The other three at the table pushed back their chairs and rose.

David's voice, low, icy, and dead level, sounded just high enough to be heard by Griswold. "Drop it and ask for your ration decently, or you'll have it all at once."

Griswold writhed, but David maintained his hold. David's knee in the back of Griswold's chair prevented the farmboy from pushing away from the table.

"Ask nicely," said David. He smiled, deceptively gentle. "Like a man with breeding."

Griswold was panting harshly. The fork dropped from between his numbed fingers. He growled, "Let me have the tray."

"Is that all?"

"Please." He spat it out.

David lowered the tray and released the other's fist from which the blood had been crushed, leaving it white. Griswold massaged it with his other hand and reached for his fork. He looked about him, mad with fury, but there was only amusement or indifference in the eyes that met his. The farms on Mars were hard; each man had to care for himself.

Makian was standing. "Williams," he called.

David approached. "Sir?"

Makian made no direct reference to what had just occurred, but he stood there for a moment, looking carefully at David, as though he were seeing him for the first time and liked what he saw. He said, "Would you like to join the checkup tomorrow?"

"The checkup, sir? What is that?" Unobtrusively he surveyed the table. Makian's steak was gone, but his peas remained behind and the mashed potatoes were scarcely touched. He had not the grit, apparently, of Hennes, who had left a clean platter.

"The checkup is the monthly drive through all the farm to check on the plant rows. It's an old farm custom. We check on possible accidental breaks in the glass, on the condition and workings of the irrigation pipes and farm machinery, also on possible poaching. We need as many good men as possible out on the checkup."

"I'd like to go, sir."

"Good! I think you'll do." Makian turned to Hennes, who had been listening throughout with cold and unemotional eyes. "I like the boy's style, Hennes. We may be able to make a farmboy out of him. And, Hennes——" His voice sank and David, moving away, could no longer catch it, but from the quick hooded glance Makian cast in the direction of Griswold's table, it could not have been very complimentary to the veteran farmboy.

David Starr caught the footstep inside his own partitioning and acted even before he was fully awake. He slipped off the far side of the bed and underneath. He caught the glimpse of bare feet glimmering whitely in the pale light of the residual fluorescents shining through the window. The residuals were allowed to burn in the farm dome during the sleeping period to avoid darkness too inconveniently black.

David waited, heard the rustle of the sheets as hands probed uselessly through the bed, then a whisper. "Earthman! Earthman! Where in Space——"

David touched one of the feet and was rewarded by a sudden withdrawal and a sharp intake of breath.

There was a pause and then a head, shapeless in the dusk, was near his. "Earthman? You there?"

"Where else would I be sleeping, Bigman? I like it here under the bed."

The little fellow fumed and whispered peevishly, "You might have squeezed a yell out of me and then I would have been in the stew to my ears. I've got to talk to you."

"Now's your chance." David chuckled softly and crawled back into bed.

Bigman said, "You're a suspicious space bug for an Earthman."

"You bet," said David. "I intend living a long life."

"If you're not careful, you won't."

"No?"

"No. I'm foolish to be here. If I'm caught, I'll never

get my reference papers. It's just that you helped me when I could use it, and it's my turn to pay back. What was it you did to this louse, Griswold?"

"Just a little mixup in the special mess."

"A little mixup? He was raving mad. It was all Hennes could do to hold him back."

"Is this what you came to tell me, Bigman?"

"Part of it. They were behind the garage just after lights-out. They didn't know I was around, and I didn't tell them. Anyway, Hennes was yanking the stuffings out of Griswold; first for starting something with you when the Old Man was watching; and second, for not having the sand to finish once he had started it. Griswold was too mad to talk sense. Near as I could judge, he was just gargling something about how he would have your gizzard. Hennes said——" He broke off. "Listen, didn't you tell me that Hennes was all clear as far as you were concerned?"

"He seems so."

"Those midnight trips——"

"You only saw him once."

"Once is enough. If it was legitimate, why can't you give me the straight stuff?"

"It's not mine to give, Bigman, but it all seems legitimate."

"If that's the case, what's he got against you? Why doesn't he call off his dogs?"

"What do you mean?"

"Well, when Griswold finished talking, Hennes said he was to hold off. He said you would be out on checkup tomorrow and that would be the time. So I thought I'd come and warn you, Earthman. Better stay off checkup."

David's voice remained unflurried. "Checkup would be time for what? Did Hennes say?"

"I didn't hear past that. They moved away and I

couldn't follow, or I would have been out in the open. But I assume it's pretty plain."

"Maybe. But suppose we try to find out for sure exactly what they're after."

Bigman leaned close, as though he were trying to extract a reading from David's face despite the gloom. "How do you mean?"

David said, "How do you suppose. I'll be at the checkup and give the boys a chance to show me."

"You can't do that," gasped Bigman. "You couldn't handle yourself on a checkup against them. You don't know anything about Mars, you poor Earthman you."

"Then," said David phlegmatically, "it could mean suicide, I suppose. Let's wait and see." He patted Bigman on the shoulder, turned over, and went to sleep again.

6

"Sand Away!"

Checkup excitement began within the farm dome as soon as the main fluorescents were turned on. There was a wild noise and a mad scurry. Sand-cars were brought out in rows, each farmboy tending his own.

Makian was here and there, never too long at any one point. Hennes, in his flat, efficient voice, assigned the parties and set the routes across the farm's vast expanse. He looked up as he passed David and stopped.

"Williams," he said, "are you still of a mind to be on the checkup?"

"I wouldn't miss it."

"All right then. Since you haven't any car of your own, I'll assign you one out of general stock. Once it's assigned, it's yours to take care of and keep in working condition. Any repairs or damage which we consider avoidable will come out of your pay. Understood?"

"Fair enough."

"I'll put you on Griswold's team. I know that you and he don't get along, but he's our best man in the fields and you're an Earthie without experience. I wouldn't care to load you onto a lesser man. Can you drive a sand-car?"

"I think I can handle any moving vehicle with a little practice."

"You can, eh? We'll give you your chance to make good on that." He was about to step away when his eyes caught something. He barked, "And where do you think you're going?"

Bigman had just stepped into the assembly room. He was in a new outfit and his boots had been polished to mirror-shine. His hair was slicked down and his face was scrubbed and pink. He drawled, "On the checkup, Hennes—*Mister* Hennes. I'm not on detention and I still have my rating as licensed farmboy even though you have put me on chow detail. That means I can go on checkup. It also means I have a right to my old car and my old squad."

Hennes shrugged. "You read the rule books a lot, and that's what they say, I suppose. But one more week, Bigman, one more week. After that, if you ever show your nose anywhere on Makian territory I'll have a real man step on you and squash you."

Bigman made a threatening gesture at Hennes's retreating back and then turned to David. "Ever used a nosepiece, Earthman?"

"Never actually. I've heard about them, of course."

"Hearing isn't using. I've checked an extra one out for you. Look, let me show you how to get it on. No, no, get your thumbs out of there. Now watch how I hold my hands. That's right. Now over the head and make sure the straps aren't twisted in the back of the neck, or you'll end with a headache. Now can you see through them?"

The upper part of David's face was transformed into a plastic-encased monstrosity, and the double hose leading from the oxygen cylinders up each side of his chin subtracted further from any appearance of humanity.

"Do you have trouble breathing?" asked Bigman.

David was struggling, fighting to suck in air. He yanked the nosepiece off. "How do you turn it on? There's no gauge."

Bigman was laughing. "That's the return for the scare you gave me last night. You don't need a gauge. The cylinders automatically feed oxygen as soon as the warmth and pressure of your face trip a contact; and it automatically closes off when you take it off."

"Then there's something wrong with it. I——"

"Nothing wrong with it. It feeds at a gas pressure of one fifth normal to match the pressure of the Mars atmosphere, and you can't suck it in out here when you're fighting the pressure of a normal Earth atmosphere. Out there in the desert it will be fine. And it will be enough too, because even though it's one fifth normal, it's all oxygen. You'll have as much oxygen as you always had. Just remember one thing: breathe in through your nose but breathe out through your mouth. If you breathe out through your nose, you'll fog up your eyepieces, and that won't be good."

He strutted about David's tall, straight body and shook his head. "Don't know what to do about your boots. Black and white! You look like a garbage detail or something." He glanced down at his own chartreuse-and-vermilion creations with more than a little complacency.

David said, "I'll manage. You'd better get to your car. It looks as though they're getting ready to move."

"You're right. Well, take it easy. Watch out for the gravity change. That's hard to take if you're not used to it. And, Earthman——"

"Well."

"Keep your eyes open. You know what I mean."

"Thanks. I shall."

The sand-cars were lining up now in squares of nine. There were more than a hundred all told, each with its farmboy peering over its tires and controls. Each vehicle had its handmade signs intended as humor. The sand-car trundled out for David was speckled with such signs from half-a-dozen previous owners, beginning with a "Watch Out, Girls" circling the bullet-like prow of the car and ending with a "This Ain't No Dust Storm, This Is Me," on the rear bumper.

David climbed in and closed the door. It fit tightly. Not even a seam showed. Immediately above his head there was the filtered and refiltered vent that allowed equalization of air pressure within and without the car. The glass was not quite clear. It had a faint misting that was proof of dozens of dust storms met and weathered. David found the controls familiar enough. They were standard for ground cars, for the most part. The few unfamiliar buttons explained themselves upon manipulation.

Griswold came past, gesturing at him furiously. He opened his door.

Griswold yelled, "Get your front flaps down, you jerk. We're not heading into any storm."

David searched for the proper button and found it on the steering-wheel shaft. The windshields, which looked as though they were welded to metal, disengaged themselves and sank down into sockets. Visibility improved. Of course, he thought. Mars's atmosphere would scarcely raise wind enough to disturb them, and this was Martian summer. It would not be too cold.

A voice called, "Hey, Earthman!" He looked up. Bigman was waving at him. He was in Griswold's group of nine also. David waved back.

A section of the dome lifted up. Nine cars trundled in, moving sluggishly. The section closed behind them. Minutes passed, then it opened, empty, and nine more moved in.

Griswold's voice sounded suddenly and loudly next to

David's ear. David turned and saw the small receiver in the car top just behind his head. The small grilled opening at the head of the steering-wheel shaft was a mouthpiece.

"Squad eight, ready?"

The voices sounded consecutively: "Number one, ready." "Number two, ready." "Number three, ready." There was a pause after number six. Just a few seconds. David then called, "Number seven, ready." There followed "Number eight, ready." Bigman's reedy tones came last. "Number nine, ready."

The dome section was raising again and the cars ahead of David began moving. David slowly stepped on the resistor, cutting the coils, allowing electricity to pour into the motor. His sand-car leaped ahead, all but crashing into the rear of the one in front. He let out the resistor with a jerk and felt the car tremble beneath him. Gently he babied it along. The section enclosed them like a small tunnel, shutting off behind.

He became conscious of the hiss of air being pumped out of the section back into the dome proper. He felt his heart begin to pound, but his hands were steady upon the wheel.

His clothing bellied away from him and the air was seeping out along the cylindrical line where boots met thigh. There was a tingling in his hands and chin, a feeling of puffiness, of distention. He swallowed repeatedly, to relieve the gathering pain in his ears. After five minutes he found himself panting in an effort to gather enough oxygen for his needs.

The others were slipping on their nosepieces. He did the same, and this time oxygen slid smoothly up his nostrils. He breathed deeply, puffing it out through his mouth. His arms and feet still tingled, but the feeling was beginning to die away.

And now the section was opening ahead of them, and the flat, ruddy sands of Mars glittered in the sun's feeble light. There was a yell in unison from eight farmboy throats as the section lifted.

"Sand awa-a-a-ay!" and the first cars in line began to move.

It was the traditional farmboy cry, made thin and almost soprano in the thin air of Mars.

David let in the resistor and crawled across the line that marked the boundary between dome metal and Martian soil.

And it hit him!

The sudden gravity change was like a sharp fall of a thousand feet. One hundred and twenty pounds of his two hundred disappeared as he crossed the line, and it left him by way of the pit of his stomach. He clutched at the wheel as the sensation of fall, fall, *fall* persisted. The sandcar veered wildly.

There was the sound of Griswold's voice, which maintained its hoarseness even in the incongruous hollowness forced upon it by the thin air which carried sound waves so poorly. "Number seven! Back in line!"

David fought with the wheel, fought with his own sensations, fought to make himself see clearly. He dragged at the oxygen through his nosepiece and slowly the worst passed.

He could see Bigman looking anxiously in his direction. He took one hand away from the wheel momentarily to wave, then concentrated on the road.

The Martian desert was almost flat, flat and bare. Not even a scrub of vegetation existed here. This particular area had been dead and deserted for who knew how many thousands or millions of years. The thought suddenly struck him that perhaps he was wrong. Perhaps the desert sands had been coated with blue-green microorganisms until Earthmen had come and burned them away to make room for their farms.

The cars ahead trailed faint dust that rose slowly, as if it were part of a motion-picture film that had been slowed down. It settled as slowly.

David's car was trailing badly. He added speed and still more speed, and found that something was going wrong. The others, ahead of him, were hugging the ground but he, himself, was bounding like a jackrabbit. At every trifling imperfection in the ground surface, at every projecting line of rock, his car took off. It drifted lazily up into the air, inches high, its wheels whining against nothing. It came down as gently, then lurched forward with a jerk as the straining wheels caught hold.

It caused him to lose ground, and when he poured the juice on to gain again, the jumping grew worse. It was the low gravity that did it, of course, but the others managed to compensate for it. He wondered how.

It was getting cold. Even at Martian summer, he guessed the temperature to be barely above freezing. He could look directly at the sun in the sky. It was a dwarfed sun in a purple sky in which he could make out three or four stars. The air was too thin to blank them out or to scatter light in such a manner as to form the sky-blue of Earth.

Griswold's voice was sounding again: "Cars one, four, and seven to the left. Cars two, five, and eight to the center. Cars three, six, and nine to the right. Cars two and three will be in charge of their subsections."

Griswold's car, number one, was beginning to curl to the left, and David, following it with his eyes, noticed the dark line on the leftward horizon. Number four was following one, and David turned his wheel sharply left to match the angle of veer.

What followed caught him by surprise. His car went into a rapid skid, scarcely allowing him time to realize it. He yanked desperately at the wheel, spinning it in the direction of skid. He shut off all power and felt the wheels rasp as the car whirled onward. The desert circled before him, so that only its redness could make any impression.

And then there was Bigman's thin cry through the receiver, "Stamp on the emergency traction. It's just to the right of the resistors."

David probed desperately for the emergency traction, whatever it was, but his aching feet found nothing. The dark line on the horizon appeared before him and then vanished. It was much sharper now, and broader. Even in that rapid flash, its nature became appallingly evident. It was one of the fissures of Mars, long and straight. Like the far more numerous ones on Earth's Moon, they were cracks in the planetary surface, made as the world dried through millions of years. They were up to a hundred feet across and no man had plumbed their depth.

"It's a pink, stubby button," yelled Bigman. "Stamp everywhere."

David did so, and there was a sudden slight yielding beneath his toes. The swift motion of his sand-car became a rebellious grinding that tore at him. The dust came up in clouds, choking him and obscuring everything.

He bent over the wheel and waited. The car was definitely slowing. And then, finally, it stopped.

He sat back and breathed quietly for a moment. Then he withdrew his nosepiece, wiped the inner surfaces while the cold air stung at nose and eyes, and replaced it. His clothes were ruddy gray with dust and his chin was caked with it. He could feel its dryness upon his lips, and the interior of his car was filthy with it.

The two other cars of his sub-section had pulled up next to him. Griswold was climbing out of one, his stubbled face made monstrously ugly by the nosepiece. David was suddenly aware of the reason for the popularity of beards and stubble among the farmboys. They were protection against the cold, thin wind of Mars.

Griswold was snarling, showing yellowed and broken teeth. He said, "Earthman, the repairs for this sand-car will come right out of your wages. You had Hennes's warning."

David opened the door and climbed out. From outside, the car was a worse wreck still, if that were possible. The tires were torn and from them projected the huge teeth which were obviously the "emergency traction."

He said, "Not one cent comes out of my wages, Griswold. There was something wrong with the car."

"That's for sure. The driver. A stupid, dumb-lug driver, that's what's wrong with the car."

Another car came squealing up, and Griswold turned to it.

His stubble seemed to bristle. "Get the blast out of here, you cinch-bug. Get on with your job."

Bigman jumped out of his car. "Not till I take a look at the Earthman's car."

Bigman weighed less than fifty pounds on Mars, and in one long, flat leap he was at David's side. He bent for a moment, then straightened. He said, "Where are the weight-rods, Griswold?"

David said, "What are the weight-rods, Bigman?"

The little fellow spoke rapidly. "When you take these sand-cars out into low gravity, you put foot-thick beams over each of the axles. You take them out when you're on high grav. I'm sorry, fella, but I never once thought that this might be what——"

David stopped him. His lips drew back. It would explain why his car had floated upward at each bump while the others were glued to the soil. He turned to Griswold. "Did you know they were gone?"

Griswold swore. "Each man is responsible for his own car. If you didn't notice they were gone, that's your negligence."

All the cars were now on the scene. A circle of hairy men were forming around the three, quiet, attentive, not interfering.

Bigman stormed. "You big hunk of silica, the man's a tenderfoot. He can't be expected to——"

"Quiet, Bigman," said David. "This is my job. I ask you again, Griswold. Did you know about this in advance?"

"And I told you, Earthie. In the desert a man has to watch himself. I'm not going to mother you."

"All right. In that case I'll watch myself right now." David looked about. They were almost at the edge of the fissure. Another ten feet and he would have been a dead man. "However, you'll have to watch yourself too, because I'm taking your car. You can drive mine back to the farm dome or you can stay here for all I care."

"By Mars!" Griswold's hand shot to his hip and there was a sudden rough cry from the circle of watching men.

"Fair fight! Fair fight!"

The code of the Martian deserts was a hard one, but it drew the line at advantages considered unfair. That was understood and *enforced*. Only by such mutual precautions could any man be protected from an eventual force-knife in the back or blast-gun in the belly.

Griswold looked at the hard faces about him. He said, "We'll have it out back in the dome. On your jobs, men."

David said, "I'll see you in the dome if you wish. Meanwhile, step aside."

He walked forward unhurriedly, and Griswold stepped back. "You stupid greenhorn. We can't have a fistfight with nosepieces on. Do you have anything but bone inside your skull?"

"Take your nosepiece off, then," said David, "and I'll take mine off. Stop me in fair fight, if you can."

"Fair fight!" came the approving shout from the crowd, and Bigman yelled, "Put up or back down, Griswold." He leaped forward, ripping Griswold's blaster from his hip.

David put his hand to his nosepiece. "Ready?"

Bigman called, "I'll count three."

The men yelled confusedly. They were waiting now, in keen anticipation. Griswold glanced wildly about him.

Bigman was counting, "One——"

And at the count of "Three" David quietly removed his nosepiece, and tossed it, with the attached cylinders, to one side. He stood there, unprotected, holding his breath against the unbreathable atmosphere of Mars.

7

Bigman Makes a Discovery

Griswold did not stir, and his nosepiece remained in place. There was a threatening growl from the spectators.

David moved as quickly as he dared, gauging his steps against the light gravity. He lunged clumsily (it was almost as though water were holding him up) and caught Griswold about the shoulder. He twisted sideways, avoiding the farmboy's knee. One hand reached to Griswold's chin, caught the nosepiece and yanked it up and off.

Griswold grabbed for it with the beginning of a thin yell, but caught himself and clamped his mouth shut against the loss of any air. He broke away, staggering a bit. Slowly he circled David.

Nearly a minute had passed since David had drawn his last breath. His lungs felt the strain. Griswold, eyes bloodshot, crouched and sidled toward David. His legs were springy, his motions graceful. He was used to low gravity and could handle himself. David realized grimly that he himself probably could not. One quick, injudicious move and he might find himself sprawling.

Each second took its strain. David kept out of reach

and watched the twisting grimace on Griswold's face tauten and grow tortured. He would have to outwait the farmboy. He himself had an athlete's lungs. Griswold ate too much and drank too much to be in proper shape. The fissure caught his eye. It was some four feet behind him now, a sheer cliff, dropping perpendicularly. It was toward it that Griswold was maneuvering him.

He halted his retreat. In ten seconds Griswold would have to charge. He would have to.

And Griswold did.

David let himself drop to one side, and caught the other with his shoulder. He whirled under the impact and allowed the force of the whirl to add itself to his own thrusting fist which caught Griswold's jawbone at its socket.

Griswold staggered blindly. He let out his breath in a huge puff and filled his lungs with a mixture of argon, neon, and carbon dioxide. Slowly, dreadfully, he crumpled. With a last effort he tried to raise himself, half succeeded, started falling again, tottered forward in an attempt to maintain his balance——

There was a confused yelling in David's ears. On trembling legs, deaf and blind to everything but his nosepiece on the ground, he walked back to the car. Forcing his tortured, oxygen-craving body to work slowly and with dignity, he buckled on his cylinders with care and adjusted his nosepiece. Then, finally, he took a shuddering drag of oxygen that poured into his lungs like the rush of cold water into a desiccated stomach.

It was a full minute before he could do anything but breathe, his huge chest rising and falling in large, rapid sweeps. He opened his eyes.

"Where's Griswold?"

They were around him, all of them, Bigman in the very fore.

Bigman looked surprised. "Didn't you see?"

"I knocked him down." David looked about sharply. Griswold was nowhere.

Bigman made a down-sweeping motion with his hand. "Into the fissure."

"What?" David frowned beneath the nosepiece. "This is a bad joke."

"No, no." "Over the edge like a diver." "By Space, it was his own fault." "Clear case of self-defense for you, Earthie." They were all talking at once.

David said, "Wait, what happened? Did *I* throw him over?"

"No, Earthie," Bigman clamored. "It wasn't your doing. You hit him and the bug went down. Then he tried to get up. He started going down again, and when he tried to keep his balance, he sort of hopped forward, too blind to see what lay ahead of him. We tried to get him, but there wasn't enough time, and over he went. If he hadn't been so busy maneuvering you to the edge of the fissure so he could throw you over, it wouldn't have happened."

David looked at the men. They looked at him.

Finally one of the farmboys thrust out a hard hand. "Good show, farmboy."

It was calmly said, but it meant acceptance, and it broke the log jam.

Bigman yelled a triumph, jumped six feet into the air, and sank slowly down, with legs twiddling under him in a maneuver no ballet dancer, however expert, could have duplicated under Earth gravity. The others were crowding close now. Men who had addressed David only as "Earthie" or "You," or not at all, were clapping him on the back and telling him he was a man Mars could be proud of.

Bigman shouted, "Men, let's continue the checkup. Do we need Griswold to show us how?"

They howled back, "No!"

"Then how about it?" He vaulted into his car.

"Come on, farmboy," they yelled at David, who jumped into what had been Griswold's car fifteen minutes before and set it in motion.

Once again the call of "Sand awa-a-a-ay!" shrilled and ululated through the Martian wisps.

The news spread by sand-car radio, leaping across the empty spaces between the glass-enclosed stretches of farm lands. While David maneuvered his vehicle up and down the corridors between the glass walls, word of Griswold's end made its way across all the expanse of the farm.

The eight remaining farmboys of what had been Griswold's sub-section gathered together once again in the dying ruddy light of Mars's sinking sun and retraced the early-morning drive back to the farm dome. When David returned, he found himself already notorious.

There was no formal evening meal that day. It had been eaten out in the desert before the return, so in less than half an hour of the completion of the checkup, men had gathered before the Main House, waiting.

There was no doubt that by now Hennes and the Old Man himself had heard of the fight. There were enough of the "Hennes crowd," that is, men who had been hired since Hennes had become foreman and whose interests were tied thoroughly to those of Hennes, to insure the fact that the news had spread in that direction. So the men waited with pleased anticipation.

It was not that they had any great hate for Hennes. He was efficient and no brute. But he was not liked. He was cold and aloof, lacked the quality of easy mixing which had marked earlier foremen. On Mars, with its lack of social distinctions, that was a serious shortcoming and one which the men could not help but resent. And Griswold himself had been anything but popular.

All in all, it was more excitement than the Makian farm had seen in three Martian years, and a Martian year is just one month short of being two Earth-years long.

When David appeared, a considerable cheer went up and way was made for him, though a small group well to one side looked glum and hostile.

Inside, the cheers must have been heard, for Makian, Hennes, Benson, and a few others stepped out. David walked up the foot of the ramp which led to the doorway and Hennes moved forward to the head of the ramp, where he stood, looking down.

David said, "Sir, I have come to explain today's incident."

Hennes said evenly, "A valuable employee of the Makian farms died today as the result of a quarrel with you. Can your explanation remove that fact?"

"No, sir, but the man Griswold was beaten in fair fight."

A voice called out from the crowd, "Griswold tried to kill the boy. He forgot to have the weight-rods included in the boy's car by *accident.*" There were several scattered squawks of laughter at the final sarcastic word.

Hennes paled. His fist clenched. "Who said that?"

There was silence, and then from the very front of the crowd a small, subdued voice said, "Please, teacher, it wasn't I." Bigman was standing there, hands clasped before him, eyes looking modestly down.

The laughter came again, and this time it was a roar.

Hennes suppressed fury with an effort. He said to David, "Do you claim an attempt on your life?"

David said, "No, sir. I claim only a fair fight, witnessed by seven farmboys. A man who enters a fair fight must be willing to come out as best he can. Do you intend to set up new rules?"

A yell of approval went up from the audience. Hennes looked about him. He cried, "I am sorry that you men are being misled and agitated into actions you will regret. Now get back to your work, all of you, and be assured that your attitude this evening will not be forgotten. As for you, Williams, we will consider the case. This is not the end."

He slammed back into Main House and, after a moment's hesitation, the rest followed him.

David was called to Benson's office early the next day. It had been a long night of celebration, which David could neither avoid nor break away from, and he yawned prodigiously as he stooped to avoid hitting the lintel.

Benson said, "Come in, Williams." He was dressed in a white smock and the air in the office had a characteristic animal odor that came from the cages of rats and hamsters. He smiled. "You look sleepy. Sit down."

"Thanks," said David. "I *am* sleepy. What can I do for you?"

"It's what I can do for you, Williams. You're in trouble and you could be in worse trouble. I'm afraid you don't know what conditions on Mars are like. Mr. Makian has the full legal authority to order you blasted if he believes the death of Griswold can be considered murder."

"Without a trial?"

"No, but Hennes could find twelve farmboys who would think his way easily enough."

"He'd have trouble with the rest of the farmboys if he tried to do that, wouldn't he?"

"I know. I told Hennes that over and over again last night. Don't think that Hennes and I get along. He's too dictatorial for me; too fond, by far, of his own ideas, such as that private detective work of his which I mentioned to you the other time. And Mr. Makian agreed with me completely. He must let Hennes take charge of all direct dealings with the men, of course, which is why he didn't interfere yesterday, but he told Hennes afterward, to his face, that he wasn't going to sit by and see his farm destroyed over a stupid rascal such as Griswold, and Hennes had to promise to let the matter stew for a while. Just the same, he won't forget this in a hurry, and Hennes is a bad enemy to have here."

"I'll have to risk it, won't I?"

"We can run the risk to a minimum. I've asked Makian if I may use you here. You could be quite useful, you know, even without scientific training. You can help feed the animals and clean the cages. I could teach you how to anesthetize them and give injections. It won't be much, but it will keep you out of Hennes's way and prevent disruption of farm morale which is something we can't afford now, as you should know. Are you willing?"

With the utmost gravity David said, "It would be rather a social comedown for a man who's been told he's an honest-to-goodness farmboy now."

The scientist frowned. "Oh, come now, Williams. Don't take seriously what those fools tell you. Farmboy! Huh! It's a fancy name for a semi-skilled agricultural laborer and nothing more. You'd be silly to listen to their upside-down notions of social status. Look, if you work with me you might be helping to work out the mystery of the poisonings; help avenge your sister. That's why you came to Mars, wasn't it?"

"I'll work for you," said David.

"Good." Benson's round face stretched in a smile of relief.

•   •   •

Bigman looked through the door cautiously. He half whispered, "Hey!"

David turned around and closed the cage door. "Hello, Bigman."

"Is Benson around?"

"No. He's gone for the day."

"Okay." Bigman entered, walking carefully, as though to prevent even an accidental contact between his clothing and any object in the laboratories.

"Don't tell me you have something against Benson."

"Who, me? No. He's just a bit—you know." He tapped his temple a few times. "What kind of a grown man would come to Mars to fool around with little animals? And then he's always telling us how to run the planting and harvesting. What does he know? You can't learn anything about Mars farming in some Earth college. At that, he tries to make himself seem better than we are. You know what I mean? We have to slap him down sometimes."

He looked gloomily at David. "And now look at you. He's got you all spiffed out in a nightgown too, playing nursemaid to a mouse. Why do you let him?"

"It's just for a while," said David.

"Well." Bigman pondered a moment, then thrust out his hand awkwardly. "I want to say good-by."

David took it. "Leaving?"

"My month's up. I have my papers so now I'll be getting a job somewhere else. I'm glad I met up with you, Earthie. Maybe when your own time's up we can meet again. You won't want to stay under Hennes."

"Hold on." David did not release the little fellow's hand. "You'll be going to Wingrad City now, won't you?"

"Till I find a job. Yes."

"Good. I've been waiting for this for a week. I can't leave the farm, Bigman, so will you do an errand for me?"

"You bet. Just name it."

"It's a little risky. You'd have to come back here."

"All right. I'm not afraid of Hennes. Besides, there are ways for us to meet he doesn't know a thing about. I've been on Makian farms a lot longer than he has."

David forced Bigman into a seat. He squatted next to him, and his voice was a whisper. "Look, there's a library at the corner of Canal and Phobos streets in Wingrad City. I want you to get some book films for me along with a viewer. The information that will get you the proper films is in this sealed——"

Bigman's hand clawed out sharply, seizing David's right sleeve, forcing it upward.

"Here, what are you doing?" demanded David.

"I want to see something," panted Bigman. He had bared David's wrist now, holding it, inner surface upward, watching it breathlessly.

David made no move to withdraw it. He watched his own wrist without concern. "Well, what's the idea?"

"Wrong one," muttered Bigman.

"Really?" David took his wrist away from Bigman's clutch effortlessly and exposed the other wrist. He held them both before him. "What are you looking for?"

"You know what I'm looking for. I thought your face was familiar ever since you came here. Couldn't place it. I could kick myself. What kind of an Earthman would come here and be rated as good as any native farmboy in less than a month? And I have to wait for you to send me to the library at the Council of Science before I tumble."

"I still don't understand you, Bigman."

"I think you do, David Starr." He nearly shouted the name in his triumph.

8

Night Meeting

David said, "Quiet, man!"

Bigman's voice sank. "I've seen you in video reels often enough. But why don't your wrists show the mark? I've heard all the members of the Council were marked."

"Where did you hear this? And who told you the library at Canal and Phobos is the Council of Science?"

Bigman flushed. "Don't look down at the farmboy, mister. I've lived in the city. I've even had schooling."

"My apologies. I didn't mean it that way. Will you still help me?"

"Not until I understand about your wrists."

"That's not hard. It's a colorless tattoo that will turn dark in air, but only if I want it to."

"How's that?"

"It's a matter of emotion. Each human emotion is accompanied by a particular hormone pattern in the blood. One and only one such pattern activates the tattoo. I happen to know the emotion that fits."

David did nothing visibly, but slowly a patch on the inner surface of his right wrist appeared and darkened. The golden dots of the Big Dipper and Orion glowed momentarily and then the whole faded rapidly.

Bigman's face glowed and his hands came down for that automatic smack against his boots. David caught his arms roughly.

"Hey," said Bigman.

"No excitement, please. Are you with me?"

"Sure I'm with you. I'll be back tonight with the stuff you want and I'll tell you where we can meet. There's a place outside, near the Second Section——" He went on, whispering directions.

David nodded. "Good. Here's the envelope."

Bigman took it and inserted it between his hip boot and thigh. He said, "There's a pocket on the inside top of the better-quality hip boots, Mr. Starr. Do you know that?"

"I do. Don't look down at this farmboy, either. And my name, Bigman, is still Williams. That leaves just one last statement. The Council librarians will be the only ones who will be able to open that envelope safely. If anyone else tries, he'll be hurt."

Bigman drew himself up. "No one else will open it. There are people who are bigger than I am. Maybe you think I don't know that, but I do. Just the same, bigger or not, nobody, and I mean nobody, will take this from me without killing me. What's more, I wasn't thinking of opening it myself, either, if you've given that any thought."

"I have," said David. "I try to give all possibilities some thought, but I didn't give that one very much."

Bigman smiled, made a mock pass with his fist at David's chin, and was gone.

It was almost dinnertime when Benson returned. He looked unhappy and his plump cheeks were drooping.

He said listlessly, "How are you, Williams?"

David was washing his hands by dipping them into the special detergent solution which was universally used on Mars for this purpose. He withdrew his hands into the stream of warm air for drying, while the wash water flushed away into the tanks where it could be purified and returned to the central supply. Water was expensive on Mars and was used and reused wherever possible.

David said, "You look tired, Mr. Benson."

Benson closed the door carefully behind him. He blurted it out. "Six people died yesterday of the poisoning. That's the highest number yet for a single day. It's getting worse all the time and there's nothing we seem to be able to do."

He glowered at the lines of animal cages. "All alive, I suppose."

"All alive," said David.

"Well, what can I do? Every day Makian asks me if I have discovered anything. Does he think I can find discoveries under my pillow in the morning? I was in the grain bins today, Williams. It was an ocean of wheat, thousands and thousands of tons all set for shipment to Earth. I dipped into it a hundred times. Fifty grains here; fifty grains there. I tried every corner of every bin. I had them dip twenty feet down for samples. But what good is it? Under present conditions it would be a generous estimate to suppose that one out of a billion grains is infected."

He nudged at the suitcase he had brought with him. "Do you think the fifty thousand grains I've got here have the one in a billion among them? One chance in twenty thousand!"

David said, "Mr. Benson, you told me that no one ever died on the farm here, even though we eat Martian food almost exclusively."

"Not as far as I know."

"How about Mars as a whole?"

Benson frowned. "I don't know. I suppose not or I would have heard of it. Of course life isn't as tightly organized here on Mars as it is on Earth. A farmboy dies and usually he is simply buried without formality. There are few questions." Then, sharply, "Why do you ask?"

"I was just thinking that if it were a Martian germ, people on Mars might be more accustomed to it than Earth people. They might be immune."

"Well! Not a bad thought for a non-scientist. In fact, it's a good idea. I'll keep it in mind." He reached up to pat David's shoulder. "You go on and eat. We'll begin feeding the new samples tomorrow."

As David left, Benson turned to his suitcase and was lifting out the carefully labeled little packets, one of which might hold the all-important poisoned kernel. By tomorrow those samples would be ground, each little pile of powder carefully mixed and painstakingly divided into twenty sub-samples, some for feeding and some for testing.

By tomorrow! David smiled tightly to himself. He wondered where he would be tomorrow. He even wondered if he would be alive tomorrow.

The farm dome lay asleep like a giant prehistoric monster curled upon the surface of Mars. The residual fluorescents were pale glimmers against the dome roof. Amid the silence the ordinarily unheard vibrations of the dome's atmospherics, which compressed Martian atmosphere to the normal Earth level and added moisture and oxygen from the quantities supplied by the growing plants of the vast greenhouses, sounded in a low grumble.

David was moving quickly from shadow to shadow with a caution that was, to a large extent, not necessary. There was no one watching. The hard composition of the dome was low overhead, bending rapidly to the ground, when he reached Lock 17. His hair brushed it.

The inner door was open and he stepped inside. His

pencil flashlight swept the walls within and found the controls. They weren't labeled, but Bigman's directions had been clear enough. He depressed the yellow button. There was a faint click, a pause, and then the soughing of air. It was much louder than it had been on the day of the checkup, and since the lock was a small one designed for three or four men rather than a giant one designed for nine sand-cars, the air pressure dropped much more quickly.

He adjusted his nosepiece, waited for the hissing to die away, the silence indicating pressure equilibrium. Only then did he depress the red button. The outer section lifted and he stepped out.

This time he was not trying to control a car. He lowered himself to the hard, cold sands and waited for the stomach-turning sensations to pass as he accustomed himself to the gravity change. It took scarcely two minutes for that to happen. A few more gravity-change passages, David thought grimly, and he would have what the farmboys called "gravity legs."

He rose, turned to get his bearings, and then found himself, quite involuntarily, frozen in fascination!

It was the first time he had ever seen the Martian night sky. The stars themselves were the old familiar ones of Earth, arranged in all the familiar constellations. The distance from Mars to Earth, great though it was, was insufficient to alter perceptibly the relative positions of the distant stars. But though the stars were unchanged in position, how vastly they were changed in brilliance.

The thinner air of Mars scarcely softened them, but left them hard and gem-bright. There was no moon, of course, not one such as Earth knew. Mars's two satellites, Phobos and Deimos, were tiny things only five or ten miles across, simply mountains flying loose in space. Even though they were much closer to Mars than the Moon was to Earth, they would show no disk and be only two more stars.

He searched for them, even though he realized they might easily both be on the other side of Mars. Low on the western horizon he caught something else. Slowly he turned to it. It was by far the brightest object in the sky, with a faint blue-green tinge to it that was matched for beauty by nothing else in the heavens he watched. Separated from it by about the width of Mars's shrunken sun was another object, yellower, bright in itself but dwarfed by the much greater brilliance of its neighbor.

David needed no star map to identify the double object. They were the Earth and the Moon, the double "evening star" of Mars.

He tore his eyes away, turned toward the low outcropping of rock visible in the light of his pencil flash, and began walking. Bigman had told him to use those rocks as a guide. It was cold in the Martian night, and David was regretfully aware of the heating powers of even the Martian sun, one hundred and thirty million miles away.

The sand-car was invisible, or nearly so, in the weak starlight, and he heard the low, even purr of its engines long before he saw it.

He called, "Bigman!" and the little fellow popped out of it.

"Space!" said Bigman. "I was beginning to think you were lost."

"Why is the engine running?"

"That's easy. How else do I keep from freezing to death? We won't be heard, though. I know this place."

"Do you have the films?"

"*Do* I? Listen, I don't know what you had in the message you sent but they had five or six scholars circling me like satellites. It was 'Mr. Jones this' and 'Mr. Jones that.' I said, 'My name's Bigman,' I said. And then it was 'Mr.

Bigman, if you please.' Anyway"—Bigman ticked items off on his fingers—"before the day was gone, they had four films for me, two viewers, a box as big as myself which I haven't opened, and the loan (or maybe the gift for all I know) of a sand-car to carry it all in."

David smiled but made no answer. He entered into the welcome warmth of the car and quickly, in a race to outrun the fleet night, adjusted the viewers for projection and inserted a film in each. Direct viewing would have been quicker, more preferable, but even in the warm interior of the sand-car his nosepiece was still a necessity, and the bulbous transparent covering of his eyes made direct viewing impossible.

Slowly the sand-car lurched forward through the night, repeating almost exactly the route of Griswold's subsection on the day of the checkup.

"I don't get it," said Bigman. He had been muttering under his breath uselessly for fifteen minutes and now he had to repeat his louder statement twice before the brooding David would respond.

"Don't get what?"

"What you're doing. Where you're going. I figure this is my business because I'm going to stay with you from here on. I've been thinking today, Mr. St—Williams, thinking a lot. Mr. Makian's been in a kind of biting temper for months now, and he wasn't a bad joe at all before that. Hennes came in at that time, with a new shuffle for all hands. And Schoolboy Benson gets *his* licks in all of a sudden. Before it all started he was nobody, and now he's real pally with the big shots. Then, to top it off, you're here, with the Council of Science ready to put up anything you want. It's something big, I know, and I want to be in on it."

"Do you?" said David. "Did you see the maps I was viewing?"

"Sure. Just old maps of Mars. I've seen them a million times."

"How about the ones with the crosshatched areas? Do you know what those areas stood for?"

"Any farmboy can tell you that. There are supposed to be caverns underneath, except that I don't believe it. My point is this. How in Space can anyone tell there are holes two miles underneath the ground if no one's been down there to see? Tell me that."

David did not bother to describe the science of seismography to Bigman. Instead, he said, "Ever hear of Martians?"

Bigman began, "Sure. What kind of a question——" and then the sand-car screeched and trembled as the little fellow's hands moved convulsively on the wheels. "You mean *real* Martians? *Mars* Martians; not *people* Martians like us? Martians living here before people came?"

His thin laugh rattled piercingly inside the car and when he caught his breath again (it is difficult to laugh and breathe at the same time with a nosepiece on), he said, "You've been talking to that guy Benson."

David remained gravely unruffled at the other's glee. "Why do you say that, Bigman?"

"We once caught him reading some kind of book about it, and we ribbed the pants off him. Jumping Asteroids, he got sore. He called us all ignorant peasants, and I looked up the word in the dictionary and told the boys what it meant. There was talk of mayhem for a while, and he got shoved around sort of by accident, if you know what I mean, for a while after that. He never mentioned anything about Martians to *us* after that; wouldn't have had the nerve. I guess, though, he figured you were an Earthman and would fall for that kind of comet gas."

"Are you sure it's comet gas?"

"Sure. What else can it be? People have been on Mars for hundreds and hundreds of years. No one's ever seen Martians."

"Suppose they're down in the caverns two miles underneath."

"No one's seen the caverns either. Besides, how would the Martians get there in the first place? People have been over every inch of Mars and there sure aren't staircases going down anywhere. Or elevators, either."

"Are you certain? I saw one the other day."

"What?" Bigman looked back over his shoulder. He said, "Kidding me?"

"It wasn't a staircase, but it was a hole. And it was at *least* two miles deep."

"Oh, you mean the *fissure*. Nuts, that doesn't mean anything. Mars is full of fissures."

"Exactly, Bigman. And I've got detailed maps of the fissures on Mars too. Right here. There's a funny thing about them which, as nearly as I can tell from the geography you brought me, hasn't been noticed before. Not a single fissure crosses a single cavern."

"What does that prove?"

"It makes sense. If you were building airtight caverns, would you want a hole in the roof? And there's another coincidence. Each fissure cuts close to a cavern, but without ever touching, as though the Martians used them as points of entrance into the caverns they were building."

The sand-car stopped suddenly. In the dim light of the viewers, which were still focused on two maps projected simultaneously upon the flat white surface of the built-in screens, Bigman's face blinked somberly at David in the back seat.

He said, "Wait a minute. Wait a jumping minute. Where are we going?"

"To the fissure, Bigman. About two miles past the place where Griswold went over. That's where it gets nearest the cavern under the Makian farms."

"And once we get there?"

David said calmly, "Once we get there, why, I'll climb down into it."

9

Into the Fissure

"Are you serious?" asked Bigman.

"Quite serious," said David.

"You mean"—he tried to smile—"there really *are* Martians?"

"Would you believe me if I said there were?"

"No." He came to a sudden decision. "But that doesn't matter. I said I wanted to be in on this, and I don't back out." Once again the car moved forward.

The feeble dawn of the Martian heavens was beginning to light the grim landscape when the car approached the fissure. It had been creeping for half an hour previous, its powerful headlights probing the darkness, lest, as Bigman had put it, they find the fissure a little too quickly.

David climbed out of the car and approached the giant crack. No light penetrated it as yet. It was a black and ominous hole in the ground, stretching out of sight in either direction, with the opposing lip a featureless gray prominence. He pointed his flash downward and the beam of light faded into nothing.

Bigman came up behind him. "Are you sure this is the right place?"

David looked about him. "According to the maps, this is the closest approach to a cavern. How far are we from the nearest farm section?"

"Two miles easy."

The Earthman nodded. Farmboys were unlikely to touch this spot except possibly during checkup.

He said, "No use waiting then."

Bigman said, "How are you going to do it, anyway?"

David had already lifted the box which Bigman had obtained in Wingrad City out of the car. He tore it open and took out the contents. "Ever see one of these?" he asked.

Bigman shook his head. He twiddled a piece of it between gloved thumb and forefinger. It consisted of a pair of long ropes with a silky sheen connected at twelve-inch intervals by crosspieces.

"It's a rope ladder, I suppose," he said.

"Yes," said David, "but not rope. This is spun silicone, lighter than magnesium, stronger than steel, and barely affected by any temperatures we're likely to meet on Mars. Mostly, it's used on the Moon, where the gravity is really low and the mountains really high. On Mars, there's not much use for it because it's a rather flat world. In fact, it was a stroke of luck that the Council could locate one in the city."

"What good will this do you?" Bigman was running the length of it through his hands until the ladder ended in a thick bulb of metal.

"Careful," said David. "If the safety catch isn't on, you can damage yourself pretty badly."

He took it gently out of Bigman's hand, encircled the metal bulb with his own strong hands, and twisted each hand in opposing directions. There was a sharp little click, but when he released his hold, the bulb seemed unchanged.

"Now look." The soil of Mars thinned and vanished at the approaches of the fissure, and the cliff edge was naked rock. David bent and, with a light pressure, touched the bulb end of the ladder to the crag, faintly ruddy in the flushing sky of morning. He took his hand away, and it remained there, balanced at an odd angle.

"Lift it up," he said.

Bigman looked at him, bent, and lifted. For a moment he looked puzzled as the bulb remained where it was; then he yanked with all his might and still nothing happened.

He looked up angrily. "What did you do?"

David smiled. "When the safety is released, any pressure at the tip of the bulb releases a thin forcefield about twelve inches long that cuts right into the rock. The end of the field then expands outward in each direction about six inches, to make a 'T' of force. The limits of the field are blunt, not sharp, so you can't loosen it by yanking it from side to side. The only way you can pull out the bulb is to break the rock clean off."

"How do you release it?"

David ran the hundred-foot length of ladder through his hands and came up with a similar bulb at the other end. He twisted it, then pushed it at the rock. It remained there, and after some fifteen seconds the first bulb fell on its side.

"If you activate one bulb," he said, "the other is automatically deactivated. Or, of course, if you adjust the safety catch of an activated bulb"—he bent down and did so—"it is deactivated"—he lifted it up—"and the other remains unaffected."

Bigman squatted. Where the two bulbs had been there were now narrow cuts about four inches long in the living rock. They were too narrow for him to insert his fingernail.

David Starr was speaking. He said, "I've got water and food for a week. I'm afraid my oxygen won't last more than two days, but you wait a week anyway. If I'm not back then, this is the letter you're to deliver to the Council headquarters."

"Hold on. You don't really think these fairy-tale Martians——"

"I mean lots of things. I mean I may slip. The rope ladder may be faulty. I may accidentally anchor it to a point at which there is a fault in the rock. Anything. So can I rely on you?"

Bigman looked disappointed. "But that's a fine situation. Am I supposed to sit around up here while you take all the risks?"

"It's the way a team works, Bigman. You know that."

He was stooping at the lip of the fissure. The sun was edging over the horizon before them and the sky had faded from black to purple. The fissure, however, remained a forbidding dusky abyss. The sparse atmosphere of Mars did not scatter light very well, and only when the sun was directly overhead was the eternal night of the fissure dispelled.

Stolidly David tossed the ladder into the fissure. Its fiber made no noise as it swung against the rock, upheld by the knob which held tightly to the stony lip. A hundred feet below they could hear the other knob thump once or twice.

David yanked at the rope to test its hold, then, seizing the topmost rung with his hands, he vaulted into the abyss himself. It was a feathery feeling floating down at less than half the speed one would have on Earth, but there it ended. His actual weight was not far below Earth normal, considering the two oxygen cylinders he carried, each the largest size available at the farm.

His head projected above surface. Bigman was staring

at him, wide-eyed. David said, "Now get away and take the car with you. Return the films and viewers to the Council and leave the scooter."

"Right," said Bigman. All cars carried emergency four-wheeled platforms that could travel fifty miles under their own power. They were uncomfortable and no protection at all against cold or, worse still, against dust storms. Still, when a sand-car broke down miles from home, scooters were better than waiting to be found.

David Starr looked downward. It was too dark to see the end of the ladder, the sheen of which glimmered into grayness. Allowing his legs to dangle free, he scrambled down the face of the cliff rung by rung, counting as he did so. At the eightieth rung he reached for the free end of the ladder and reeled it in after hooking an arm about and through a rung, leaving both hands free.

When the lower bulb was in his hand, he reached to the right and thrust it at the face of the cliff. It remained there. He yanked hard at it, and it held. Quickly he swung himself from his previous position to the branch of the rope ladder now dangling from the new anchor. One hand remained on the portion of the ladder he had left, waiting for it to give. When it did so, he swung it outward, so that the bulb from above would swing wide of himself as it fell.

He felt a slight pendulum effect upon himself as the bulb, which had been at the lip of the fissure thirty seconds before, now lashed back and forth some one hundred and eighty feet below the surface of Mars. He looked up. There was a broad swath of purple sky to be seen, but he knew it would get narrower with each rung he descended.

Down he went, and at every eighty rungs he set himself a new anchor, first to the right of the old one and then to the left, maintaining in general a straight passage downward.

Six hours had passed, and once again David paused for a bite of concentrated ration and a swig of water from his canteen. Catching his feet in rungs and relaxing the pressure on his arms was all he could do in the way of resting. Nowhere in all the descent had there been a horizontal ledge large enough for him to catch his breath upon. At least nowhere within the reach of his flashlight.

That was bad in other ways. It meant that the trip upward, supposing that there ever was to be a trip upward, would have to be made by the slow method of jabbing each bulb, in turn, at a spot as high as one could reach. It could be done and had been—on the Moon. On Mars the gravity was more than twice what it was on the Moon, and progress would be horribly slow, far slower than the journey down was. And that, David realized grimly, was slow enough. He could not be much more than a mile below surface.

Downward there was only black. Above, the now narrow streak of sky had brightened. David decided to wait. It was past eleven by his Earth-time watch, and that had fair significance on Mars, where the period of rotation was only half an hour longer than on Earth. The sun would soon be overhead.

He thought soberly that the maps of the Martian caverns were at best only rough approximations from the action of vibration waves under the planet's surface. With very slight errors existing he could be miles away from the true entrance into the caverns.

And then, too, there might be no entrances at all. The caverns might be purely natural phenomena, like the Carlsbad Caverns on Earth. Except, of course, that these Martian caverns were hundreds of miles across.

He waited, almost drowsily, hanging loosely over nothing, in darkness and silence. He flexed his numbed fingers. Even under the gloves, the Martian cold nipped.

When he was descending, the activity kept him warm; when he waited, the cold burrowed in.

He had almost decided to renew his climbing to keep from freezing when he caught the first approach of dim light. He looked up and saw the slowly descending dim yellow of sunlight. Over the lip of the fissure, into the small streak of sky that remained to his vision, the sun came. It took ten minutes for the light to increase to maximum, when the entire burning globe had become visible. Small though it was to an Earthman's eyes, its width was one quarter that of the fissure opening. David knew the light would last half an hour or less and that the darkness would return for twenty-four hours thereafter.

He looked about rapidly, swinging as he did so. The wall of the fissure was by no means straight. It was jagged, but it was everywhere vertical. It was as though a cut had been made into the Martian soil with a badly crimped knife, but one which cut straight down. The opposite wall was considerably closer than it had been at the surface, but David estimated that there would be at least another mile or two of descent before it would be close enough to touch.

Still, it all amounted to nothing. Nothing!

And then he saw the patch of blackness. David's breath whistled sharply. There was considerable blackness elsewhere. Wherever an outcropping of rock cast a shadow, there was blackness. It was just that this particular patch was rectangular. It had perfect, or what seemed to be perfect, right angles. It *had* to be artificial. It was like a door of some sort set into the rock.

Quickly he caught up the lower knob of the ladder, set it as far out in the direction of the patch as he could reach, gathered in the other knob as it fell, and set it still farther out in the same direction. He alternated them as rapidly as he could, hoping savagely that the sun would hold out, that the patch itself was not, somehow, an illusion.

The sun had crossed the fissure and now touched the lip of the wall from which he dangled. The rock he faced, which had been yellow-red, turned gray again. But there was still light upon the other wall, and he could see well enough. He was less than a hundred feet away, and each alternation of ladder knobs brought him a yard closer.

Glimmering, the sunlight traveled up the opposite wall, and the dusk was closing in when he reached the edge of the patch. His gloved fingers closed upon the edge of a cavity set into the rock. *It was smooth.* The line had neither fault nor flaw. It *had* to be made by intelligence.

He needed sunlight no longer. The small beam of the flashlight would be enough. He swung his ladder into the inset, and when he dropped a knob he felt it clunk sharply on rock beneath. A horizontal ledge!

He descended quickly, and in a few minutes found himself standing on rock. For the first time in more than six hours he was standing on something solid. He found the inactive bulb, thrust it into rock at waist level, brought down the ladder, then adjusted the safety latch and pulled out the bulb. For the first time in more than six hours both ends of the ladder were free.

David looped the ladder around his waist and arm and looked about. The cavity in the face of the cliff was about ten feet high and six across. With his flashlight pointing the way, he walked inward and came face to face with a smooth and quite solid stone slab that barred farther progress.

It, too, was the work of intelligence. It had to be. But it remained an effective barrier to further exploration just the same.

There was a sudden pain in his ears, and he spun

sharply. There could be only one explanation. Somehow the air pressure about himself was increasing. He moved back toward the face of the cliff and was not surprised to find that the opening through which he had come was barred by rock which had not previously been there. It had slid into place without a sound.

His heart beat quickly. He was obviously in an air lock of some sort. Carefully he removed his nosepiece and sampled the new air. It felt good in his lungs, and it was warm.

He advanced to the inner slab of rock and waited confidently for it to lift up and away.

It did exactly that; but a full minute before it did so David felt his arms compressed suddenly against his body as though a steel lasso had been thrown about him and tightened. He had time for one startled cry, and then his legs pushed one against the other under similar pressure.

And so it was that when the inner door opened and the way to enter the cavern was clear before him, David Starr could move neither hand nor foot.

10

Birth of the Space Ranger

David waited. There was no use in speaking to empty air. Presumably the entities who had built the caverns and who could so immobilize him in so immaterial a fashion would be perfectly capable of playing all the cards.

He felt himself lift from the ground and slowly tip backward until the line of his body was parallel with the floor. He tried to crane his head upward but found it to be nearly immovable. The bonds were not so strong as those which had tightened about his limbs. It was rather like a harness of velvety rubber that gave, but only so far.

He moved inward smoothly. It was like entering warm, fragrant, breathable water. As his head left the air lock, the last portion of his body to do so, a dreamless sleep closed over him.

David Starr opened his eyes with no sensation of any passage of time but, with the sensation of life near by. Exactly what form that sensation took he could not say. He was first conscious of the heat. It was that of a hot summer day on Earth. Second, there was the dim red light that surrounded him and that scarcely sufficed for vision. By it he could barely make out the walls of a small room as he turned his head. Nowhere was there motion; nowhere life.

And yet somewhere near there must be the working of a powerful intelligence. David felt that in a way he could not explain.

Cautiously he tried to move a hand, and it lifted without hindrance. Wonderingly he sat upright and found himself on a surface that yielded and gave but whose nature he could not make out in the dimness.

The voice came suddenly. "The creature is aware of its surroundings . . ." The last part of the statement was a jumble of meaningless sound. David could not identify the direction from which the voice came. It was from all directions and no direction.

A second voice sounded. It was different, though the difference was a subtle one. It was gentler, smoother, more feminine, somehow. "Are you well, creature?"

David said, "I cannot see you."

The first voice (David thought of it as a man's) sounded again. "It is then as I told . . ." Again the jumble. "You are not equipped to see mind."

The last phrase was blurred, but to David it sounded like "see mind."

"I can see matter," he said, "but there is scarcely light to see by."

There was a silence, as though the two were conferring apart, and then there was the gentle thrusting of an object into David's hand. It was his flashlight.

"Has this," came the masculine voice, "any significance to you with regard to light?"

"Why, certainly. Don't you see?" He flashed it on and quickly splashed the light beam about himself. The room *was* empty of life, and quite bare. The surface he rested upon was transparent to light and some four feet off the floor.

"It is as I said," said the feminine voice excitedly. "The creature's sight sense is activated by short-wave radiation."

"But most of the radiation of the instrument is in the infrared. It was that I judged by," protested the other. The light was brightening even as the voice sounded, turning first orange, then yellow, and finally white.

David said, "Can you cool the room too?"

"But it has been carefully adjusted to the temperature of your body."

"Nevertheless, I would have it cooler."

They were co-operative, at least. A cool wind swept over David, welcome and refreshing. He let the temperature drop to seventy before he stopped them.

David thought, "I think you are communicating directly with my mind. Presumably that is why I seem to hear you speaking International English."

The masculine voice said, "The last phrase is a jumble, but certainly we are communicating. How else would that be done?"

David nodded to himself. That accounted for the occasional noisy blur. When a proper name was used that had no accompanying picture for his own mind to interpret, it could only be received as a blur. Mental static.

The feminine voice said, "In the early history of our race there are legends that our minds were closed to one another and that we communicated by means of symbols for the eye and ear. From your question I cannot help but wonder if this is the case with your own people, creature."

David said, "That is so. How long is it since I was brought into the cavern?"

The masculine voice said, "Not quite a planetary rotation. We apologize for any inconvenience we caused you, but it was our first opportunity to study one of the new surface creatures alive. We have salvaged several before this, one only a short while ago, but none were functional, and the amount of information obtained from such is, of necessity, limited."

David wondered if Griswold had been the recently salvaged corpse. He said cautiously, "Is your examination of myself over?"

The feminine voice responded quickly. "You fear harm. There is a distinct impression in your mind that we may be so savage as to interfere with your life functions in order to gain knowledge. How horrible!"

"I'm sorry if I have offended you. It is merely that I am unacquainted with your methods."

The masculine voice said, "We know all we need. We are quite capable of making a molecule-by-molecule investigation of your body without the need of physical contact at all. The evidence of our psycho-mechanisms is quite sufficient."

"What are these psycho-mechanisms you mention?"

"Are you acquainted with matter-mind transformations?"

"I am afraid not."

There was a pause, and then the masculine voice said curtly, "I have just investigated your mind. I am afraid, judging by its texture, that your grasp of scientific principles is insufficient for you to understand my explanations."

David felt put in his place. He said, "My apologies."

The masculine voice went on. "I would ask you some questions."

"Proceed, sir."

"What was the last part of your statement?"

"It was merely a manner of honorable address."

A pause. "Oh yes, I see. You complicate your communication symbols in accordance with the person you address. An odd custom. But I delay. Tell me, creature, you radiate an enormous heat. Are you ill or can this be normal?"

"It is quite normal. The dead bodies you examined were undoubtedly at the temperature of their environment, whatever it was. But while functioning, our bodies maintain a constant temperature that best suits us."

"Then you are not natives of this planet?"

David said, "Before I answer this question, may I ask you what your attitude would be toward creatures like myself if we originated from another planet?"

"I assure you that you and your fellow creatures are a matter of indifference to us except in so far as you arouse our curiosity. I see from your mind that you are uneasy with regard to our motives. I see that you fear our hostility. Remove such thoughts."

"Can you not read in my mind, then, the answer to your questions? Why do you question me specifically?"

"I can only read emotions and general attitudes in absence of precise communication. But, then, you are a creature and would not understand. For precise information, communication must involve an effort of will. If it will help to ease your mind, I will inform you that we have every reason to believe you to be a member of a race not native to this planet. For one thing, the composition of your tissues is utterly different from that of any living thing ever known to have existed on the face of the world. Your body heat indicates also that you come from another world, a warmer one."

"You are correct. We come from Earth."

"I do not understand the last word."

"From the planet next nearer the sun than this one."

"So! That is most interesting. At the time our race retired to the caverns some half a million revolutions ago we knew your planet to possess life, though probably not intelligence. Was your race intelligent then?"

"Scarcely," said David. One million Earth-years had passed since the Martians had left the surface of their planet.

"It is indeed interesting. I must carry this report to the Central Mind directly. Come, ———."

"Let me remain behind, ———. I would like to communicate further with this creature."

"As you please."

The feminine voice said, "Tell me of your world."

David spoke freely. He felt a pleasant, almost delicious, languor. Suspicion departed and there was no reason he could not answer truthfully and in full. These beings were kind and friendly. He bubbled with information.

And then she released her hold on his mind and he stopped abruptly. Angrily he said, "What have I been saying?"

"Nothing of harm," the feminine voice assured him. "I have merely repressed the inhibitions of your mind. It is unlawful to do so, and I would not have dared do it if —— were here. But you are only a creature and I am so curious. I knew that your suspicion was too deep to let you talk without a little help from me and your suspicion is so misplaced. We would never harm you creatures as long as you do not intrude upon us."

"We have already done so, have we not?" asked David. "We occupy your planet from end to end."

"You are still testing me. You mistrust me. The surface of the planet is of no interest to us. *This* is home. And yet," the feminine voice seemed almost wistful, "there must be a certain thrill in traveling from world to world. We are well aware that there are many planets in space and many suns. To think that creatures like yourself are inheriting all that. It is all so interesting that I am thankful again and again that we sensed you making your clumsy way down toward us in time to make an opening for you."

"What!" David could not help but shout, although he knew that the sound waves his vocal cords created went unheeded and that only the thoughts of his mind were sensed. "You *made* that opening?"

"Not I alone. —— helped. That is why we were given the chance to investigate you."

"But how did you do it?"

"Why, by willing it."

"I don't understand."

"But it is simple. Can you not see it in my mind? But I forget. You are a creature. You see, when we retired to the caverns we were forced to destroy many thousands of cubic miles of matter to make space for ourselves under the surface. There was nowhere to store the matter as such, so we converted it to energy and —— —— —— ——."

"No, no, I don't follow you."

"You don't understand? In that case, all I can say is that the energy was stored in such a way that it could be tapped by an effort of the mind."

"But if all the matter that was once in these vast caverns were converted into energy——"

"There would be a great deal. Certainly. We have lived on that energy for half a million revolutions, and it is calculated that we have enough for twenty million more revolutions. Even before we left the surface we had studied the relation of mind and matter and since we have come to the caverns we have perfected the science to such a degree that we have abandoned matter entirely as far as our personal use is concerned. We are creatures of pure mind and energy, who never die and are no longer born. I am here with you, but since you cannot sense mind, you are not aware of me except with your mind."

"But surely people such as yourselves can make themselves heir to all the universe."

"You fear that we shall contest the universe with poor material creatures such as yourself? That we shall fight for a place among the stars? That is silly. All the universe is here with us. We are sufficient to ourselves."

David was silent. Then slowly he put his hands to his head as he had the sensation of fine, very fine tendrils gently touching his mind. It was the first time the feeling had come, and he shrank from its intimacy.

She said, "My apologies again. But you are such an interesting creature. Your mind tells me that your fellow creatures are in great danger and you suspect that we might be the cause. I assure you, creature, it is not so."

She said it simply. David had no course but to believe.

He said, "Your companion said my tissue chemistry was entirely different from that of any life on Mars. May I ask how?"

"It is composed of a nitrogenous material."

"Protein," explained David.

"I do not understand that word."

"What are your tissues composed of?"

"Of ——— ——— ———. It is entirely different. There is practically no nitrogen in it."

"You could offer me no food, then?"

"I am afraid not. ——— says any organic matter of our planet would be quickly poisonous to you. We could manufacture simple compounds of your life type that you might feed on, but the complex nitrogenous material that forms the bulk of your tissue is quite beyond us without much study. Are you hungry, creature?" There was no mistaking the sympathy and concern in her thoughts. (David persisted in thinking of it as a voice.)

He said, "For the moment I have still my own food."

The feminine voice said, "It seems unpleasant for me

to think of you simply as a creature. What is your name?"
Then, as though she feared she might not be understood,
"How do your fellow creatures identify you?"

"I am called David Starr."

"I do not understand that except that there seems a
reference to the suns of the universe. Do they call you
that because you are a traveler through space?"

"No. Many of my people travel through space. 'Starr'
has no particular meaning at present. It is simply a sound
to identify me, as your names are simply sounds. At least
they make no picture; I cannot understand them."

"What a pity. You should have a name which would
indicate your travels through space; the way in which you
range from one end of the universe to the other. If I were
a creature such as yourself, it seems to me that it would
be fitting I should be called 'Space Ranger.'"

And so it was that from the lips of a living creature he
did not see and could never see in its true form David
Starr heard, for the first time, the name by which, eventually, all the Galaxy would know him.

11

The Storm

A deeper, slower voice now took form in David's mind. It said gravely, "I greet you, creature. It is a good name ———— has just given you."

The feminine voice said, "I make way for you ———— ————."

By the loss of a faint touch upon his mind David became unmistakably aware that the owner of the feminine voice was no longer in mental contact. He turned warily, laboring once more under the illusion that there was direction to these voices and finding his untried mind still attempting to interpret in the old inadequate ways something with which it had never before come in contact. The voice came from no direction, of course. It was within his mind.

The creature of the deep voice gauged the difficulty. It said, "You are disturbed by the failure of your sense equipment to detect me and I do not wish you to be disturbed. I could adopt the outward physical appearance of a creature such as yourself but that would be a poor and undignified imposture. Will this suffice?"

David Starr watched the glimmer appear in the air

before him. It was a soft streak of blue-green light about seven feet high and a foot wide.

He said calmly, "That is quite sufficient."

The deep voice said, "Good! And now let me explain who I am. I am the Administrator of ——— ———. The report of the capture of a live specimen of the new surface life came to me as a matter of course. I will examine your mind."

The office of the new being had been a jumble of sound, and nothing more, to David, but he had caught the unmistakable sense of dignity and responsibility that accompanied it. Nevertheless he said firmly, "I would much prefer that you remained outside my mind."

"Your modesty," said the deep voice, "is quite understandable and praiseworthy. I should explain that my inspection would be confined most carefully to the outer fringes only. I would avoid very scrupulously any intrusion on your inner privacy."

David tensed his muscles uselessly. For long minutes there was nothing. Even the illusive feathery touch upon his mind, that had been present when the owner of the feminine voice had probed it, was absent from this new and more experienced inspection. And yet David was aware, without knowing how he could possibly be aware, of the compartments of his mind being delicately opened, then closed, without pain or disturbance.

The deep voice said, "I thank you. You will be released very shortly and returned to the surface."

David said defiantly, "What have you found in my mind?"

"Enough to pity your fellows. We of the Inner Life were once like yourselves so we have some comprehension of it. Your people are out of balance with the universe. You have a questioning mind that seeks to understand what it dimly senses, without possessing the truer, deeper senses that alone can reveal reality to you. In your futile seeking after the shadows that encompass you, you drive through space to the outermost limits of the Galaxy. It is as I have said; —— has named you well. You are a race of Space Rangers indeed.

"Yet of what use is your ranging? The true victory is within. To understand the material universe, you must first become divorced from it as we are. We have turned away from the stars and toward ourselves. We have retreated to the caverns of our one world and abandoned our bodies. With us there is no longer death, except when a mind would rest; or birth, except when a mind gone to rest must be replaced."

David said, "Yet you are not all-sufficient to yourselves. Some of you suffer from curiosity. The being who spoke to me before wished to know of Earth."

"—— is recently born. Her days are not equal to a hundred revolutions of the planet about the sun. Her control of thought patterns is imperfect. We who are mature can easily conceive all the various designs into which your Earth history could have been woven. Few of them would be comprehensible to yourself, and not in an infinity of years could we have exhausted the thoughts possible in the consideration of your one world, and each thought would have been as fascinating and stimulating as the one thought which happens to represent reality. In time —— will learn that this is so."

"Yet you yourself take the trouble to examine my mind."

"In order that I may make certain of that which I previously merely suspected. Your race has the capacity for growth. Under the best circumstances a million revolutions of our planet—a moment in the life of the Galaxy —may see it achieve the Inner Life. That would be good.

My race would have a companion in eternity and companionship would benefit us mutually."

"You say we *may* achieve it," said David cautiously.

"Your species have certain tendencies my people never had. From your mind I can see easily that there are tendencies against the welfare of the whole."

"If you speak of such things as crime and war, then see in my mind that the vast majority of humans fights the anti-social tendencies and that though our progress against them is slow, it is certain."

"I see that. I see more. I see that you yourself are eager for the welfare of the whole. You have a strong and healthy mind, the essence of which I would not be sorry to see made into one of ours. I would like to help you in your strivings."

"How?" demanded David.

"Your mind is full of suspicion again. Relieve your tension. My help would not be through personal interference in the activities of your people, I assure you. Such interference would be incomprehensible to yourselves and undignified for myself. Let me suggest instead the two inadequacies which you are most aware of in yourself.

"First, since you are composed of unstable ingredients, you are a creature of no permanence. Not only will you decompose and dissolve in a few revolutions of the planet, but if before then you are subjected to any of a thousand different stresses, you will die. Secondly, you feel that you can work best in secrecy, yet not long ago a fellow creature recognized your true identity although you had pretended to a different identity altogether. Is what I have said true?"

David said, "It is true. But what can you do about it?"

The deep voice said, "It is already done and in your hand."

And there was a soft-textured something in David

Starr's hand. His fingers almost let it drop before they realized they were holding it. It was a nearly weightless strip of—— Well, of what?

The deep voice answered the unspoken thought placidly. "It is neither gauze, nor fiber, nor plastic, nor metal. It is not matter at all as your mind understands matter. It is ——. Put it over your eyes."

David did as he was told, and it sprang from his hands as though it had a primitive life of its own, folding softly and warmly against every fold of structure of his forehead, eyes, and nose; yet it did not prevent him from breathing or from blinking his eyes.

"What has been accomplished?" he asked.

Before the words were out of his mouth there was a mirror before him, manufactured out of energy as silently and quickly as thought itself. In it he could see himself but dimly. His farmboy costume, from hip boots to wide lapels, appeared out of focus through a shadowy mist that changed continuously, as though it were a thin smoke that drifted yet never vanished. From his upper lip to the top of his head all was lost in a shimmer of light that blazed without blinding and through which nothing could be seen. As he stared, the mirror vanished, returning to the store of energy from which it had been momentarily withdrawn.

David asked wonderingly, "Is that how I would appear to others?"

"Yes, if those others had only the sensory equipment you yourself have."

"Yet I can see perfectly. That means that light rays enter the shield. Why may they not leave then and reveal my face?"

"They do leave, as you say, but they are changed in the passage and reveal only what you see in the mirror. To explain that properly, I must use concepts lacking in your mind's understanding."

"And the rest?" David's hands moved slowly over the smoke that encircled him. He felt nothing.

The deep voice again answered the voiceless thought. "*You* feel nothing. Yet what appears to you as smoke is a barrier which is resistant to short-wave radiation and impassable to material objects of larger than molecular size."

"You mean it is a personal force-shield?"

"That is a crude description, yes."

David said, "Great Galaxy, it's impossible! It has been definitely proven that no force-field small enough to protect a man from radiation and from material inertia can be generated by any machine capable of being carried by a man."

"And so it is to any science of which your fellows are capable of evolving. But the mask you wear is not a power source. It is instead a storage device of energy which, for instance, can be derived from a few moments' exposure to a sun radiating as strongly as ours is from the distance of this planet. It is, further, a mechanism for releasing that energy at mental demand. Since your own mind is incapable of controlling the power, it has been adjusted to the characteristics of your mind and will operate automatically as needed. Remove the mask now."

David lifted his hand to his eyes and, again responsive to his will, the mask fell away and was only a strip of gauze in his hand.

The deep voice spoke for a last time. "And now you must leave us, Space Ranger."

And as gently as can be imagined, consciousness left David Starr.

Nor was there any transition in his return to consciousness. It came back in its entirety. There wasn't even a moment's uncertainty as to his whereabouts; none of the "Where am I?" attitude.

He knew with surety that he was standing on his good two legs upon the surface of Mars; that he was wearing the nosepiece again and breathing through it; that behind him was the exact place at the lip of the fissure where he had thrust the rope ladder's anchor for the beginning of the descent; that to his left, half-hidden among the rocks, was the scooter which Bigman had left behind.

He even knew the exact manner in which he had been returned to the surface. It was not memory; it was information deliberately inserted in his mind, probably as a final device to impress him with the power of the Martians over matter-energy interconversions. They had dissolved a tunnel to the surface for him. They had lifted him against gravity at almost rocket speed, turning the solid rock to energy before him and congealing the energy to rock once more behind him, until he was standing on the planet's outer skin once more.

There were even words in his mind that he had never consciously heard. They were in the feminine voice of the caverns, and the words were simply these: "Have no fear, Space Ranger!"

He stepped forward and was aware that the warm, Earth-like surroundings that had been prepared for him in the cavern below no longer existed. He felt the cold the more for the contrast and the wind was stronger than any he had felt yet on Mars. The sun was low in the east as it had been when he first descended the fissure. Was that the previous dawn? He had no way of judging the passage of time during his unconscious intervals, but he felt certain his descent had not been more than two dawns before anyway.

There was a difference to the sky. It seemed bluer and the sun was redder. David frowned thoughtfully for a mo-

ment, then shrugged. He was becoming accustomed to
the Martian landscape, that was all. It was beginning to
seem more familiar and, through habit, he was interpret-
ing it in the old Earthly patterns.

Meanwhile it would be better to begin the return to
the farm dome immediately. The scooter was by no means
so quick as a sand-car nor as comfortable. The less time
spent on it the better.

He took approximate sightings among the rock formations and felt like an old hand because of it. The farmboys
found their way across what seemed trackless desert by
just this method. They would sight along a rock that
"looked like a watermelon on a hat," proceed in that direction until level with one that "looked like a spaceship
with two off-center jets" and head between it and a farther rock that "looked like a box with its top stove in." It
was a crude method but it required no instruments other
than a retentive memory and a picturesque imagination,
and the farmboys had those in plenty.

David was following the route Bigman had recom-
mended for speediest return with the least chance of going wrong among the less spectacular formations. The
scooter jounced along, leaping crazily when it struck
ridges and kicking up the dust when it turned. David rode
with it, digging his heels firmly into the sockets provided
for them and holding a metal steering leash tightly in each
hand. He made no effort to cut his speed. Even if the
vehicle turned over, there would be little chance for
much harm to himself under Martian gravity.

It was another consideration that stopped him: the
queer taste in his mouth and the itch along the side of his
jawbone and down the line of his backbone. There was a
faint grittiness in his mouth, and he looked back with
distaste at the plume of dust that jetted out behind him

like rocket exhaust. Strange that it should work its way forward and around him to fill his mouth as it did.

Forward and around! *Great Galaxy!* The thought that came to him at that moment clamped a cold, stifling hand upon his heart and throat.

He slowed the scooter and headed for a rocky ridge where it could stir up no dust. There he stopped it and waited for the air to grow clear. But it didn't. His tongue worked about, tasting the inside of his mouth and shrinking from the increasing roughness that came of fine grit. He looked at the redder sun and bluer sky with new understanding. It was the general dust in the air that was scattering more light, taking the blue from the sun and adding it to the sky in general. His lips were growing dry and the itching was spreading.

There was no longer doubt about it, and with a grim intensity of purpose he flung himself upon his scooter and dashed at top speed across the rocks, gravel, and dust.

Dust!

Dust!

Even on Earth men knew intimately of the Martian dust storm, which resembled only in sound the sandstorm of the Earthly deserts. It was the deadliest storm known to the inhabited Solar System. No man, caught as David Starr was now, without a sand-car as protection, miles from the nearest shelter, had ever, in all the history of Mars, survived a dust storm. Men had rolled in death throes within fifty feet of a dome, unable to make the distance while observers within neither dared nor could sally to the rescue without a sand-car.

David Starr knew that only minutes separated him from the same agonizing death. Already the dust was creeping remorselessly between his nosepiece and the skin of his face. He could feel it in his watering, blinking eyes.

12

The Missing Piece

The nature of the Martian dust storm is not well understood. Like Earth's Moon, the surface of Mars is, to a large extent, covered by fine dust. Unlike the Moon, Mars possesses an atmosphere capable of stirring up that dust. Usually this is not a serious matter. The Martian atmosphere is thin and winds are not long-sustained.

But occasionally, for reasons unknown, though possibly connected with electron bombardments from space, the dust becomes electrically charged and each particle repels its neighbors. Even without wind they would tend to lift upward. Each step would raise a cloud that would refuse to settle, but would drift and wisp out through the air.

When to this a wind is added, a fully developed dust storm might be said to exist. The dust is never thick enough to obscure vision; that isn't its danger. It is rather the pervasiveness of the dust that kills.

The dust particles are extremely fine and penetrate everywhere. Clothes cannot keep them out; the shelter of a rocky ledge means nothing; even the nosepiece with its broad gasket fitting against the face is helpless to prevent the individual particle from working its way through.

At the height of a storm two minutes would suffice to arouse an unbearable itching, five minutes would virtually blind a man, and fifteen minutes would kill him. Even a mild storm, so gentle that it may not even be noticed by the people exposed, is sufficient to redden exposed skin in what are called dust burns.

David Starr knew all this and more. He knew that his own skin was reddening. He was coughing without its having any effect on clearing his caking throat. He had tried clamping his mouth shut, blowing his breath out during exhalations through the smallest opening he could manage. It didn't help. The dust crept in, working its way past his lips. The scooter was jerking irregularly now as the dust did to its motor what it was doing to David.

His eyes were swollen nearly closed now. The tears that streamed out were accumulating against the gasket at the bottom of the nosepiece and were fogging the eyepieces, through which he could see nothing anyway.

Nothing could stop those tiny dust particles but the elaborately machined seams of a dome or a sand-car. Nothing.

Nothing?

Through the maddening itch and the racking cough he was thinking desperately of the Martians. Would they have known that a dust storm was brewing? *Could* they have? Would they have sent him to the surface if they had known? From his mind they must have gleaned the information that he had only a scooter to carry him back to the dome. They might have as easily transported him to the surface just outside the farm dome, or, for that matter, even inside the dome.

They *must* have known conditions were right for a dust storm. He remembered how the being with the deep voice had been so abrupt in his decision to return David to the surface, as though he hurried in order that time might be allowed for David to be caught in the storm.

And yet the last words of the feminine voice, the words he had not consciously heard and which, therefore, he was certain had been inserted in his mind while he was being borne through rock to the surface, were: "Have no fear, Space Ranger."

Even as he thought all this he knew the answer. One hand was fumbling in his pocket, the other at his nosepiece. As the nosepiece lifted off, the partially protected nose and eyes received a fresh surge of dust, burning and irritating.

He had the irresistible desire to sneeze, but fought it back. The involuntary intake of breath would fill his lungs with quantities of the dust. That in itself might be fatal.

But he was bringing up the strip of gauze he had taken from his pocket, letting it wrap about his eyes and nose, and then over it he slapped the nosepiece again.

Only then did he sneeze. It meant he drew in vast quantities of Mars's useless atmospheric gases, but no dust was coming. He followed that by force-breathing, gasping in as much oxygen as he could and puffing it out, flinging the dust of his mouth away; alternating that with deliberate inhalations through the mouth to prevent any oncoming of oxygen drunkenness.

Gradually, as the tears washed the dust out of his eyes and no new dust entered, he found he could see again. His limbs and body were obscured by the smokiness of the force-shield that surrounded him, and he knew the upper part of his head to be invisible in the glow of his mask.

Air molecules could penetrate the shield freely, but, small though they were, the dust particles were large enough to be stopped. David could see the process with the naked eye. As each dust particle struck the shield, it was halted and the energy of its motion converted into light, so that at its point of attempted penetration a tiny sparkle showed. David found his body an ocean of such sparkles crowding one another, all the brighter as the Martian sun, red and smokily dim through the dust, allowed the ground below to remain in semi-darkness.

David slapped and brushed at his clothing. Dust clouds arose, too fine to see even if the cloudiness of the shield had not prevented sight in any case. The dust left but could not return. Gradually he became almost clear of the particles. He looked dubiously at the scooter and attempted to start its motor. He was rewarded only by a short, grating noise and then silence. It was to be expected. Unlike the sand-cars, scooters did not, *could* not, have enclosed motors.

He would have to walk. The thought was not a particularly frightening one. The farm dome was little more than two miles away and he had plenty of oxygen. His cylinders were full. The Martians had seen to that before sending him back.

He thought he understood them now. They *did* know the dust storm was coming. They might even have helped it along. It would be strange if, with their long experience with Martian weather and their advanced science, they had not learned the fundamental causes and mechanisms of dust storms. But in sending him out to face the storm, they knew he had the perfect defense in his pocket. They had not warned him of either the ordeal that awaited him or of the defense he carried. It made sense. If he were the man who deserved the gift of the force-shield, he would, or should, think of it himself. If he did not, he was the wrong man for the job.

David smiled grimly even as he winced at the touch of his clothing against inflamed skin as he stretched his legs across the Martian terrain. The Martians were coldly unemotional in risking his life, but he could almost sympathize with them. He had thought quickly enough to save himself, but he denied himself any pride in that. He should have thought of the mask much sooner.

The force-shield that surrounded him was making it easier to travel. He noted that the shield covered the soles of his boots so that they never made contact with the Martian surface but came to rest some quarter inch above it. The repulsion between himself and the planet was an elastic one, as though he were on many steel springs. That, combined with the low gravity, enabled him to devour the distance between himself and the dome in swinging giant strides.

He was in a hurry. More than anything else at the moment he felt the need of a hot bath.

By the time David reached one of the outer locks of the farm dome the worst of the storm was over and the light flashes on his force-shield had thinned to occasional sparks. It was safe to remove the mask from his eyes.

When the locks had opened for him, there were first of all stares, and then cries, as the farmboys on duty swarmed about him.

"Jumping Jupiter, it's Williams!"

"Where've you been, boy?"

"What happened?"

And above the confused cries and simultaneous questioning there came the shrill cry, "How did you get through the dust storm?"

The question penetrated, and there was a short silence.

Someone said, "Look at his face. It's like a peeled tomato."

That was an exaggeration, but there was enough truth to it to impress all who were there. Hands were yanking at his collar which had been tightly bound about his neck in the fight against the Martian cold. They shuffled him into a seat and put in a call for Hennes.

Hennes arrived in ten minutes, hopping off a scooter and approaching with a look that was compounded of annoyance and anger. There were no visible signs of any relief at the safe return of a man in his employ.

He barked, "What's this all about, Williams?"

David lifted his eyes and said coolly, "I was lost."

"Oh, is that what you call it? Gone for two days and you were just lost. How did you manage it?"

"I thought I'd take a walk and I walked too far."

"You thought you needed a breath of air, so you've been walking through two Martian nights? Do you expect me to believe that?"

"Are any sand-cars missing?"

One of the farmboys interposed hastily as Hennes reddened further. "He's knocked out, Mr. Hennes. He was out in the dust storm."

Hennes said, "Don't be a fool. If he were out in the dust storm, he wouldn't be sitting here alive."

"Well, I know," the farmboy said, "but look at him."

Hennes looked at him. The redness of his exposed neck and shoulders was a fact that could not be easily argued away.

He said, "Were you in the storm?"

"I'm afraid so," said David.

"How did you get through?"

"There was a man," said David. "A man in smoke and light. The dust didn't bother him. He called himself the Space Ranger."

The men were gathering close. Hennes turned on them furiously, his plump face working.

"Get the Space out of here!" he yelled. "Back to your work. And you, Jonnitel, get a sand-car out here."

It was nearly an hour before the hot bath he craved was allowed David. Hennes permitted no one else to approach him. Over and over again, as he paced the floor of his private office, he would stop in midstride, whirl in sudden fury, and demand of David, "What about this Space Ranger? Where did you meet him? What did he say? What did he do? What's this smoke and light you speak of?"

To all of which David would only shake his head slightly and say, "I took a walk. I got lost. A man calling himself the Space Ranger brought me back."

Hennes gave up eventually. The dome doctor took charge. David got his hot bath. His body was anointed with creams and injected with the proper hormones. He could not avoid the injection of Soporite as well. He was asleep almost before the needle was withdrawn.

He woke to find himself between clean, cool sheets in the sick bay. The reddening of the skin had subsided considerably. They would be at him again, he knew, but he would have to fight them off but a little while longer.

He was sure he had the answer to the food-poisoning mystery now; almost the whole answer. He needed only a missing piece or two, and, of course, legal proof.

He heard the light footstep beyond the head of his bed and stiffened slightly. Was it going to begin again so soon? But it was only Benson who moved into his line of vision. Benson, with his plump lips pursed, his thin hair in disarray, his whole face a picture of worry. He carried something that looked like an old-fashioned clumsy gun.

He said, "Williams, are you awake?"

David said, "You see I am."

Benson passed the back of his hand across a perspiring forehead. "They don't know I'm here. I shouldn't be, I suppose."

"Why not?"

"Hennes is convinced you're involved with this food poisoning. He's been raving to Makian and myself about it. He claims you've been out somewhere and have nothing to say about it now other than ridiculous stories. Despite anything I can do, I'm afraid you're in terrible trouble."

"Despite anything you can do? You don't believe Hennes's theory about my complicity in all this?"

Benson leaned forward, and David could feel his breath warm on his face as he whispered, "No, I don't. I don't because I think your story is true. That's why I've come here. I must ask you about this creature you speak of, the one you claim was covered with smoke and light. Are you sure it wasn't a hallucination, Williams?"

"I saw him," said David.

"How do you know he was human? Did he speak English?"

"He didn't speak, but he was shaped like a human." David's eyes fastened upon Benson. "Do you think it was a Martian?"

"Ah"—Benson's lips drew back in a spasmodic smile —"you remember my theory. Yes, I think it was a Martian. Think, man, *think!* They're coming out in the open now and every piece of information may be vital. We have so little time."

"Why so little time?" David raised himself to one elbow.

"Of course you don't know what's happened since you've been gone, but frankly, Williams, we are all of us in despair now." He held up the gun-like affair in his hand and said bitterly, "Do you know what this is?"

"I've seen you with it before."

"It's my sampling harpoon; it's my own invention. I take it with me when I'm at the storage bins in the city. It shoots a little hollow pellet attached to it by a metal-mesh cord into a bin of, let us say, grain. At a certain time after shooting an opening appears in the front of the pellet long enough to allow the hollow within to become packed with grain. After that the pellet closes again. I drag it back and empty out the random sample it has accumulated. By varying the time after shooting in which the pellet opens, samples can be taken at various depths in the bin."

David said, "That's ingenious, but why are you carrying it now?"

"Because I'm wondering if I oughtn't to throw it into the disposal unit after I leave you. It was my only weapon for fighting the poisoners. It has done me no good so far, and can certainly do me no good in the future."

"What has happened?" David seized the other's shoulder and gripped it hard. "Tell me."

Benson winced at the pain. He said, "Every member of the farming syndicates has received a new letter from whoever is behind the poisoning. There's no doubt that the letters and the poisonings are caused by the same men, or rather, entities. The letters admit it now."

"What do they say?"

Benson shrugged. "What difference do the details make? What it amounts to is a demand for complete surrender on our part or the food-poisoning attacks will be multiplied a thousandfold. I believe it can and will be done, and if that happens, Earth and Mars, the whole system, in fact, will panic."

He rose to his feet. "I've told Makian and Hennes that I believe you, that your Space Ranger is the clue to the whole thing, but they won't believe me. Hennes, I think, even suspects that I'm in it with you."

He seemed absorbed in his own wrongs.

David said, "How long do we have Benson?"

"Two days. No, that was yesterday. We have thirty-six hours now."

Thirty-six hours!

David would have to work quickly. Very quickly. But maybe there would yet be time. Without knowing it Benson had given him the missing piece to the mystery.

13

The Council Takes Over

Benson left some ten minutes later. Nothing that David told him satisfied him with regard to his theories connecting Martians and poisoning, and his uneasiness grew rapidly.

He said, "I don't want Hennes catching me. We've had—words."

"What about Makian? He's on our side, isn't he?"

"I don't know. He stands to be ruined by day after tomorrow. I don't think he has enough spine left to stand up to the fellow. Look, I'd better go. If you think of anything, anything at all, get it to me somehow, will you?"

He held out a hand. David took it briefly, and then Benson was gone.

David sat up in bed. His own uneasiness had grown since he had awakened. His clothes were thrown over a chair at the other end of the room. His boots stood upright by the side of the bed. He had not dared inspect them in Benson's presence; had scarcely dared look at them.

Perhaps, he thought pessimistically, they had not tampered with them. A farmboy's hip boots are inviolate.

Stealing from a farmboy's hip boots, next to stealing his sand-car in the open desert, was the unforgivable crime. Even in death, a farmboy's boots were buried with him, with the contents unremoved.

David groped inside the inner pocket of each boot in turn, and his fingers met nothingness. There had been a handkerchief in one, a few odd coins in the other. Undoubtedly they had gone through his clothing; he had expected that. But apparently they had not drawn the line at his boots. He held his breath as his arm dived into the recesses of one boot. The soft leather reached to his armpit and crumpled down as his fingers stretched out to the toes. A surge of pure gladness filled him as he felt the soft gauze-like material of the Martian mask.

He had hidden it there on general principles before the bath, but he had not anticipated the Soporite. It was luck, purely, that they had not searched the toes of his boots. He would have to be more careful henceforward.

He put the mask into a boot pocket and clipped it shut. He picked up the boots; they had been polished while he slept, which was good of someone, and showed the almost instinctive respect which the farmboy had for boots, anyone's boots.

His clothes had been put through the Refresher Spray as well. The shining plastic fibers of which they were composed had a brand-new smell about them. The pockets were all empty, of course, but underneath the chair all the contents were in a careless heap. He sorted them out. Nothing seemed to be missing. Even the handkerchief and coins from his boot pockets were there.

He put on underclothes and socks, the one-piece overall, and then the boots. He was buckling his belt when a brown-bearded farmboy stepped in.

David looked up. He said coldly, "What do you want, Zukis?"

The farmboy said, "Where do you think you're going, Earthie?" His little eyes were glaring viciously, and to David the other's expression was much the same as it had been the first day he had laid eyes on him. David could recall Hennes's sand-car outside the Farm Employment Office, himself just settling into the seat, and the bearded angry face glowering at him, while a weapon fired before he could move to defend himself.

"Nowhere," said David, "that I need ask your permission."

"That so? You're wrong, mister, because you're staying right here. Hennes's orders." Zukis blocked the door with his body. Two blasters were conspicuously displayed at either side of his drooping belt.

Zukis waited. Then, his greasy beard splitting in two as he smiled yellowly, he said, "Think maybe you've changed your mind, Earthie?"

"Maybe," said David. He added, "Someone got in to see me just now. How come? Weren't you watching?"

"Shut up," snarled Zukis.

"Or were you paid off to look the other way for a while? Hennes might not like that."

Zukis spat, missing David's boots by half an inch.

David said, "You want to toss out your blasters and try that again?"

Zukis said, "Just watch out if you want any feeding, Earthie."

He closed and locked the door behind him as he left. A few minutes passed and there was the sound of clattering metal against it as it opened again. Zukis carried a tray. There was the yellow of squash on it and the green of something leafy.

"Vegetable salad," said Zukis. "Good enough for you."

A blackened thumb showed over one end of the tray.

The other end balanced upon the back of his wrist so that
the farmboy's hand was not visible.

David straightened, leaping to one side, bending his
legs under him and bringing them down upon the mattress of the bed. Zukis, caught by surprise, turned in
alarm, but David, using the springs of the mattress as
extra leverage, launched into the air.

He collided heavily with the farmboy, brought down
one hand flatly on the tray, ripping it out of the other's
grasp and hurling it to the ground while twining his other
hand in the farmboy's beard.

Zukis dropped, yelling hoarsely. David's booted foot
came down on the farmboy's hand, the one that had been
hidden under the tray. The other's yell became an ago-
nized scream as the smashed fingers flew open, releasing
the cocked blaster they had been holding.

David's hand whipped away from the beard and
caught the other's unharmed wrist as it groped for the
second blaster. He brought it up roughly, across the
prone chest, under the head and out again. He pulled.

"Quiet," he said, "or I'll tear your arm loose from its
socket."

Zukis subsided, his eyes rolling, his breath puffing out
wetly. He said, "What are you after?"

"Why were you hiding the blaster under the tray?"

"I had to protect myself, didn't I? In case you jumped
me while my hands were full of tray?"

"Then why didn't you send someone else with the tray
and cover him?"

"I didn't think of that," whined Zukis.

David tightened pressure a bit and Zukis's mouth
twisted in agony. "Suppose you tell the truth, Zukis."

"I—I was going to kill you."

"And what would you have told Makian?"

"You were—trying to escape."

"Was that your own idea?"

"No. It was Hennes's. Get Hennes. I'm just following orders."

David released him. He picked up one blaster and flicked the other out of its holster. "Get up."

Zukis rolled over on one side. He groaned as he tried to lift his weight on a mashed right hand and nearly torn left shoulder.

"What are you going to do? You wouldn't shoot an unarmed man, would you?"

"Wouldn't you?" asked David.

A new voice broke in. "Drop those guns, Williams," it said crisply.

David moved his head quickly. Hennes was in the doorway, blaster leveled. Behind him was Makian, face gray and etched with lines. Hennes's eyes showed his intentions plainly enough and his blaster was ready.

David dropped the blasters he had just torn from Zukis.

"Kick them over," said Hennes.

David did so.

"Now. What happened?"

David said, "You know what happened. Zukis tried a little assassination at your orders and I didn't sit still and take it."

Zukis was gabbling. "No, sir, Mr. Hennes. No, sir. It was no such thing. I was bringing in his lunch when he jumped me. My hands were full of tray; I had no chance to defend myself."

"Shut up," said Hennes contemptuously. "We'll have a talk about that later. Get out of here and be back with a couple of pinions in less than no time."

Zukis scrambled out.

Makian said mildly, "Why the pinions, Hennes?"

"Because this man is a dangerous impostor, Mr.

Makian. You remember I brought him in because he seemed to know something about the food poisoning."

"Yes. Yes, of course."

"He told us a story about a younger sister being poisoned by Martian jam, remember? I checked on that. There haven't been too many deaths by poisoning that have reached the authorities the way this man claimed his sister's death had. Less than two hundred and fifty, in fact. It was easy to check them all and I had that done. None on record involved a twelve-year-old girl, with a brother of Williams' age, who died over a jar of jam."

Makian was startled. "How long have you known this, Hennes?"

"Almost since he came here. But I let it go. I wanted to see what he was after. I set Griswold to watching him——"

"To trying to kill me, you mean," interrupted David.

"Yes, you would say that, considering that you killed him because he was fool enough to let you suspect him." He turned back to Makian. "Then he managed to wiggle himself in with that soft-headed sap, Benson, where he could keep close check on our progress in investigating the poisoning. Then, as the last straw, he slipped out of the dome three nights ago for a reason he won't explain. You want to know why? He was reporting to the men who hired him—the ones who are behind all this. It's more than just a coincidence that the ultimatum came while he was gone."

"And where were you?" demanded David suddenly. "Did you stop keeping tabs on me after Griswold died? If you knew I was gone on the kind of deal you suspected, why wasn't a party sent out after me?"

Makian looked puzzled, and began, "Well——"

But David interrupted. "Let me finish, Mr. Makian. I think that maybe Hennes wasn't in the dome the night I left and even the day and night after I left. Where were you, Hennes?"

Hennes stepped forward, his mouth twisting. David's cupped hand was near his face. He did not believe Hennes would shoot, but he was ready to use the shield-mask if he had to.

Makian placed a nervous hand on Hennes's shoulder. "I suggest we leave him for the Council."

David said quickly, "What is this about the Council?"

"None of your business," snarled Hennes.

Zukis was back with the pinions. They were flexible plastic rods that could be bent in any way and then frozen in position. They were infinitely stronger than ropes or even metal handcuffs.

"Hold out your hands," ordered Hennes.

David did so without a word. The pinion was wrapped twice about his wrists. Zukis, leering, drew them savagely tight then drew out the pin, which action resulted in an automatic molecular rearrangement that hardened the plastic. The energy developed in that rearrangement made the plastic warm to the touch. Another pinion went about David's ankles.

David sat quietly down upon the bed. In one hand he still had the shield-mask. Makian's remark about the Council was proof enough to David that he would not remain pinioned long. Meanwhile he was content to allow matters to develop further.

He said again, "What's this about the Council?"

But he need not have asked. There was a yell from outside, and a catapulting figure hurled itself through the door with the cry of, "Where's Williams?"

It was Bigman himself, as large as life, which wasn't very large. He was paying no attention to anything but David's seated figure. He was speaking rapidly and breathlessly. "I didn't hear you were through a dust storm till I landed inside the dome. Sizzling Ceres, you must have been fried. How did you get through it? I——I——"

He noticed David's position for the first time, and turned furiously. "Who in Space has the boy tied up like this?"

Hennes had caught his breath by now. One of his hands shot out and caught Bigman's overall collar in a brutal grip that lifted his slight body off the floor. "I told you what would happen, slug, if I caught you here again."

Bigman yelled, "Let go, you pulp-mouth jerk! I've got a right in here. I give you a second and a half to let me go or you'll answer to the Council of Science."

Makian said, "For Mars' sake, Hennes, let him go."

Hennes let him drop. "Get out of here."

"Not on your life. I'm an accredited employee of the Council. I came here with Dr. Silvers. Ask him."

He nodded at the tall, thin man just outside the door. His name suited him. His hair was silver-white and he had a mustache of the same shade.

"If you'll pardon me," said Dr. Silvers, "I would like to take charge of matters. The government at International City on Earth has declared a state of System Emergency and all the farms will be under the control of the Council of Science henceforward. I have been assigned to take over the Makian Farms."

"I expected something like this," muttered Makian unhappily.

"Remove this man's pinions," ordered Dr. Silvers.

Hennes said, "He's dangerous."

"I will take full responsibility."

Bigman jumped and clicked his heels. "On your way, Hennes."

Hennes paled in anger, but no words came.

· · ·

Three hours had passed when Dr. Silvers met Makian and Hennes again in Makian's private quarters.

He said, "I'll want to go over all the production records of this farm for the last six months. I will have to see your Dr. Benson with regard to whatever advances he has made in connection with solving this food-poisoning problem. We have six weeks to break this matter. No more."

"Six weeks," exploded Hennes. "You mean one day."

"No, sir. If we haven't the answer by the time the ultimatum expires, all exports of food from Mars will be stopped. We will not give in while a single chance remains."

"By Space," said Hennes. "Earth will starve."

"Not for six weeks," said Dr. Silvers. "Food supplies will last that long, with rationing."

"There'll be panic and rioting," said Hennes.

"True," said Dr. Silvers grimly. "It will be most unpleasant."

"You'll ruin the farm syndicates," groaned Makian.

"It will be ruined anyway. Now, I intend to see Dr. Benson this evening. We will have a four-way conference tomorrow at noon. Tomorrow midnight, if nothing breaks anywhere on Mars or at the Moon's Central Laboratories, the embargo goes into effect and arrangements will be made for an all-Mars conference of the various syndicate members."

"Why?" asked Hennes.

"Because," said Dr. Silvers, "there is reason to think that whoever is behind this mad crime must be connected with the farms closely. They know too much about the farms for any other conclusion to be arrived at."

"What about Williams?"

"I've questioned him. He sticks to his story, which is,

I'll admit, queer enough. I've sent him to the city, where
he'll be questioned further; under hypnosis, if necessary."

The door signal flashed.

Dr. Silvers said, "Open the door, Mr. Makian."

Makian did so, as though he were not owner of one of
the largest farms on Mars and, by virtue of that fact, one
of the richest and most powerful men in the Solar System.

Bigman stepped in. He looked at Hennes challeng-
ingly. He said, "Williams is on a sand-car heading back for
the city under guard."

"Good," said Dr. Silvers, his thin lips set tightly.

A mile outside the farm dome the sand-car stopped.
David Starr, nosepiece in place, stepped out. He waved to
the driver, who leaned out and said, "Remember! Lock 7!
We'll have one of our men there to let you in."

David smiled and nodded. He watched the sand-car
continue its trip toward the city and then turned back on
foot to the farm dome.

The men of the Council co-operated, of course. They
had helped him in his desire to leave openly and to return
secretly, but none of them, not even Dr. Silvers, knew the
purpose of his request.

He had the pieces to the puzzle, but he still needed
the proof.

14

"I Am the Space Ranger!"

Hennes entered his bedroom in a haze compounded equally of weariness and anger. The weariness was simple. It was nearing 3 A.M. He had not had too much rest the last two nights or, for that matter, much relief of tension in the last six months. Yet he had felt it necessary to sit through the session this Dr. Silvers of the Council had had with Benson.

Dr. Silvers had not liked that, and that accounted for one bit of the anger that drenched and drowned him. Dr. Silvers! An old incompetent who came bustling down from the city thinking he could get to the bottom of the trouble in a day and a night when all the science of Earth and Mars had been exerting itself for months to no avail. And Hennes was angry at Makian as well for becoming as limp as well-oiled boots and nothing more than the simple lackey of the white-headed fool. Makian! Two decades ago he had been almost a legend as the toughest owner of the toughest farm on Mars.

There was Benson too, and his interference with Hennes's plans for settling the interfering greenhorn, this Williams, in the quickest and easiest way. And Griswold and

Zukis, who were too stupid to carry through the necessary steps that would have won over the weakness of Makian and the sentimentality of Benson.

He pondered briefly the advisability of a Soporite pill. On this night he wanted rest for the necessary keenness of the next day and yet his anger might keep sleep away.

He shook his head. No. He could not risk drugged helplessness in the event of some crucial turn of events in the night.

He compromised by throwing the toggle switch that magnetically bound the door in place. He even tested the door briefly to make sure the electromagnetic circuits worked. Personal doors, in the totally masculine and informal life of a farm dome, were so infrequently locked that it was not uncommon to have insulation wear through, wires fall loose, without anyone being the wiser over the years. His own door had not been locked, to his knowledge, since he had first taken the job.

The circuit was in order. The door did not even tremble as he pulled at it. So much for that.

He sighed heavily, sat down upon the bed, and removed his boots, first one, then the other. He rubbed his feet wearily, sighed again, then stiffened; stiffened so suddenly that he shot off the bed without really being aware of moving.

His stare was one of complete bewilderment. It couldn't be. *It couldn't be!* It would mean that William's foolish story was true. It would mean that Benson's ridiculous mouthings about Martians might, after all, turn out to be——

No, he refused to believe that. It would be easier to believe that his lack-sleep mind was having a private joke.

Yet the dark of the room was alight with the cold blue-white brilliance that carried no glare with it. By it he could see the bed, the walls, the chair, the dresser, even his boots, standing where he had just placed them. And he could see the man creature with only a blaze of light where a head ought to be and no distinct feature elsewhere; rather a kind of smoke instead.

He felt the wall against his back. He had not been conscious of his retreat backward.

The object spoke, and the words were hollow and booming as though they carried an echo with them.

The object said, "I am the Space Ranger!"

Hennes drew himself up. First surprise over, he forced himself into calmness. In a steady voice he said, "What do you want?"

The Space Ranger did not move or speak, and Hennes found his eyes fastened upon the apparition.

The foreman waited, his chest pumping, and still the thing of smoke and light did not move. It might have been a robot geared to make the one statement of identity. For a moment Hennes wondered if that might be the case, and surrendered the thought as soon as it was born. He was standing next to the chest of drawers, and not all his wonder allowed him to forget that fact. Slowly his hand was moving.

In the light of the thing itself his motion was not invisible, but it paid no attention. Hennes's hand was resting lightly on the surface of the bureau in a pretense of innocent gesture. The robot, Martian, man, whatever it was, Hennes thought, would not know the secret of the bureau. It had hidden in the room, waiting, but it had not searched the room. Or if it had done so, it had been a most skillful job, since even now Hennes's flicking eye could note no single abnormal thing about the room; nothing misplaced; nothing where it should not be, except for the Space Ranger itself.

His fingers touched a little notch in the wood. It was a common mechanism and few farm managers on Mars lacked one. In a way it was old-fashioned, as old-fashioned as the imported wooden bureau itself, a tradition dating back to the lawless old days of the farming pioneers, but tradition dies hard. The little notch moved slightly under his fingernail and a panel in the side of the chest dropped outward. Hennes was ready for it, and the hand was a blur of motion toward the blaster which the moving panel had revealed.

He held the blaster now, aimed dead center, and in all that time the creature had not moved. What passed for arms dangled emptily.

Hennes found confidence sweeping back. Robot, Martian, or man, the object could not withstand a blaster. It was a small weapon, and the projectile it hurled was almost contemptible in size. The old-fashioned "guns" of ancient days carried metal slugs that were rocks in comparison. But the small projectile of the blaster was far more deadly. Once set in motion, anything that stopped it tripped a tiny atomic trigger that converted a sub-microscopic fraction of its mass into energy, and in that conversion the object that stopped it, whether rock, metal, or human flesh, was consumed to the accompaniment of a tiny noise like the flick of a fingernail against rubber.

Hennes said in a tone that borrowed menace from the blaster he held, "Who are you? What do you want?"

Once again the object spoke, and once again it said slowly, "I am the Space Ranger!"

Hennes's lips curved in cold ferocity as he fired.

The projectile left the muzzle, raced squarely at the object of smoke, reached it, and stopped. It stopped instantaneously, without touching the body that was still one quarter of an inch beyond its final penetration. Even the concussion of collision was not carried beyond the force-shield barrier which absorbed all the projectile's momentum, converting it into a flare of light.

That flare of light was never seen. It was drowned out in the intense blaze that was the blaster projectile exploding into energy as it stopped with no surrounding matter to shield the blast of light. It was as though a pin-sized sun existed in the room for a tiny fraction of a second.

Hennes, with a wild yell, threw his hands to his eyes as though to protect them against a physical blow. It was too late. Minutes later, when he dared open his eyelids, his aching, burning eyes could tell him nothing. Open or closed, he saw only red-studded blackness. He could not see the Space Ranger whirl into motion, pounce upon his boots, search their pockets with flying fingers, break the door's magnetic circuit, and slip out of the room seconds before the inevitable crowd of people with their confused cries of alarm had begun to gather.

Hennes's hand still covered his eyes when he heard them. He called, "Get the thing! Get him! He's in the room. Tackle him, you Mars-forsaken, black-booted cowards."

"There's no one in the room," half-a-dozen voices called, and someone added, "Smells like a blaster, though."

A firmer, more authoritative voice said, "What's wrong, Hennes?" It was Dr. Silvers.

"Intruders," said Hennes, shaking in frustration and wrath. "Doesn't anyone see him? What's the matter with all of you? Are you——" He couldn't say the word. His blinking eyes were watering and blurred light was just beginning to make its way into them again. He couldn't say "blind."

Silvers asked, "Who was the intruder? Can you describe him?"

And Hennes could only shake his head helplessly. How could he explain? Could he tell them of a nightmare of smoke that could speak and against which a blaster bullet could only explode prematurely and without damage except to the man who sped it on its way?

Dr. James Silvers made his way back to his room in dull gloom. This disturbance that had routed him out of his room before he had completed preparation for bed, this aimless running about of men, the tongue-tied lack of explanation on the part of Hennes, all were to him nothing but a series of pinpricks. His eyes were fixed on tomorrow.

He had no faith in victory, no faith in the efficacy of any embargo. Let the food shipments stop. Let even a few on Earth find out why, or, worse still, invent their own theories therefore, and the results might be more frightful than any mass poisoning.

This young David Starr expressed confidence, but so far his actions inspired none in himself. His story of a Space Ranger was a poorly calculated one, fit only to arouse the suspicions of men such as Hennes and bringing him almost to his death. It was fortunate for the youngster that he, Silvers, had arrived at the proper time. Nor had he explained the reasons for such a story. He had merely expounded his plans for leaving the city and then secretly returning. Yet when Silvers had first received Starr's letter, brought by the little fellow, the one that called himself Bigman in tremendous defiance of the truth, he had quickly checked with Council headquarters on Earth. It had confirmed that David Starr was to be obeyed in all particulars.

Yet how could such a young man——

Dr. Silvers halted. That was strange! The door to his room, which he had left ajar in his haste, was still ajar, but no light shone out into the hall. Yet he had not put it out before leaving. He could remember its glow behind him as he had hastened down the hall toward the stairs.

Had someone put it out for him on some strange impulse toward economy? It seemed hardly likely.

There was no sound within the room. He drew his blaster, threw the door open, and stepped firmly to where he knew the light switch to be located.

A hand dropped over his mouth.

He squirmed, but the arm was a large and muscular one, and the voice in his ear was familiar.

"It's all right, Dr. Silvers. I just didn't want you to give me away by yelling in surprise."

The arm dropped away. Dr. Silvers said, "Starr?"

"Yes. Close the door. It seemed your room would be the best hiding place while the search goes on. In any case, I must speak to you. Did Hennes say what had happened?"

"No, not really. Were you involved in that?"

David's smile was lost in the darkness. "In a way, Dr. Silvers. Hennes was visited by the Space Ranger, and in the confusion I was able to reach your room with no one, I hope, having seen me."

The old scientist's voice rose despite himself. "What are you saying? I am in no mood for jokes."

"I am not joking. The Space Ranger exists."

"That will not do. The story did not impress Hennes and I deserve the truth."

"It impresses Hennes now, I am sure, and you will have the truth when tomorrow is done. Meanwhile, listen to me. The Space Ranger, as I say, exists, and he is our great hope. The game we play is a rickety one and though I know who is behind the poisoning, the knowledge may be useless. It is not a criminal or two, intending to gain a few millions by colossal blackmail, that we face, but rather a well-organized group that intends to gain control of the entire Solar System. It can carry on, I am convinced, even if we pick off the leaders, unless we learn enough of the details of the conspiracy to stop its workings cold."

"Show me the leader," said Dr. Silvers grimly, "and the Council will learn all necessary details."

"Never quickly enough," said David, just as grimly. "We must have the answer, *all* the answer, in less than twenty-four hours. Victory after that will not stop the death of millions upon Earth."

Dr. Silvers said, "What do you plan then?"

"In theory," said David, "I know who the poisoner is and how the poisoning was accomplished. To be met with anything but a flat denial on the part of the poisoner I need a bit of material proof. That I will have before the evening is over. To gain from him, even then, the necessary information, we must break his morale completely. There we must use the Space Ranger. Indeed, he has begun the process of morale-cracking already."

"The Space Ranger again. You are bewitched by this thing. If he does exist, if this is not a trick of yours in which even I must be a victim, who is he and what is he? How do you know he is not deceiving you?"

"I can tell no one the details of that. I can only tell you that I know him to be on the side of humanity. I trust him as I would myself, and I will take full responsibility for him. You must do as I say, Dr. Silvers, in this matter, or I warn you we will have no choice but to proceed without you. The importance of the game is such that even you may not stand in my way."

There was no mistaking the firm resolution of the voice. Dr. Silvers could not see the expression of David's face in the darkness, but somehow he did not have to. "What is it you wish me to do?"

"Tomorrow noon you will meet with Makian, Hennes, and Benson. Bring Bigman with you as a personal bodyguard. He is small, but he is quick and knows no fear.

Have the Central Building protected by Council men, and I would advise that you have them armed with repeater blasters and gas pellets just in case. Now remember this, between twelve-fifteen and twelve-thirty leave the rear entrance unguarded and unobserved. I will guarantee its safety. Show no surprise at whatever happens thereafter."

"Will you be there?"

"No. My presence will not be necessary."

"Then?"

"There will be a visit from the Space Ranger. He knows what I know, and from him the accusations will be more shattering to the criminal."

Dr. Silvers felt hope arising in spite of himself. "Do you think, then, that we'll succeed?"

There was a long silence. Then David Starr said, "How can I tell? I can only hope so."

There was a longer silence. Dr. Silvers felt a tiny draft as though the door had opened. He turned to the light switch. The room flooded with light, and he found himself alone.

15

The Space Ranger Takes Over

David Starr worked as quickly as he dared. Not much was left of the night. Some of the excitement and tension were beginning to fade, and the utter weariness that he had been refusing to acknowledge for hours was soaking in just a bit.

His small pencil flash flickered here and there. He hoped earnestly that what he sought for would not be behind still additional locks. If it were, he would have to use force, and he was in no mood to attract attention just then. There was no safe that he could see; nothing equivalent to such an object. That was both good and bad. What he looked for would not be out of reach, but then again it might not be in the room at all.

That would be a pity after the carefully planned manner in which he had obtained the key to this room. Hennes would not recover quickly from the working out of that plan.

David smiled. He himself had been almost as surprised as Hennes at the very first. His words, "I am the Space Ranger," had been the first he had spoken through the force-shield since his emergence from the Martian caverns. He could not remember what his voice had sounded like there. Perhaps he had not truly heard it. Perhaps, under Martian influence, he had simply sensed his own thoughts as he did theirs.

Here on the surface, however, the sound of his own voice had left him thunderstruck. Its hollowness and booming depth had been entirely unexpected. He recovered, of course, and understood almost immediately. Although the shield let air molecules pass, it probably slowed them. Such interference would naturally affect sound waves.

David was not exactly sorry for that. The voice, as it was, would be helpful.

The shield had worked well against the blaster radiation. The flash had not been stopped entirely; he had seen it clearly. At least the effect upon himself had been nothing compared to that upon Hennes.

Methodically, even as his weary mind turned these things over, he was inspecting the contents of shelves and cabinets.

The light beam held steady for a moment. David reached past other gadgets to pick up a small metal object. He turned it over and over in the small light. He wound a little button which set at different positions and observed what happened afterward.

His heart bounded.

It was the final proof. The proof of all his speculations —the speculations that had been so reasonable and so complete and yet had rested upon nothing more than logic. Now the logic had been borne out by something made of molecules, something that could be touched and felt.

He put it in his hip-boot pocket to join his mask and the keys he had taken from Hennes's boots earlier in the night.

He locked the door behind him and stepped out into the open. The dome above was beginning to gray visibly. Soon the main fluorescents would go on and day would officially begin. The last day, either for the poisoners or for Earth civilization as it then was.

Meanwhile there would be a chance for sleep.

The Makian farm dome lay in a frozen quiet. Few of the farmboys could even guess at what was going on. That it was something serious was, of course, obvious, but further than that it was impossible to see. Some few whispered that Makian had been caught in serious financial irregularities, but no one could believe it. It wasn't even logical, since why would they send in an army just for that?

Certainly hard-faced men in uniform circled Central Building with repeater blasters cradled in their arms. On the roof of the building two artillery pieces had been set up. And the area around it was deserted. All farmboys, except those necessary for the maintenance of essential utilities, had been restricted to barracks. Those few excepted were ordered to remain strictly at their jobs.

At 12:15 P.M. exactly, the two men patrolling the rear of the building separated, moved away, leaving that area unguarded. At twelve-thirty they returned and took up their patrols. One of the artillerymen on the roof afterward stated that he had seen someone enter the building in that interval. He admitted he had caught only a brief glimpse and his description did not make very much sense, since he said it seemed to be a man on fire.

Nobody believed him at the time.

Dr. Silvers was not certain of anything. Not at all certain. He scarcely knew how to begin the session. He looked at the other four that sat about the table.

Makian. He looked as if he hadn't slept in a week.

Probably hadn't, either. He hadn't spoken a word so far. Silvers wondered if he was completely aware of his surroundings.

Hennes. He was wearing dark glasses. He took them off at one time and his eyes were bloodshot and angry. Now he sat there muttering to himself.

Benson. Quiet and unhappy. Dr. Silvers had spent several hours with him the night before and there was no doubt in his mind that the failures of his investigations were an embarrassment and a grief to him. He had spoken about Martians, native Martians, as causes of the poisonings, but Silvers had known better than to take that seriously.

Bigman. The only happy one of the lot. To be sure he understood only a fragment of the real crisis. He was leaning back in his chair, obviously pleased at being at the same table with important people, savoring his role to the full.

And there was one additional chair that Silvers had brought to the table. It stood there, empty and waiting. No one commented on the fact.

Dr. Silvers kept the conversation going somehow, making insubstantial remarks, trying to mask his own uncertainties. Like the empty chair, he was waiting.

At twelve-sixteen he looked up and rose slowly to his feet. No words came. Bigman pushed his chair back and it went over with a crash. Hennes's head turned sharply and he grasped the table with fingers that became white with strain. Benson looked about and whimpered. Only Makian seemed unmoved. His eyes lifted, then, apparently, took in the sight merely as another incomprehensible element in a world that had grown too large and strange for him.

The figure in the doorway said, "I am the Space Ranger!"

In the bright lights of the room the glow that surrounded his head was somewhat subdued, the smoke that
concealed his body somewhat more substantial than Hennes had seen it the night before.

The Space Ranger moved in. Almost automatically the
seated men pushed their chairs away, clearing a place at
the table, so that the one empty chair stood in lonely
isolation.

The Space Ranger sat down, face invisible behind
light, smoky arms extended before him, resting on the
table, and yet not resting upon it. Between the table and
the arms one quarter of an inch of empty space existed.

The Space Ranger said, "I have come to speak to
criminals."

It was Hennes who broke the sticky silence that followed. He said, in a voice that dripped with husky venom,
"You mean burglars?"

His hand went momentarily to his dark glasses but did
not remove them. His fingers shook visibly.

The Space Ranger's voice was a monotone of slow,
hollow words. "It is true I am a burglar. Here are the keys
I abstracted from your boots. I need them no longer."

Slivers of metal flashed across the table toward Hennes, who did not pick them up.

The Space Ranger went on, "But the burglary took
place in order to prevent a greater crime. There is the
crime of the trusted foreman, for instance, who periodically spent nights in Wingrad City on a one-man search
for poisoners."

Bigman's little face puckered in glee. "Hey, Hennes,"
he called, "sounds like you're being paged."

But Hennes had eyes and ears only for the apparition
across the table. He said, "What is the crime in that?"

"The crime," said the Space Ranger, "of a fast trip out
in the direction of the Asteroids."

"Why? What for?"

"Is it not from the Asteroids that the poisoners' ultimata have come?"

"Are you accusing me of being behind the food poisoning? I deny it. I demand your proof. That is, if you think you need any proof. Perhaps you think that your masquerade can force me to admit a lie."

"Where were you the two nights before the final ultimatum was received?"

"I will not answer. I deny your right to question me."

"I will answer the question for you then. The machinery of the vast poisoning combine is located in the Asteroids, where what is left of the old pirate bands have gathered. The brains of the combine is here at Makian Farms."

Here Makian rose unsteadily to his feet, his mouth working.

The Space Ranger waved him down with a firm motion of his smoky arm and continued, "You, Hennes, are the go-between."

Hennes did remove his glasses now. His plump, sleek face, somewhat marred by his red-rimmed eyes, was set into a hard mold.

He said, "You bore me, Space Ranger, or whatever you call yourself. This conference, as I understand it, was for the purpose of discussing means of combating the poisoners. If it is being converted into a forum for the stupid accusations of a play actor, I am leaving."

Dr. Silvers reached across Bigman to grasp Hennes's wrist. "Please stay, Hennes. I want to hear more of this. No one will convict you without ample proof."

Hennes dashed Silvers's hand away and rose from his chair.

Bigman said quietly, "I'd love to see you shot, Hennes, which is exactly what you will be if you go out the door."

"Bigman is right," said Silvers. "There are armed men outside, with instructions to allow no one to leave without orders from me."

Hennes's fists clenched and unclenched. He said, "I will not contribute another word to this illegal procedure. You are all witnesses that I am being detained by force." He sat down again and folded his arms across his chest.

The Space Ranger began again, "And yet Hennes is only the go-between. He is too great a villain to be the real villain."

Benson said faintly, "You speak in contradictions."

"Only apparently. Consider the crime. You can learn a great deal about a criminal from the nature of the crime he commits. First, there is the fact that few people, comparatively, have died so far. Presumably the criminals could have gained what they wanted more quickly by beginning with wholesale poisonings, instead of merely threatening for six months during which they risked capture and gained nothing. What does this mean? It would seem that the leader somehow hesitates to kill. That is certainly not in character for Hennes. I have obtained most of my information from Williams, who is not among us now, and from him I know that after his arrival at the farm Hennes tried several times to arrange his murder."

Hennes forgot his resolve. He shouted, "A lie!"

The Space Ranger went on, unheeding, "So Hennes would have no compunction against killing. We would have to find someone of gentler mold. Yet what would force an essentially gentle person to kill people he has never seen, who have done him no harm? After all, though an insignificant percentage of Earth's population has been poisoned, the dead number several hundred. Fifty of them were children. Presumably, then, there is a strong drive for wealth and power which overcomes his gentleness. What lies behind that drive? A life of frustration, perhaps, which has driven him into a morbid hatred of humanity as a whole, a desire to show those who despised him how great a man he really is. We look for a man, then, who might be expected to have an advanced inferiority complex. Where can we find such a one?"

All were watching the Space Ranger now with an intentness that burned in every eye. Something of keenness had returned even to Makian's expression. Benson was frowning in thought, and Bigman had forgotten to grin.

The Space Ranger continued, "Most important as a clue is what followed the arrival of Williams at the farm. He was at once suspected of being a spy. His story of the poisoning of his sister was easily shown to be false. Hennes, as I have said, was for outright murder. The leader, with his softer conscience, would take another method. He tried to neutralize the dangerous Williams by developing a friendship for him and pretending to unfriendliness with Hennes.

"Let us summarize. What do we know about the leader of the poisoners? He is a man with a conscience who has *seemed* friendly to Williams and unfriendly to Hennes. A man with an inferiority complex resulting from a life of frustration because he was different from others, less of a man, smaller——"

There was a rapid movement. A chair was thrust from the table, and a figure backed rapidly away, a blaster in his hand.

Benson rose to his feet and yelled, "Great Space. *Bigman!*"

Dr. Silvers cried helplessly, "But—but I was to bring him here as a bodyguard. He's armed."

For a moment Bigman stood there, blaster ready, watching each of them out of his sharp little eyes.

16

Solution

Bigman said, his high voice firm, "Don't let's draw any quick conclusions now. It may sound as if the Space Ranger is describing me, but he hasn't said so yet."

They watched him. No one spoke.

Bigman flipped his blaster suddenly, caught it by the muzzle, and tossed it onto the table where it skimmed noisily across in the direction of the Space Ranger. "I say I'm not the man, and there's my weapon to show I mean it."

The Space Ranger's smoke-obscured fingers reached for it.

"I also say you're not the man," he said, and the blaster skimmed back to Bigman.

Bigman pounced upon it, shoved it back in his holster, and sat down once more. "Now suppose you keep on talking, Space Ranger."

The Space Ranger said, "It might have been Bigman, but there are many reasons why it could not have been. In the first place, the enmity between Bigman and Hennes arose long before Williams appeared on the scene."

Dr. Silvers protested. "But look here. If the leader

was pretending to be on the outs with Hennes, it might not have been just for Williams' sake. It might have been a long-standing scheme."

The Space Ranger said, "Your point is well taken, Dr. Silvers. But consider this. The leader, whoever he is, must be in complete control of the gang's tactics. He must be able to enforce his own squeamishness about killing upon a group of what are probably the most desperate outlaws in the system. There is only one way he can do that, and that is by arranging it so that they cannot possibly continue without him. How? By controlling the supply of poison and the method of poisoning. Surely Bigman could do neither."

"How do you know that?" demanded Dr. Silvers.

"Because Bigman doesn't have the training that would enable him to develop and produce a new poison more virulent than any known. He doesn't have the laboratory or the botanical and bacteriological training. He doesn't have access to the food bins at Wingrad City. All of which, however, *does apply to Benson*."

The agronomist, perspiring profusely, raised his voice in a weak yell. "What are you trying to do? Test me as you tested Bigman just now?"

"I didn't test Bigman," said the Space Ranger. "I never accused him. I do accuse you, Benson. You are the brains and leader of the food-poisoning combine."

"No. You're mad."

"Not at all. Quite sane. Williams first suspected you and passed his suspicions on to me."

"He had no reason to. I was perfectly frank with him."

"Too frank. You made the mistake of telling him that it was your opinion that Martian bacteria growing upon farm products were the source of the poison. As an agronomist, you must have known that was impossible. Martian life is not protein in nature and could no more feed on

Earth plants than we could feed on rocks. So you told a deliberate lie, and that made everything else about you suspect. It made Williams wonder if perhaps you had yourself made an extract of Martian bacteria. The extract would be poisonous. Don't you think so?"

Benson cried wildly, "But how could I possibly spread the poison? You don't make sense."

"You had access to the Makian farm shipments. After the first few poisonings you could arrange to obtain samples from the storage bins at the city. You told Williams how you carefully took samples from different bins, from different levels of a single bin. You told him how you used a harpoon-like affair you invented yourself."

"But what is there wrong with that?"

"A good deal. Last night I obtained keys from Hennes. I used them to get into the one place in the farm dome which is consistently kept locked—your laboratory. There I found this." He held the small metal object up to the light.

Dr. Silvers said, "What is it, Space Ranger?"

"It is Benson's sample taker. It fits at the end of his food harpoon. Observe how it works."

The Space Ranger adjusted a small knob at one end. "Firing the harpoon." he said, "trips this safety catch. So! Now watch."

There was the faintest buzzing noise. It ended after five seconds, and the fore end of the sampler gaped open, remained so for a second, then closed.

"That's the way it's supposed to work," cried Benson. "I made no secret of it."

"No, you didn't," said the Space Ranger sternly. "You and Hennes had been quarreling for days over Williams. You hadn't the stomach to have him killed. At the very last you brought the harpoon with you to Williams' bedside to see if the sight of it would surprise him into some action that would give him away. It didn't, but Hennes would wait no longer, anyway. Zukis was sent in to kill him."

"But what's wrong with the sampler?" demanded Benson.

"Let me show its workings again. But this time, Dr. Silvers, please observe the side of the sampler toward yourself now."

Dr. Silvers leaned across the table, watching closely. Bigman, blaster out once more, divided his attention between Benson and Hennes. Makian was on his feet, leathery cheeks flushed.

Once again the sampler was set, once again the little mouth flew open, and this time, as they watched the neutral side indicated, a covering sliver of metal withdrew there as well, revealing a shallow depression that glistened gummily.

"There," said the Space Ranger, "you can see what happened. Each time Benson took a sample, a few grains of wheat, a piece of fruit, a leaf of lettuce was smeared with that colorless gum, a poisonous extract of Martian bacteria. It is a simple poison, no doubt, that is not affected by subsequent food processing and eventually turns up in a loaf of bread, a jar of jam, a can of baby food. It was a clever and diabolical trick."

Benson was beating on the table. "It's all a lie, a rotten lie!"

"Bigman," said the Space Ranger, "gag the man. Stand near him and don't let him move."

"Really," protested Dr. Silvers, "you're making a case, Space Ranger, but you must let the man defend himself."

"There is no time," said the Space Ranger, "and proof that will satisfy even you will be forthcoming quickly."

Bigman used his handkerchief as a gag. Benson struggled and then sat in sweating stillness as the butt of Bigman's blaster collided noisily with his skull.

"The next time," said Bigman, "it will be hard enough to knock you out; maybe fix you up with a concussion."

The Space Ranger rose. "You all suspected, or pretended to suspect, Bigman when I spoke of a man with an inferiority complex because he was small. There are more ways of being small than in size. Bigman compensates for his size by belligerence and loud assertion of his own opinions. The men here respect him because of this. Benson, however, living here on Mars among men of action finds himself despised as a 'college farmer,' ignored as a weakling, and looked down upon by men whom he considers much his inferiors. To be unable to compensate for this except by murder of the most cowardly sort is another and worse kind of smallness.

"But Benson is mentally sick. To get a confession out of him would be difficult; perhaps impossible. However, Hennes would do almost as well as a source of knowledge about the future activities of the poisoners. He could tell us exactly where in the Asteroids we could find his various henchmen. He could tell us where the supply of poison, for use at midnight tonight, is kept. He could tell us many things."

Hennes sneered. "I could tell you nothing, and I will tell you nothing. If you shoot Benson and myself right now, matters will proceed exactly as they would if we were alive. So do your worst."

"Would you talk," said the Space Ranger, "if we guaranteed your personal safety?"

"Who would believe in your guarantee?" said Hennes. "I'll stick to my story. I'm an innocent man. Killing us will do you no good."

"You realize that if you refuse to talk, millions of men, women, and children may die."

Hennes shrugged.

"Very well," said the Space Ranger. "I have been told

something about the effects of the Martian poison Benson has developed. Once in the stomach, absorption is very quick; the nerves to the chest muscles are paralyzed; the victim can't breathe. It is painful strangulation stretched over five minutes. Of course that is when the poison has been introduced into the stomach."

The Space Ranger, as he spoke, drew from his pocket a small glass pellet. He opened the sampler and drew it across the gummed surface until the glitter of the glass had been obscured by a sticky coating.

"Now if," he said, "the poison were placed just within the lips, matters would be different. It would be absorbed much more slowly and would take effect much more gradually. Makian," he called suddenly, "there's the man who betrayed you, used your farm to organize the poisoning of men and the ruin of the farm syndicates. Grab his arms and pinion them."

The Space Ranger tossed a pinion upon the table.

Makian, with a cry of long-pent rage, threw himself on Hennes. For a moment wrath restored to him some of the strength of his youth and Hennes struggled in vain against him.

When Makian stepped away, Hennes was strapped to his chair, his arms drawn painfully behind and around its back, his wrists pinioned tightly.

Makian said between rasping pants, "After you talk, it will be my pleasure to take you apart with my ten fingers."

The Space Ranger circled the table now, approaching Hennes slowly, the smeared glass pellet held in two fingers before him. Hennes shrank away. At the other end of the table Benson writhed desperately, and Bigman kicked him into stillness.

The Space Ranger pinched Hennes's lower lip and drew it out, exposing his teeth. Hennes tried to snap his head away, but the Space Ranger's fingers pinched together and Hennes let out a muffled scream.

The Space Ranger dropped the pellet in the space between lip and teeth.

"I believe it will take about ten minutes before you absorb enough poison through the mouth membranes to begin taking noticeable effect," said the Space Ranger. "If you agree to talk before then, we will remove the pellet and let you rinse your mouth. Otherwise, the poison will take effect slowly. Gradually it will become more and more difficult and painful to breathe, and finally, in about an hour, you will die of very slow strangulation. And if you do die, you will have accomplished nothing, because the demonstration will be very educational for Benson and we will proceed to sweat the truth out of him."

The perspiration trickled down Hennes's temples. He made choking noises in the back of his throat.

The Space Ranger waited patiently.

Hennes cried, "I'll talk. I'll talk. Take it out! *Take it out!*"

The words were muffled through his distorted lips, but their intent and the hideous terror in every line of his face were plain enough.

"Good! You had better take notes, Dr. Silvers."

It was three days before Dr. Silvers met David Starr again. He had had little sleep in that interval and he was tired, but not too tired to greet David gladly. Bigman, who had not left Silvers in all that interval, was equally effusive in his greetings.

"It worked," said Silvers. "You've heard about it, I'm sure. It worked unbelievably well."

"I know," said David, smiling. "The Space Ranger told me all about it."

"Then you've seen him since."

"Only for a moment or two."

"He disappeared almost immediately afterward. I mentioned him in my report; I had to, of course. But it certainly made me feel foolish. In any case, I have Bigman here and old Makian as witnesses."

"And myself," said David.

"Yes, of course. Well, it's over. We located the poison stores and cleaned out the Asteroids. There'll be two dozen men up for life sentences and Benson's work will actually be beneficial in the end. His experiments on Martian life were, in their way, revolutionary. It's possible a whole new series of antibiotics may be the final results of his attempts to poison Earth into submission. If the poor fool had aimed at scientific eminence, he would have ended a great man. Thank Hennes's confession for stopping him."

David said, "That confession was carefully planned for. The Space Ranger had been working on him since the night before."

"Uh, well, I doubt that any human could have withstood the danger of poisoning that Hennes was subject to. In fact, what would have happened if Hennes had been really innocent? The chance the Space Ranger took was a big one."

"Not really. There was no poison involved. Benson knew that. Do you suppose Benson would have left his sampler in his laboratory smeared with poison as evidence against himself? Do you suppose he kept any poison where it might be found by accident?"

"But the poison on the pellet."

". . . was simple gelatin, unflavored. Benson would have known it would be something like that. That's why the Space Ranger did not try to get a confession out of him. That's why he had him gagged, to prevent a warning. Hennes might have figured it out for himself, if he hadn't been in blind panic."

"Well, I'll be tossed out into Space," said Dr. Silvers blankly.

He was still rubbing his chin when he finally made his excuses and went off to bed.

David turned to Bigman.

"And what will you be doing now, Bigman?"

Bigman said, "Dr. Silvers has offered me a permanent job with the Council. But I don't think I'll take it."

"Why not?"

"Well, I'll tell you, Mr. Starr. I sort of figure on going with you, wherever you happen to be going after this."

"I'm just going to Earth," said David.

They were alone, yet Bigman looked cautiously over his shoulder before he spoke. "It seems to me you'll be going lots of places besides Earth—Space Ranger."

"*What?*"

"Sure. I knew that when I first saw you come in with all that light and smoke. That's why I didn't take you serious when it looked as if you were accusing me of being the poisoner." His face was broken out in a giant grin.

"Do you know what you're talking about?"

"I sure do. I couldn't see your face, or the details of your costume, but you were wearing hip boots and you were the right height and build."

"Coincidence."

"Maybe. I couldn't see the design on the hip boots but I made out a little of them, the colors, for instance. And you're the only farmboy I ever heard of that was willing to wear simple black and white."

David Starr threw his head back and laughed. "You win. Do you really want to join forces with me?"

"I'd be proud to," said Bigman.

David held out his hand and the two shook.

"Together then," said David, "wherever we go."

Lucky Starr
and the
Pirates of the Asteroids

DEDICATION

To Frederik Pohl,
That contradiction in terms—
A lovable agent.

CONTENTS

1

The Doomed Ship

Fifteen minutes to zero time! The *Atlas* waited to take off. The sleek, burnished lines of the space-ship glittered in the bright Earthlight that filled the Moon's night sky. Its blunt prow pointed upward into empty space. Vacuum surrounded it and the dead pumice of the Moon's surface was under it. The number of its crew was zero. There wasn't a living person aboard.

Dr. Hector Conway, Chief Councilor of Science, said, "What time is it, Gus?"

He felt uncomfortable in the Moon offices of the Council. On Earth he would have been at the very top of the stone and steel needle they called Science Tower. He would have been able to look out the window toward International City.

Here on the Moon they did their best. The offices had mock windows with brilliantly designed Earth scenes behind them. They were colored naturally, and lights within them brightened and softened during the day, simulating morning, noon, and evening. During the sleep periods they even shone a dim, dark blue.

It wasn't enough, though, for an Earthman like Conway. He knew that if he broke through the glass of the windows there would be only painted miniatures before his eyes, and if he got behind that, then there would be just another room, or maybe the solid rock of the Moon.

Dr. Augustus Henree, whom Conway had addressed, looked at his wrist. He said, between puffs at his pipe, "There's still fifteen minutes. There's no point in worrying. The *Atlas* is in perfect shape. I checked it myself yesterday."

"I know that." Conway's hair was pure white and he looked older than the lank, thin-faced Henree, though they were the same age. He said, "It's Lucky I'm worried about."

"Lucky?"

Conway smiled sheepishly. "I'm catching the habit, I'm afraid. I'm talking about David Starr. It's just that everyone calls him Lucky these days. Haven't you heard them?"

"Lucky Starr, eh? The name suits him. But what about him? This is all his idea, after all."

"Exactly. It's the sort of idea he gets. I think he'll tackle the Sirian Consulate on the Moon next."

"I wish he would."

"Don't joke. Sometimes I think you encourage him in his idea that he ought to do everything as a one-man job. It's why I came here to the Moon, to keep an eye on him, not to watch the ship."

"If that's what you came here for, Hector, you're not on the job."

"Oh well, I can't follow him about like a mother hen. But Bigman is with him. I told the little fellow I would skin him alive if Lucky decided to invade the Sirian Consulate singlehanded."

Henree laughed.

"I tell you he'd do it," grumbled Conway. "What's worse, he'd get away with it, of course."

"Well, then."

"It would just encourage him, and then someday he'll take one risk too many, and he's too valuable a man to lose!"

John Bigman Jones teetered across the packed clay flooring, carrying his stein of beer with the utmost care. They didn't extend the pseudo-gravity fields outside the city itself, so that out here at the space-port you had to do the best you could under the Moon's own gravity field. Fortunately John Bigman Jones had been born and bred on Mars, where the gravity was only two fifths normal anyway, so it wasn't too bad. Right now he weighed twenty pounds. On Mars he would have weighed fifty, and on the Earth one hundred and twenty.

He got to the sentry, who had been watching him with amused eyes. The sentry was dressed in the uniform of the Lunar National Guard, and he was used to the gravity.

John Bigman Jones said, "Hey. Don't stand there so gloomylike. I brought you a beer. Have it on me."

The sentry looked surprised, then said regretfully, "I can't. Not when I'm on duty, you know."

"Oh well. I can handle it myself, I guess. I'm John Bigman Jones. Call me Bigman." He only came up to the sentry's chin and the sentry wasn't particularly tall, but Bigman held out his hand as though he were reaching down with it.

"I'm Bert Wilson. You from Mars?" The sentry looked at Bigman's scarlet and vermilion hip boots. Nobody but a Martian farmboy would let himself be caught dead in space with them.

Bigman looked down at them proudly. "You bet. I'm stuck here for about a week. Great space, what a rock the

Moon is. Don't any of you guys ever go out on the surface?"

"Sometimes. When we have to. There isn't much to see there."

"I sure wish I could go. I hate being cooped up."

"There's a surface lock back there."

Bigman followed the thumb that had been jerked back across the sergeant's shoulder. The corridor (rather poorly lit at this distance from Luna City) narrowed into a recess in the wall.

Bigman said, "I don't have a suit."

"You couldn't go out even if you had one. No one's allowed out without a special pass for a while."

"How come?"

Wilson yawned. "They've got a ship out there that's getting set to go," he looked at his watch, "in about twelve minutes. Maybe the heat will be off after it's gone. I don't know the story on it."

The sentry rocked on the balls of his feet and watched the last of the beer drain down Bigman's throat. He said, "Say, did you get the beer at Patsy's Port Bar? Is it crowded?"

"It's empty. Listen, tell you what. It'll take you fifteen seconds to get in there and have one. I've got nothing to do. I'll stay right here and make sure nothing happens while you're gone."

Wilson looked longingly in the direction of the Port Bar. "I better not."

"It's up to you."

Neither one of them, apparently, was conscious of the figure that drifted past behind them along the corridor and into the recess where the space-lock's huge door barred the way to the surface.

Wilson's feet took him a few steps toward the Bar, as

though they were dragging the rest of him. Then he said, "Nah! I better not."

Ten minutes to zero time.

It had been Lucky Starr's idea. He had been in Conway's home office the day the news arrived that the T.S.S. *Waltham Zachary* had been gutted by pirates, its cargo gone, its officers frozen corpses in space and most of the men captives. The ship itself had put up a pitifully futile fight and had been too damaged to be worth the pirate's salvage. They had taken everything movable though, the instruments, of course, and even the motors.

Lucky said, "It's the asteroid belt that's the enemy. One hundred thousand rocks."

"More than that." Conway spat out his cigarette. "But what can we do? Ever since the Terrestrial Empire has been a going concern, the asteroids have been more than we could handle. A dozen times we've gone in there to clean out nests of them, and each time we've left enough to breed the troubles again. Twenty-five years ago, when—"

The white-haired scientist stopped short. Twenty-five years ago Lucky's parents had been killed in space and he himself, a little boy, had been cast adrift.

Lucky's calm brown eyes showed no emotion. He said, "The trouble is we don't even know where all the asteroids are."

"Naturally not. It would take a hundred ships a hundred years to get the necessary information for the sizable asteroids. And even then the pull of Jupiter would be forever changing asteroidal orbits here and there."

"We might still try. If we sent out one ship, the pirates might not know it was an impossible job and fear the consequences of a real mapping. If the word got out that we had started a mapping survey, the ship would be attacked."

"And then what?"

"Suppose we sent out an automatic ship, completely equipped, but with no human personnel."

"It would be an expensive thing to do."

"It might be worth it. Suppose we equipped it with lifeboats automatically designed to leave the ship when its instruments recorded the energy pattern of an approaching hyperatomic motor. What do you suppose the pirates would do?"

"Shoot the lifeboats into metal drift, board the ship, and take it to their base."

"Or one of their bases. Right. And if they see the lifeboats try to get away, they won't be surprised at finding no crew aboard. After all, it would be an unarmed survey ship. You wouldn't expect the crew to attempt resistance."

"Well, what are you getting at?"

"Suppose further that the ship is wired to explode once its temperature is raised to more than twenty degrees absolute, as it certainly would if it were brought into an asteroid hangar."

"You're proposing a booby trap, then?"

"A gigantic one. It would blow an asteroid apart. It might destroy dozens of pirate ships. Furthermore, the observatories at Ceres, Vesta, Juno, or Pallas might pick up the flash. Then, if we could locate surviving pirates, we might get information that would be very useful indeed."

"I see."

And so they started work on the *Atlas.*

The shadowy figure in the recess leading to the Moon's surface worked with sure quickness. The sealed controls of the air-lock gave under the needle beam of a micro-heatgun. The shielding metal disc swung open. Busy, black-gloved fingers flew for a moment. Then the disc was replaced and fused tightly back by a wider and cooler beam from the same heatgun.

The cave door of the lock yawned. The alarm that rang routinely whenever it did so was silent this time, its circuits behind the tampered disc disarranged. The figure entered the lock and the door closed behind him. Before he opened the surface door that faced out into the vacuum, he unrolled the pliant plastic he carried under his arm. He scrambled into it, the material covering him wholly and clinging to him, broken only by a strip of clear silicone plastic across his eyes. A small cylinder of liquid oxygen was clamped to a short hose that lead to the headpiece and was hooked on to the belt. It was a semi-spacesuit, designed for the quick trip across an airless surface, not guaranteed to be serviceable for stretches of more than half an hour.

Bert Wilson, startled, swiveled his head. "Did you hear that?"

Bigman gaped at the sentry. "I didn't hear anything."

"I could swear it was a lock door closing. There isn't any alarm, though."

"Is there supposed to be?"

"Sure. You've got to know when one door is open. It's a bell where there's air and a light where there isn't. Otherwise someone is liable to open the other door and blow all the air out of a ship or corridor."

"All right. If there's no alarm, there's nothing to worry about."

"I'm not so sure." With flat leaps, each one covering twenty feet in the Moon's baby gravity, the sentry passed up the corridor to the air-lock recess. He stopped at a wall panel on the way and activated three separate banks of ceiling Floressoes, turning the area into a noonday of light.

Bigman followed, leaping clumsily and in perpetual danger of overbalancing into a slow nose landing.

Wilson had his blaster out. He inspected the door, then turned to look up the corridor again. "Are you sure you didn't hear anything?"

"Nothing," said Bigman. "Of course, I wasn't listening."

Five minutes to zero time.

Pumice kicked up as the space-suited figure moved slow-motion toward the *Atlas*. The space-ship glittered in the Earthlight, but on the Moon's airless surface the light did not carry even an inch into the shadow of the ridge that hemmed in the port.

In three long leaps the figure moved across the lighted portion and into the pitchy shadow of the ship itself.

He moved up the ladder hand over hand, flinging himself into an upward drift that carried him ten rungs at a time. He came to the ship's air-lock. A moment at the controls and it yawned open, then closed.

The *Atlas* had a passenger. One passenger!

The sentry stood before the corridor air-lock and considered its appearance dubiously.

Bigman was rattling on. He said, "I been here nearly a week. I'm supposed to follow my side-kick around and make sure he doesn't get into trouble. How's that for a space wrangler like me. I haven't had a chance to get away—"

The anguished sentry said, "Give it a rest, friend. Look, you're a nice kid and all that, but let's have it some other time."

For a moment he stared at the control seal. "That's funny," he said.

Bigman was swelling ominously. His little face had reddened. He seized the sentry by the elbow and swung him about, almost overbalancing himself as he did so.

"Hey, bud, who're you calling a kid?"

"Look, go away!"

"Just a minute. Let's get something straight. Don't think I let myself get pushed around because I'm not as tall as the next fellow. Put 'em up. Go ahead. Get your fists up or I'll splatter your nose all over your face."

He was sparring and slipping about.

Wilson looked at him with astonishment. "What's got into you? Stop being foolish."

"Scared?"

"I can't fight on duty. Besides, I didn't mean to hurt your feelings. I've just got a job to do and I haven't got any time for you."

Bigman lowered his fists. "Hey, I guess the ship's taking off."

There was no sound, of course, since sound would not travel through a vacuum, but the ground under their feet vibrated softly in response to the hammer blows of a rocket exhaust lifting a ship off a planet.

"That's it, all right." Wilson's forehead creased. "Guess there's no use making a report. It's too late anyway." He had forgotten about the control seal.

Zero time!

The ceramic-lined exhaust pit yawned under the *Atlas* and the main rockets blasted their fury into it. Slowly and majestically the ship lifted and moved upward ponderously. Its speed increased. It pierced the black sky, shrinking until it was only a star among stars, and then it was gone.

• • •

Dr. Henree looked at his watch for the fifth time and said, "Well, it's gone. It must be gone now." He pointed with the stem of his pipe to the dial.

Conway said, "Let's check with the port authorities."

Five seconds later they were looking at the empty space-port on the visiscreen. The exhaust pit was still open. Even in the near-ultimate frigidity of the Moon's dark side it was still steaming.

Conway shook his head. "It was a beautiful ship."

"Still is."

"I think of it in the past. In a few days it will be a rain of molten metal. It's a doomed ship."

"Let's hope that there's a pirate base somewhere that's also doomed."

Henree nodded somberly.

They both turned as the door opened. It was only Bigman.

He broke into a grin. "Oh, boy, it was sure nice coming in to Luna City. You could feel the pounds going back on with each step you took." He stamped his feet and hopped two or three times. "See," he said, "you try that out where I was and you hit the ceiling and look like one big fool."

Conway frowned. "Where's Lucky?"

Bigman said, "I know where he is. I know where he is every minute. Say, the *Atlas* has just taken off."

"I know that," said Conway. "And where is Lucky?"

"On the *Atlas*, of course. Where do you think he'd be?"

2

Vermin of Space

Dr. Henree dropped his pipe and it bounced on the linolite flooring. He paid it no attention.

"What!"

Conway reddened and his face stood out, plumply pink, against his snowy hair. "Is this a joke?"

"No. He got on five minutes before it blasted. I talked to the sentry, guy called Wilson, and kept him from interfering. I had to pick a fight with the fellow and I would have given him the old bingo-bango," he demonstrated the one-two punch with quick, hard blows at the atmosphere, "but he backed off."

"You let him? You didn't warn us?"

"How could I? I've got to do what Lucky says. He said he had to get on at the last minute and without anyone knowing, or you and Dr. Henree would have stopped him."

Conway groaned. "He did it. By space, Gus, I should have known better than to trust that pint-sized Martian. Bigman, you fool! You know that ship's a booby trap."

"Sure. Lucky knows it too. He says not to send out ships after him or things will be ruined."

"They will, will they? There'll be men after him within the hour just the same."

Henree clutched his friend's sleeve. "Maybe not, Hector. We don't know what he's planning to do, but we can trust him to scramble out safely whatever it is. Let's not interfere."

Conway fell back, trembling with anger and anxiety.

Bigman said, "He says we're to meet him on Ceres, and also, Dr. Conway, he says you're to control your temper."

"You—" began Conway, and Bigman left the room in a hurry.

The orbit of Mars lay behind and the sun was a shrunken thing.

Lucky Starr loved the silence of space. Since he had graduated and joined the Council of Science, space had been his home, rather than any planetary surface. And the *Atlas* was a comfortable ship. It had been provisioned for a full crew with only so much omitted as might be explained by consumption before reaching the asteroids. In every way the *Atlas* was intended to look as though, until the moment of the pirates' appearance, it had been fully manned.

So Lucky ate Syntho-steak from the yeast beds of Venus, Martian pastry, and boneless chicken from Earth.

I'll get fat, he thought, and watched the skies.

He was close enough to make out the larger asteroids. There was Ceres, the largest of all, nearly five hundred miles in diameter. Vesta was on the other side of the sun, but Juno and Pallas were in sight.

If he were to use the ship's telescope, he would have found more, thousands more, maybe tens of thousands. There was no end to them.

Once it had been thought that there had been a planet

between Mars and Jupiter and that geologic ages earlier it had exploded into fragments, but that wasn't so. It was Jupiter that was the villain. Its giant gravitational influence had disrupted space for hundreds of millions of miles about it in the eons when the Solar System was being formed. The cosmic gravel between itself and Mars could never coalesce into a single planet with Jupiter pulling and pulling. Instead it coalesced into myriads of little worlds.

There were the four largest, each a hundred or more miles in diameter. There were fifteen hundred more that were between ten and a hundred miles in diameter. After that there were thousands (no one knew exactly how many) that were between one and ten miles in diameter and tens of thousands that were less than a mile in diameter but still as large or larger than the Great Pyramid.

They were so plentiful that astronomers called them "the vermin of space."

The asteroids were scattered over the entire region between Mars and Jupiter, each whirling in its own orbit. No other planetary system known to man in all the Galaxy had such an asteroid belt.

In a sense it was good. The asteroids had formed steppingstones out toward the major planets. In a sense it was bad. Any criminal who could escape to the asteroids was safe from capture by all but the most improbable chance. No police force could search every one of those flying mountains.

The smaller asteroids were no man's land. There were well-manned astronomical observatories on the largest, notably on Ceres. There were beryllium mines on Pallas, while Vesta and Juno were important fueling stations. But that still left fifty thousand sizable asteroids over which the Terrestrial Empire had no control whatever. A few were large enough to harbor fleets. Some were too small for more than a single speed-cruiser with additional space, perhaps, for a six-month supply of fuel, food, and water.

And it was impossible to map them. Even in the ancient, preatomic times, before space travel, when only fifteen hundred or so were known, and those the largest, mapping had been impossible. Their orbits had been carefully calculated via telescopic observation and still asteroids were forever being "lost," then "found" again.

Lucky snapped out of his reverie. The sensitive Ergometer was picking up pulsations from the outer reaches. He was at the control board in a step.

The steady energy outpourings of the sun, whether direct or by way of the relatively tiny reflected dribbles from the planets, were canceled out on the meter. What was coming in now were the characteristically intermittent energy pulses of a hyperatomic motor.

Lucky threw in the Ergograph connection and the energy pattern traced itself out in a series of lines. He followed the graphed paper as it emerged and his jaw muscles hardened.

There had always been a chance that the *Atlas* might meet an ordinary trading ship or passenger liner, but the energy pattern was none of that. The approaching ship had motors of advanced design, and different from any of the Terrestrial fleet.

Five minutes passed before he had enough spread of measurement to be able to calculate the distance and direction of the energy source.

He adjusted the visiplate for telescopic viewing and the star field speckled enormously. Carefully he searched among the infinitely silent, infinitely distant, infinitely motionless stars until a flicker of movement caught his eyes and the Ergometer's reading dials lined up at multiple zero.

It was a pirate. No doubt! He could make out its outlines by the half that glittered in the sun and by the port lights in the shaded half. It was a thin, graceful vessel, having the look of speed and maneuverability. It had an alien look about it too.

Sirian design, thought Lucky.

He watched the ship grow slowly larger on the screen. Was it such a ship that his father and mother watched on the last day of their lives?

He scarcely remembered his father and mother, but he had seen pictures of them and had heard endless stories about Lawrence and Barbara Starr from Henree and Conway. They had been inseparable, the tall, grave Gus Henree, the choleric, persevering Hector Conway, and the quick, laughing Larry Starr. They had gone to school together, graduated simultaneously, entered the Council as one and done all their assignments as a team.

And then Lawrence Starr had been promoted and assigned to a tour of duty on Venus. He, his wife, and his four-year-old son were Venus-bound when the pirate ship attacked.

For years Lucky had unhappily imagined what that last hour upon the dying ship must have been like. First, the crippling of the main power drives at the stern of the ship while pirate and victim were still apart. Then the blasting of the air-locks and the boarding. The crew and passengers scrambling into space-suits against the loss of air when the air-locks caved in. The crew armed and waiting. The passengers huddling in the interior rooms without much hope. Women weeping. Children screaming.

His father wasn't among the hiders. His father was a Council member. He had been armed and fighting. Lucky was sure of that. He had one memory, a short one that had been burned into his mind. His father, a tall, strong man, was standing with blaster raised and face set in what must have been one of the few moments of cold rage in his life, as the door of the control room crashed inward in a cloud of black smoke. And his mother, face wet and smudged but clearly seen through the space-suit face-plate, was forcing him into a small lifeboat.

"Don't cry, David, it will be all right."

Those were the only words he remembered ever having heard his mother say. Then there was thunder behind him and he was pressed back against a wall.

They found him in the lifeboat two days later, when they followed its coldly automatic radio calls for help.

The government had launched a tremendous campaign against the asteroid pirates immediately afterward and the Council had lent that drive every last ounce of their own effort. For the pirates it turned out that to attack and kill key men of the Council of Science was bad business. Such asteroid hideouts as were located were blasted into dust, and the pirate menace was reduced to the merest flicker for twenty years.

But often Lucky wondered if they had ever located the particular pirate ship that had carried the men who had killed his parents. There was no way of telling.

And now the menace had revived in a less spectacular but far more dangerous fashion. Piracy wasn't a matter of individual jabs any longer. It bore the appearance of an organized attack on Terrestrial commerce. There was more to it. From the nature of the warfare carried on Lucky felt certain that one mind, one strategic direction, lay behind it. That one mind, he knew, he would have to find.

• • •

He lifted his eyes to the Ergometer once more. The energy recordings were strong now. The other vessel was well within the distance at which space courtesy required routine messages of mutual identification. For that matter, it was well within the distance at which a pirate might have made its initial hostile move.

The floor shuddered under Lucky. It wasn't a blaster bolt from the other ship, but rather the recoil of a departing lifeboat. The energy pulses had become strong enough to activate their automatic controls.

Another shudder. And another. Five altogether.

He watched the oncoming ship closely. Often pirates shot up such lifeboats, partly out of the perverted fun of it and partly to prevent escapees from describing the vessel, assuming they had not done so already through the sub-ether.

This time, however, the ship ignored the lifeboats altogether. It approached within locking range. Its magnetic grapples shot out, clamped on the *Atlas's* hull, and the two vessels were suddenly welded together, their motions through space well matched.

Lucky waited.

He heard the air-lock open, then shut. He heard the clang of feet and the sound of helmets being unclipped, then the sound of voices.

He didn't move.

A figure appeared in the door. Helmet and gauntlets had been removed, but the rest of the man was still swathed in ice-coated space-suit. Space-suits had a habit of doing that when one entered from the near-absolute zero of space into the warm moist air of the interior of a ship. The ice was beginning to melt.

The pirate caught sight of Lucky only when he was two full steps into the control room. He stopped, his face frozen in an almost comical expression of surprise. Lucky had time to note the sparse black hair, the long nose, and the dead white scar that ran from nostril to canine tooth, splitting the upper lip into two unequal parts.

Lucky bore the pirate's astonished scrutiny calmly. He had no fear of recognition. Councilmen on active duty always worked without publicity with the very thought that a too-well-known face would diminish their usefulness. His own father's face had appeared over the subether only after his death. With fleeting bitterness Lucky thought that perhaps better publicity during life might have prevented the pirate attack. But that was silly, he knew. By the time the pirates had seen Lawrence Starr the attack had proceeded too far to be stopped.

Lucky said, "I've got a blaster. I'll use it only if you reach for yours. Don't move."

The pirate had opened his mouth. He closed it again.

Lucky said, "If you want to call the rest, go ahead."

The pirate stared suspiciously, then, eyes firmly on Lucky's blaster, yelled, "Blinking Space, there's a ripper with a gat here."

There was laughter at that, and a voice shouted, "Quiet!"

Another man stepped into the room. "Step aside, Dingo," he said.

His space-suit was off entirely and he was an incongruous sight aboard ship. His clothing might have come out of the most fashionable tailor shop in International City, and would have suited better a dinner party back on Earth. His shirt had a silken look you got only out of the best plastex. Its iridescence was subtle rather than garish, and his tight-ankled breeches blended in so well that, but for the ornamented belt, it would have seemed one garment. He wore a wristband that matched his belt and a fluffy, sky-blue neck sash. His crisp brown hair was curly and looked as though it received frequent attention.

He was half a head shorter than Lucky, but from the way he carried himself the young Councilman could see that any assumption of softness he might make on the basis of the man's dude costume would be quite wrong.

The newcomer said pleasantly, "Anton is my name. Would you put down your gun?"

Lucky said, "And be shot?"

"You may be shot eventually, but not at the moment. I would like to question you first."

Lucky held fast.

Anton said, "I keep my word." A tiny flush appeared on his cheekbones. "It is my only virtue as men count virtue, but I hold fast to it."

Lucky put down his blaster and Anton picked it up. He handed it to the other pirate.

"Put it away, Dingo, and get out of here." He turned to Lucky. "The other passengers got away in the lifeboats? Right?"

Lucky said, "That's an obvious trap, Anton—"

"Captain Anton, *please.*" He smiled, but his nostrils flared.

"Well, then, it's a trap, Captain Anton. It was obvious that you knew there were no passengers or crew on this ship. You knew it long before you boarded."

"Indeed? How do you make that out?"

"You approached the ship without signaling and without a warning shot. You made no particular speed. You ignored the lifeboats when they shot out. Your men entered the ship carelessly, as though they expected no resistance. The man who first found me entered this room with his blaster well holstered. The conclusion follows."

"Very good. And what are you doing on a ship without crew or passengers?"

Lucky said grimly, "I came to see you, Captain Anton."

3

Duel in Word

Anton's expression did not change. "And now you see me."

"But not privately, Captain." Lucky's lips thinned and closed with great deliberation.

Anton looked quickly about. A dozen of his men in every stage of space-suit undress had crowded into the room, watching and listening with gaping interest.

He reddened slightly. His voice rose. "Get on your business, scum. I want a complete report on this ship. And keep your weapons ready. There may be more men on board and if anyone else gets caught as Dingo did, he'll be tossed out an air-lock."

There was slow, shuffling motion outward.

Anton's voice was a sudden scream. "Quickly! Quickly!" One snaking gesture, and a blaster was in his hand. "I'll count three and shoot. One . . . two . . ."

They were gone.

He faced Lucky again. His eyes glittered and his breath came and went quickly through pinched white nostrils.

"Discipline is a great thing," he breathed. "They must

fear me. They must fear me more than they fear capture
by the Terrestrial Navy. Then a ship is one mind and one
arm. *My* mind and arm."

Yes, thought Lucky, one mind and one arm, but
whose? Yours?

Anton's smile had returned, boyish, friendly, and
open. "Now tell me what you want."

Lucky jerked a thumb toward the other's blaster, still
drawn and ready. He matched the other's smile. "Do you
intend shooting? If so, get it over with."

Anton was shaken. "Space! You're a cool one. I'll shoot
when I please. I like it this way. What's your name?" The
blaster held on its line with deadly steadiness.

"Williams, Captain."

"You're a tall man, Williams. You look strong. And yet
here I sit and with just a pressure of my thumb you're
dead. I think it's very instructive. Two men and one
blaster is the whole secret of power. Did you ever think of
power, Williams?"

"Sometimes."

"It's the only meaning to life, don't you think?"

"Maybe."

"I see you're anxious to do business. Let's begin. Why
are you here?"

"I've heard of pirates."

"We're the men of the asteroids, Williams. No other
name."

"That suits me. I've come to join the men of the asteroids."

"You flatter us, but my thumb is still on the blaster
contact. Why do you want to join?"

"Life is closed on Earth, Captain. A man like myself
could settle down to be an accountant or an engineer. I
might even run a factory or sit behind a desk and vote at
stockholders' meetings. It doesn't matter. Whatever it is,

it would be routine. I would know my life from beginning to end. There would be no adventure, no uncertainty."

"You're a philosopher, Williams. Go on."

"There are the colonies, but I'm not attracted by a life as a farm boy on Mars or as a vat tender on Venus. What does attract me is the life on the asteroids. You live hard and dangerously. A man can rise to power as you have. As you say, power gives meaning to life."

"So you stow away on an empty ship?"

"I didn't know it was empty. I had to stow away somewhere. Legitimate space passage comes high and passports to the asteroids aren't being handed out these days. I knew this ship was part of a mapping expedition. The word had got around. It was headed for the asteroids. So I waited till just before it blasted off. That's when everybody would be busy getting ready for takeoff and yet the air-locks would still be open. I had a pal take a sentry out of circulation.

"I figured we'd stop at Ceres. It would be bound to be Prime Base for any asteroid expedition. Once there, it seemed to me I could get off without trouble. The crew would be astronomers and mathematicians. Snatch off their glasses and they'd be blind. Point a blaster at them and they'd die of fright. Once on Ceres I'd contact the pi—— The men of the asteroids, somehow. Simple."

"Only you got a surprise when you boarded ship? Is that it?" asked Anton.

"I'll say. No one aboard and before I could get it straight in my mind that there *wasn't* anyone aboard, it blasted off."

"What's it all about, Williams? How do you figure it?"

"I don't. It beats me."

"Well, let's see if we can find out. You and I together." He gestured with his blaster and said sharply, "Come on."

The pirate chief led the way out of the control room

into the long central corridor of the ship. A group of men came out of a door up ahead. They rumbled short comments at one another and stilled into silence when they caught Anton's eyes.

Anton said, "Come here."

They approached. One wiped a grizzled mustache with the back of his hand and said, "No one else on board this ship, Captain."

"All right. What do you think of the ship?"

There were four of them. The number increased as more men joined the group.

Anton's voice grew edgy. "What do any of you think of the ship?"

Dingo pushed his way forward. He had got rid of his space-suit and Lucky could see him as a man. It was not altogether a pleasant sight. He was broad and heavy and his arms were slightly bowed as they hung loosely from bulging shoulders. There were tufts of dark hair on the back of his fingers and the scar on his upper lip twitched. His eyes glared at Lucky.

He said, "I don't like it."

"You don't like the ship?" Anton asked sharply.

Dingo hesitated. He straightened his arms, threw back his shoulders. "It stinks."

"Why? Why do you say that?"

"I could take it apart with a can opener. Ask the rest and see if they don't agree with me. This crate is put together with toothpicks. It wouldn't hold together for three months."

There were murmurs of agreement. The man with the gray mustache said, "Beg your pardon, Captain, but the wiring is taped in place. It's a two-bit job. The insulation is almost burnt through already."

"All the welding was done in a real hurry," said another. "The seams stand out like that." He held out a thick and dirty thumb.

"What about repairs?" asked Anton.

Dingo said, "It would take a year and a Sunday. It isn't worth it. Anyway, we couldn't do it here. We'd have to take it to one of the rocks."

Anton turned to Lucky, explaining suavely, "We always refer to the asteroids as 'rocks,' you understand."

Lucky nodded.

Anton said, "Apparently my men feel that they wouldn't care to ride this ship. Why do you suppose the Earth government would send out an empty ship and such a jerry-built job to boot?"

"It keeps getting more and more confusing," said Lucky.

"Let's complete our investigation, then."

Anton walked first. Lucky followed closely. The men tagged behind silently. The back of Lucky's neck prickled. Anton's back was straight and fearless, as though he expected no attack from Lucky. He might well feel so. Ten armed men were on Lucky's heels.

They glanced through the small rooms, each designed for utmost economy in space. There was the computation room, the small observatory, the photographic laboratory, the galley and the bunk rooms.

They slipped down to the lower level through a narrow curving tube within which the pseudo-grav field was neutralized so that either direction could be "up" or "down" at will. Lucky was motioned down first, Anton following so closely that Lucky barely had time to scramble out of the way (his legs buckling slightly with the sudden access of weight) before the pirate chief was upon him. Hard, heavy space-boots missed his face by inches.

Lucky regained his balance and whirled angrily, but

Anton was standing there smiling pleasantly, his blaster lined up straight and true at Lucky's heart.

"A thousand apologies," he said. "Fortunately you are quite agile."

"Yes," muttered Lucky.

On the lower level were the engine room and the power plant; the empty berths where the lifeboats had been. There were the fuels store, the food and water stores, the air fresheners, and the atomic shielding.

Anton murmured, "Well, what do you think of it all? Shoddy, perhaps, but I see nothing out of order."

"It's hard to tell like this," said Lucky.

"But you must have lived on this ship for days."

"Sure, but I didn't spend time looking it over. I just waited for it to get somewhere."

"I see. Well, back to upper level."

Lucky was first "down" the travel tube again. This time he landed lightly and sprang six feet to one side with the grace of a cat.

Seconds passed before Anton popped out of the tube. "Jumpy?" he asked.

Lucky flushed.

One by one the pirates appeared. Anton did not wait for all of them, but started down the corridor again.

"You know," he said, "you'd think we'd been all over this ship. Most people would say so. Wouldn't you say so?"

"No," said Lucky calmly, "I wouldn't. We haven't been in the washroom."

Anton scowled and for more than just a moment the pleasantness was gone from his face, and only a tight, white anger flashed in its place.

Then it passed. He adjusted a stray lock of hair on his head then regarded the back of his hand with interest. "Well, let's look there."

Several of the men whistled and the rest exclaimed in a variety of ways when the appropriate door clicked open.

"Very nice," murmured Anton. "Very nice. Luxurious, I would say."

It was! There was no question of that. There were separate stall showers, three of them, with their plumbing arranged for sudsing water (luke-warm) and rinsing water (hot or cold). There were also half a dozen washbowls in ivory-chrome, with shampoo stands, hair driers and needle-jet skin stimulators. Nothing that was necessary was missing.

"There's certainly nothing shoddy about this," said Anton. "It's like a show on the sub-etherics, eh, Williams? What do you make of this?"

"I'm confused."

Anton's smile vanished like the fleeting flash of a speeding space-ship across a visiplate. "I'm not. Dingo, come in here."

The pirate chief said to Lucky, "It's a simple problem, you. We have a ship here with no one aboard, thrown together in the cheapest possible way, as though it were done in a hurry, but with a washroom that is the last word. Why? I think it's just in order to have as many pipes as possible *in* the washroom. And why that? So that we'd never suspect that one or two of them were dummies . . . Dingo, which pipe is it?"

Dingo kicked one.

"Well, don't kick it, you misbegotten fool. Take it apart."

Dingo did so, a micro-heatgun flashing briefly. He yanked out wires.

"What's that, Williams?" demanded Anton.

"Wires," said Lucky briefly.

"I know that, you lump." He was suddenly furious. "What else? I'll tell *you* what else. Those wires are set to explode every ounce of the atomite on board ship as soon as we take the ship back to base."

Lucky jumped. "How can you tell that?"

"You're surprised? You didn't know this was one big trap? You didn't know we were supposed to take this back to base for repairs? You didn't know we were supposed to explode ourselves and the base too, into hot dust? Why, you're here as the bait to make sure we were properly fooled. Only I'm not a fool!"

His men were crowding close. Dingo licked his lips.

With a snap Anton brought up his blaster and there was no mercy, no dream of mercy, in his eyes.

"Wait! Great Galaxy, wait! I know nothing about this. You have no right to shoot me without cause." He tensed for a jump, one last fight before death.

"No right!" Anton, eyes glaring, lowered his blaster suddenly. "How dare you say no right. I have all rights on this ship."

"You can't kill a good man. The men of the asteroids need good men. Don't throw one away for nothing."

A sudden, unexpected murmur came from some of the pirates.

A voice said, "He's got guts, Cap'n. Maybe we could use—"

It died away as Anton turned.

He turned back. "What makes you a good man, Williams? Answer that and I'll consider."

"I'll hold my own against anyone here. Bare fists or any weapon."

"So?" Anton's teeth bared themselves. "You hear that, men?"

There was an affirmative roar.

"It's your challenge, Williams. Any weapon. Good! Come out of this alive and you won't be shot. You'll be considered for membership in my crew."

"I have your word, Captain?"

"You have my word, and I never break my word. The crew hears me. *If* you come out of this alive."

"Whom do I fight?" demanded Lucky.

"Dingo here. A good man. Anyone who can beat him is a *very* good man."

Lucky measured the huge lump of gristle and sinew standing before him, its little eyes glittering with anticipation, and glumly agreed with the captain.

But he said firmly, "What weapons? Or is it bare fists?"

"Weapons! Push-tubes, to be exact. Push-tubes in open space."

For a moment Lucky found it difficult to maintain an appropriate stolidity.

Anton smiled. "Are you afraid it won't be a proper test for you? Don't be. Dingo is the best man with a push-gun in our entire fleet."

Lucky's heart plummeted. A push-gun duel required an expert. Notoriously so! Played as he had played it in college days, it was a sport. Fought by professionals, it was deadly!

And he was no professional!

4

Duel in Deed

Pirates crowded the outer skin of the *Atlas* and of their own Sirian-designed ship. Some were standing, held by the magnetic field of their boots. Others had cast themselves loose for better viewing, maintaining their place by means of a short magnetic cable attached to the ship's hull.

Fifty miles apart two metal-foil goal posts had been set. Not more than three feet square in their collapsed state aboard ship, they opened into a hundred feet either way of thin-beaten beryl-magnesium sheets. Undimmed and undamaged in the great emptiness of space, they were set spinning, and the flickering reflections of the sun on their gleaming surfaces sent beams that were visible for miles.

"You know the rules." Anton's voice was loud in Lucky's ears, and presumably in Dingo's ears as well.

Lucky could make out the other's space-suited shape as a sunlit speck half a mile away. The lifeboat that had brought them here was racing away now, back toward the pirate ship.

"You know the rules," said Anton's voice. "The one

who gets pushed back to his own goal post is the loser. If neither gets pushed back, the one whose push-gun expires first is the loser. No time limit. No off-side. You have five minutes to get set. The push-gun can't be used till the word is given."

No off-side, thought Lucky. That was the giveaway. Push duels as a legal sport could not take place more than a hundred miles from an asteroid at least fifty miles in diameter. This would place a definite, though small, gravitational pull on the players. It would not be enough to affect mobility. It would be enough, however, to rescue a contestant who found himself miles out in space with an expired push-gun. Even if not picked up by the rescue boat he had only to remain quiet and in a matter of hours or, at most, one or two days, he would drift back to the asteroid's surface.

Here, on the other hand, there was no sizable asteroid within hundreds of thousands of miles. A real push would continue indefinitely. It would end, as likely as not, in the sun, long after the unlucky contestant had smothered to death when his oxygen gave out. Under such conditions it was usually understood that, when one contestant or another passed outside certain set limits, time was called until their return.

Saying "no off-side" was saying "to the death."

Anton's voice came clear and sharp across the miles of space between himself and the radio receiver in Lucky's helmet. He said, "Two minutes to go. Adjust body signals."

Lucky brought his hand up and closed the switch set into his chest. The colored metal foil which had earlier been magnet-set into his helmet was spinning. It was a miniature goal post. Dingo's figure, a moment before merely a dim dot, now sprang into flickering ruddy life.

His own signal, Lucky knew, was a flashing green. And the goal posts were pure white.

Even now a fraction of Lucky's mind was far away. He had tried to make one objection at the very beginning. He had said, "Look, this all suits me, you understand. But while we're fooling around, a government patrol ship might——"

Anton barked contemptuously, "Forget it. No patrol ship would have the guts to get this far into the rocks. We've a hundred ships within call, a thousand rocks to hold us if we had to make a getaway. Get into your suit."

A hundred ships! A thousand rocks! If true, the pirates had never yet shown their full hand. What was going on?

"One minute left!" said Anton's voice through space.

Grimly Lucky brought up his two push-guns. They were L-shaped objects connected by springy, gummed fabric tubing to the doughnutlike gas cylinders (containing carbon dioxide liquid under great pressure) that had been adjusted about his waist. In the old days the connecting tubing had been metal mesh. But that, though stronger, had also been more massive and had added to the momentum and inertia of the guns. In push duels rapid aiming and firing was essential. Once a fluorinated silicone had been invented which could remain a flexible gum at space temperatures and yet not become tacky in the direct rays of the sun, the lighter tubing material was universally used.

"Fire when ready!" cried Anton.

One of Dingo's push-guns triggered for an instant. The liquid carbon dioxide of his gas cylinder bubbled into violent gas and spurted out through the push-gun's needlelike orifice. The gas froze into a line of tiny crystals within six inches of its point of emersion. Even in the half second allowed for release a line of crystals, miles long, had been formed. As they pushed out one way, Dingo was pushed in the other. It was a spaceship and its rocket blast in miniature.

Three times the "crystal line" flashed and faded in the distance. It pointed into space directly away from Lucky, and each time Dingo gained speed toward Lucky. The actual state of affairs was deceptive. The only change visible to the eye was the slow brightening of Dingo's suit signal, but Lucky knew that the distance between them was closing with hurtling velocity.

What Lucky did not know was the proper strategy to expect; the appropriate defense. He waited to let the other's offensive moves unfold.

Dingo was large enough now to see as a humanoid shape with head and four limbs. He was passing to one side, and making no move to adjust his aim. He seemed content to bear far to Lucky's left.

Lucky still waited. The chorus of confused cries that rang in his helmet had died down. They came from the open transmitters of the audience. Though these were too far away to see the contestants, they could still follow the passage of the body signals and the flashes of the carbon dioxide streams. They were expecting something, Lucky thought.

It came suddenly.

A blast of carbon dioxide, then another appeared to Dingo's right, and his line of flight veered toward the young Councilman's position. Lucky brought his push-gun up, ready to flash downward and avoid close quarters. The safest strategy, he thought, was to do just that, and to move as slowly and as little as possible otherwise, in order to conserve carbon dioxide.

But Dingo's flight did not continue toward Lucky. He fired straight ahead of himself, a long streak, and began to recede. Lucky watched him, and only too late the streak of light met his eyes.

The line of carbon dioxide that Dingo had last fired traveled forward, yes, but he had been moving leftward at the time and so it did likewise. The two motions together moved it directly toward Lucky and it struck his left shoulder bull's-eye.

To Lucky it felt like a sharp blow pounding him. The crystals were tiny, but they extended for miles and they were traveling at miles per second. They all hit his suit in the space of what seemed a fraction of an eyelid's flicker. Lucky's suit trembled and the roar of the audience was in his ear.

"You got him, Dingo!"

"What a blast!"

"Straight toward goal post. Look at him!"

"It was beautiful. Beautiful!"

"Look at the joker spin!"

Underneath that there were murmurs that seemed, somehow, less exuberant.

Lucky was spinning or, rather, it seemed to his eyes that the heavens and all the stars in it were spinning. Across the face plate of his helmet the stars were white streaks, as though they were sparkles of trillions of carbon dioxide crystals themselves.

He could see nothing but the numerous blurs. For a moment it was as though the blow had knocked the power of thinking out of him.

A blow in the midriff and one in the back sent him, still spinning, further on his hurtling way through space.

He had to do something or Dingo would make a football of him from one end of the Solar System to the other. The first thing was to stop the spin and get his bearings. He was tumbling diagonally, left shoulder over right hip. He pointed the push-gun in the direction counter to that twist, and in lightning releases pumped out streams of carbon dioxide.

The stars slowed until their turning was a stately march that left them sharply defined points. The sky became the familiar sky of space.

One star flickered and was too bright. Lucky knew it to be his own goal post. Almost diametrically opposed was the angry red of Dingo's body signal. Lucky could not fling himself backward beyond the goal post or the duel would be over and he would have lost. Beyond the goal post and within a mile of it was the standard rule for a goal ending. Nor, on the other hand, could he afford to get closer to his opponent.

He brought his push-gun straight up over his head, closed contact, and held it so. He counted a full minute before he released contact, and through all the sixty seconds he felt the pressure against the top of his helmet as he accelerated downward.

It was a desperate maneuver, for he threw away a half hour's supply of gas in that one minute.

Dingo, in outrage, yelled hoarsely, "You flumstered coward! You yellow mugger!"

The cries of the audience also rose to a crescendo.

"Look at him run."

"He got past Dingo. Dingo, get him."

"Hey, Williams. Put up a fight."

Lucky saw the crimson blur of his enemy again.

He had to keep on the move. There was nothing else he could do. Dingo was an expert and could hit a one-inch meteorite as it flashed by. He himself, Lucky thought ruefully, would do well to hit Ceres at a mile.

He used his push-guns alternately. To the left, to the right; then quickly, to the right, to the left and to the right again.

It made no difference. It was as though Dingo could foretell his moves, cut across the corners, move in inexorably.

Lucky felt the perspiration beading out upon his forehead, and suddenly he was aware of the silence. He could not remember the exact moment it had come, but it had come like the breaking of a thread. One moment there had been the yells and laughter of the pirates, and the next moment only the dead silence of space where sound could never be heard.

Had he passed beyond range of the ships? Impossible! Suit radios, even the simplest type, would carry thousands of miles in space. He pushed the sensitivity dial on his chest to maximum.

"Captain Anton!"

But it was Dingo's rough voice that answered. "Don't yell. I hear you."

Lucky said, "Call time! There's something wrong with my radio."

Dingo was close enough to be made out as a human figure again. A flashing line of crystals and he was closer. Lucky moved away, but the pirate followed on his heels.

"Nothing wrong," said Dingo. "Just a gimmicked radio. I've been waiting. I've been waiting. I could have knocked you past goal long ago, but I've been waiting for the radio to go. It's just a little transistor I gimmicked before you put on your suit. You can still talk to me, though. It'll still carry a mile or two. Or at least you can talk to me for a little while." He relished the joke and barked his laughter.

Lucky said, "I don't get it."

Dingo's voice turned harshly cruel. "You caught me on the ship with my blaster in its holster. You trapped me there. You made me look like a fool. No one traps me and I don't let anyone make a fool out of me in front of the captain and live very long after that. I'm not goaling you for someone else to finish. I'm finishing you here! Myself!"

Dingo was much closer. Lucky could almost make out the face behind the thick glassite of the face plate.

Lucky abandoned attempts at bobbing and weaving. That would lead, he decided, to being consistently outmaneuvered. He considered straight flight, pushing outward at increasing velocity as long as his gas held out.

But then afterward? And was he going to be content to die while running away?

He would have to fight back. He aimed the push-gun at Dingo, and Dingo wasn't there when the line of crystals passed through the spot where a moment before he *had* been. He tried again and again, but Dingo was a flitting demon.

And then Lucky felt the hard impact of the other's push-gun blast and he was spinning again. Desperately he tried to come out of the spin and before he could do so, he felt the clanging force of a body's collision with his.

Dingo held his suit in tight embrace.

Helmet to helmet. Face plate to face plate. Lucky was staring at the white scar splitting Dingo's upper lip. It spread tightly as Dingo smiled.

"Hello, chum," he said. "Pleased to meet you."

For a moment Dingo floated away, or seemed to, as he loosened the grip of his arms. The pirate's thighs held firm about Lucky's knees, their apelike strength immobilizing him. Lucky's own whipcord muscles wrenched this way and that uselessly.

Dingo's partial retreat had only been designed to free his arms. One lifted high, push-gun held butt-first. It came down directly on the face plate and Lucky's head snapped back with the sudden, shattering impact. The relentless arm swung up again, while the other curled about Lucky's neck.

"Hold your head still," the pirate snarled. "I'm finishing this."

Lucky knew that to be the literal truth unless he acted quickly. The glassite was strong and tough, but it would hold out only so long against the battering of metal.

He brought up the heel of his gauntleted hand against Dingo's helmet, straightening his arm and pushing the pirate's head back. Dingo rocked his head to one side, disengaging Lucky's arm. He brought the butt of his push-gun down a second time.

Lucky dropped both push-guns, let them dangle from their connecting tubes, and with a sure movement snatched at the connecting tubes of Dingo's guns. He threaded them between the fingers of his steel gloves. The muscles of his arms lumped and tightened painfully. His jaws clenched and he felt the blood creep to his temples.

Dingo, his mouth twisted in fierce joyful anticipation, disregarded everything but the upturned face of his victim behind the transparent face plate, contorted, as he thought, with fear. Once more the butt came down. A small cracking star appeared where the metal had struck.

Then something else gave and the universe seemed to go mad.

First one and, almost immediately afterward, the other of the connecting tubes of Dingo's two push-guns parted and an uncontrollable stream of carbon dioxide ravened out of each broken tube.

The tubes whipped like insane snakes, and Lucky was slammed against his suit first this way, then that, in violent reaction to the mad and uncontrolled acceleration.

Dingo yelled in jolted surprise and his grip loosened.

The two almost separated, but Lucky held on grimly to one of the pirate's ankles.

The carbon dioxide stream slackened and Lucky went up his opponent's leg hand over hand.

They were apparently motionless now. The chance

whippings of the stream had left them even without any perceptible spin. Dingo's push-gun tubes, now dead and flaccid, stretched out in their last position. All seemed still, as still as death.

But that was a delusion. Lucky knew they were traveling at miles per second in whatever direction that last stroke of gas had sent them. They were alone and lost in space, the two of them.

5

The Hermit on the Rock

Lucky was on Dingo's back now and it was his thighs that gripped the other's waist. He spoke softly and grimly. "You can hear me, Dingo, can't you? I don't know where we are or where we're going, but neither do you. So we need each other now, Dingo. Are you ready to make a deal? You can find out where we are because your radio will reach the ships, but you can't get back without carbon dioxide. I have enough for both of us, but I'll need you to guide us back."

"To space with you, you scupper," yelled Dingo. "When I'm done with you, I'll *have* your push-tubes."

"I don't think you will," said Lucky coolly.

"You think you'll let them loose too. Go ahead! Go ahead, you loshing ripper! What good will that do? The captain will come for me wherever I am while you're floating around with a busted helmet and frozen blood on your face."

"Not exactly, my friend. There is something in your back, you know. Maybe you can't feel it through the metal, but it's there, I assure you."

"A push-gun. So what. It doesn't mean a thing as long

as we're held together." But his arms halted their writhing attempt to seize Lucky.

"I'm not a push-gun duelist." Lucky sounded cheerful about it. "But I still know more than you do about push-guns. Push-gun shots are exchanged miles apart. There's no air resistance to slow and mess up the gas stream, but there's internal resistance. There's always some turbulence in the stream. The crystals knock together, slow up. The line of gas widens. If it misses its mark, it finally spreads out in space and vanishes, but if it finally hits, it still kicks like a mule after miles of travel."

"What in space are you talking about? What are you running off about?" The pirate twisted with bull strength, and Lucky grunted as he forced him back.

Lucky said, "Just this. What do you suppose happens when the carbon dioxide hits at two inches, before turbulence has done anything at all to cut down its velocity or to broaden the beam. Don't guess. I'll tell you. It would cut through your suit as though it were a blowtorch, and through your body too."

"You're nuts! You're talking crazy!"

Dingo swore madly, but of a sudden he was holding his body stiffly motionless.

"Try it, then," said Lucky. "Move! My push-gun is hard against your suit and I'm squeezing the trigger. Try it out."

"You're fouling me," snarled Dingo. "This isn't a clean win."

"I've got a crack in my face plate," said Lucky. "The men will know where the foul is. You have half a minute to make up your mind."

The seconds passed in silence. Lucky caught the motion of Dingo's hand.

He said, "Good-by, Dingo!"

Dingo cried thickly, "Wait! *Wait!* I'm just extending

my sending range." Then he called, "Captain Anton . . .
Captain Anton . . ."

It took an hour and a half to get back to the ships.

The *Atlas* was moving through space again in the wake of
its pirate captor. Its automatic circuits had been shifted to
manual controls wherever necessary, and a prize crew of
three controlled its power. As before, it had a passenger
list of one—Lucky Starr.

Lucky was confined to a cabin and saw the crew only
when they brought him his rations. The *Atlas's* own rations, thought Lucky. Or, at least, such as were left. Most
of the food and such equipment that wasn't necessary for
the immediate maneuvering of the ship had already been
transferred to the pirate vessel.

All three pirates brought him his first meal. They were
lean men, browned by the unsoftened rays of the sun of
space.

They gave him his tray in silence, inspected the cabin
cautiously, stood by while he opened the cans and let
their contents warm up, then carried away the remains.

Lucky said, "Sit down, men. You don't have to stand
while I eat."

They did not answer. One, the thinnest and lankest of
the three, with a nose that had once been broken and was
now bent sideways, and an Adam's-apple that jutted
sharply outward, looked at the others as though he felt
inclined to accept the invitation. He met with no response, however.

The next meal was brought by Broken Nose alone. He
put down the tray, went back to the door, which he
opened. He looked up and down the corridor, closed the
door again, and said, "I'm Martin Maniu."

Lucky smiled. "I'm Bill Williams. The other two don't
talk to me, eh?"

"They're Dingo's friends. But I'm not. Maybe you're a government man like the captain thinks, and maybe you're not. I don't know. But as far as I'm concerned, anyone who does what you did to that scupper Dingo is all right. He's a wise guy and he plays rough. He got me into a push fight once when I was new. He nearly pushed me into an asteroid. For no reason, either. He claimed it was a mistake, but listen, he doesn't make any mistakes with a pusher. You made quite a few friends, mister, when you dragged back that hyena by the seat of his pants."

"I'm glad of that, anyway."

"But watch out for him. He'll never forget it. Don't be alone with him even twenty years from now. I'm telling you. It isn't just beating him, you see. It's bluffing him with the story about cutting through an inch of metal with the carbon dioxide. Everyone's laughing at him and he's sick about it. Man, I mean sick! It's the best thing that's ever happened. Man, I sure hope the Boss gives you a clean bill."

"The Boss? Captain Anton?"

"No, the Boss. The big fellow. Say, the food you've got on board ship is good. Especially the meat." The pirate smacked his lips loudly. "You get tired of all these yeast mashes, especially when you're in charge of a vat yourself."

Lucky was brushing up the remainder of his meal. "Who *is* this guy?"

"Who?"

"The Boss."

Maniu shrugged. "Space! I don't know. You don't think a guy like me would ever meet him. Just someone the fellows talk about. It stands to reason *someone's* boss."

"The organization is pretty complicated."

"Man, you never know till you join. Listen, I was dead broke when I came out here. I didn't know what to do. I thought, well, we'll bang up a few ships and then I'll get mine and it'll be over. You know, it would be better than starving to death like I was doing."

"It wasn't that way?"

"*No.* I've never been on a raiding expedition. Hardly any of us are. Just a few like Dingo. *He* goes out all the time. He likes it, the scupper. Mostly we go out and pick up a few women sometimes." The pirate smiled. "I've got a wife and a kid. You wouldn't believe that now, would you? Sure, we've got a little project of our own. Have our own vats. Once in a while I draw space duty, like now, for instance. It's a soft life. You could do all right, if you join up. A good-looking fellow like you could get a wife in no time and settle down. Or there's plenty of excitement if that's what you want.

"Yes, sir, Bill. I hope the Boss takes you."

Lucky followed him to the door. "Where are we going, by the way? One of the bases?"

"Just to one of the rocks, I guess. Whichever is nearest. You'll stay there till the word comes through. It's what they usually do."

He added as he closed the door, "And don't tell the fellows, or anybody, I've been talking to you. Okay, pal?"

"Sure thing."

Alone again, Lucky pounded a fist slowly and softly into his palm. The Boss! Was that just talk? Scuttlebutt? Or did it mean something? And what about the rest of the conversation?

He had to wait. Galaxy! If only Conway and Henree had the good sense not to interfere for a while longer.

Lucky did not get a chance to view the "rock" as the *Atlas* approached. He did not see it until, preceded by Martin Maniu and followed by a second pirate, he stepped out of the air-lock into space and found it a hundred yards below.

The asteroid was quite typical. Lucky judged it to be two miles across the longest way. It was angular and craggy, as though a giant had torn off the top of a mountain and tossed it out into space. Its sunside glimmered gray-brown, and it was turning visibly, shadows shifting and changing.

He pushed downward toward the asteroid as he left the air-lock, flexing his leg muscles against the ship's hull. The crags floated up slowly toward himself. When his hands touched ground, his inertia forced the rest of his body on downward, tumbling him in slowest motion until he could grasp a projection and bring himself to a halt.

He stood up. There was almost the illusion of a planetary surface about the rock. The nearest jags of matter, however, had nothing behind them, nothing but space. The stars, moving visibly as the rock turned, were hard, bright glitters. The ship, which had been put into an orbit about the rock, remained motionless overhead.

A pirate led the way, some fifty feet, to a rise in rock in no way distinguished from its surroundings. He made it in two long steps. As they waited a section of the rise slipped aside, and from the opening a space-suited figure stepped out.

"Okay, Herm," said one of the pirates, gruffly, "here he is. He's in your care now."

The voice that next sounded in Lucky's receiver was gentle and rather weary. "How long will he be with me, gentlemen?"

"Till we come to get him. And don't ask questions."

The pirates turned away and leaped upward. The rock's gravity could do nothing to stop them. They dwindled steadily and after a few minutes, Lucky saw a brief flash of crystals as one of them corrected his direction of travel by means of a push-gun; a small one, routinely used for such purposes, that was part of standard suit equipment. Its gas supply consisted of a built-in carbon dioxide cartridge.

Minutes passed and the ship's rear jets gleamed redly. It, too, began dwindling.

It was useless to try to check the direction in which it was leaving, Lucky knew, without some knowledge of his own location in space. And of that, except that he was somewhere in the asteroid belt, he knew nothing.

So intense was his absorption that he was almost startled at the soft voice of the other man on the asteroid.

He said, "It *is* beautiful out here. I come out so rarely that sometimes I forget. Look there!"

Lucky turned to his left. The small Sun was just poking above the sharp edge of the asteroid. In a moment it was too bright to look at. It was a gleaming twenty-credit gold piece. The sky, black before, remained black, and the stars shone undiminished. That was the way on an airless world where there was no dust to scatter sunlight and turn the heavens a deep, masking blue.

The man of the asteroid said, "In twenty-five minutes or so it will be setting again. Sometimes, when Jupiter is at its closest, you can see it too, like a little marble, with its four satellites like sparks lined up in military formation. But that only happens every three and a half years. This isn't the time."

Lucky said bluntly, "Those men called you Herm. Is that your name? Are you one of them?"

"You mean am I a pirate? No. But I'll admit I may be an accessory after the fact. Nor is my name Herm. That's just a term they use for hermits in general. My name, sir, is Joseph Patrick Hansen, and since we are to be companions at close quarters for an indefinite period, I hope we shall be friends."

He held out a metal-sheathed hand, and Lucky grasped it.

"I'm Bill Williams," he said. "You say you're a hermit? Do you mean by that that you live here all the time?"

"That's right."

Lucky looked about the poor splinter of granite and silica and frowned. "It doesn't look very inviting."

"Nevertheless I'll try to do my best to make you comfortable."

The hermit touched a section of the slab or rock out of which he had come and a piece of it wheeled open once again. Lucky noted that the edges had been beveled and lined with lastium or some similar material to insure air tightness.

"Won't you step inside, Mr. Williams?" invited the hermit.

Lucky did so. The rock slab closed behind them. As it closed, a small Fluoro lit up and shone away the obscurity. It revealed a small air-lock, not much larger than was required to hold two men.

A small red signal light flickered, and the hermit said, "You can open your face-plate now. We've got air." He did so himself as he spoke.

Lucky followed suit, dragging in lungfuls of clear, fresh air. Not bad. Better than the air on shipboard. Definitely.

But it was when the inner door of the air-lock opened that the wind went out of Lucky in one big gasp.

6

What the Hermit Knew

Lucky had seen few such luxurious rooms even on Earth. It was thirty feet long, twenty wide, and thirty high. A balcony circled it. Above and below the walls were lined with bookfilms. A wall projector was set on a pedestal, while on another was a gemlike model of the Galaxy. The lighting was entirely indirect.

As soon as he set foot within the room, he felt the tug of pseudo-grav motors. It wasn't set at Earth normal. From the feel of it it seemed somewhere between Earth and Mars normal. There was a delightful sensation of lightness and yet enough pull to allow full muscular coordination.

The hermit had removed his space-suit and suspended it over a white plastic trough into which the frost that had collected thickly over it when they stepped out of frozen space and into the warm, moist air of the room might trickle as it melted.

He was tall and straight, his face was pink and unlined, but his hair was quite white, as were his bushy eyebrows, and the veins stood out on the back of his hands.

He said politely, "May I help you with your suit?"

Lucky came to life. "That's all right." He clambered out quickly. "This is an unusual place you have here."

"You like it?" Hansen smiled. "It took many years to make it look like this. Nor is this all there is to my little home." He seemed filled with a quiet pride.

"I imagine so," said Lucky. "There must be a power-plant for light and heat as well as to keep the pseudo-grav field alive. You must have an air purifier and replacer, water supplies, food stores, all that."

"That's right."

"A hermit's life is not bad."

The hermit was obviously both proud and pleased. "It doesn't have to be," he said. "Sit down, Williams, sit down. Would you like a drink?"

"No, thank you." Lucky lowered himself into an arm-chair. Its apparently normal seat and back masked a soft diamagnetic field that gave under his weight only so far, then achieved a balance that molded itself to every curve of his body. "Unless you can scare up a cup of coffee?"

"Easily!" The old man stepped into an alcove. In seconds he was back with a fragrant and steaming cup, plus a second for himself.

The arm of Lucky's chair unfolded into a narrow ledge at the proper touch of Hansen's toe and the hermit set down one cup into an appropriate recess. As he did so he paused to stare at the younger man.

Lucky looked up. "Yes?"

Hansen shook his head. "Nothing. Nothing."

They faced one another. The lights in the more distant parts of the large room faded until only the area immediately surrounding the two men was clear to vision.

"And now if you'll pardon an old man's curiosity," said the hermit, "I'd like to ask you why you've come here."

"I didn't come. I was brought," said Lucky.

"You mean you're not one of——" Hansen paused.

"No, I'm not a pirate. At least, not yet."

Hansen put down his cup and looked troubled. "I don't understand. Perhaps I've said things I shouldn't have."

"Don't worry about it. I'm going to be one of them soon enough."

Lucky finished his coffee and then, choosing his words carefully, began with his boarding of the *Atlas* on the Moon and carried through to the moment.

Hansen listened in absorption. "And are you sure this is what you want to do, young man, now that you've seen a little of what the life is like?"

"I'm sure."

"Why, for Earth's sake?"

"Exactly. For the sake of Earth and what it did to me. It's no place to live. Why did *you* come out here?"

"It's a long story, I'm afraid. You needn't look alarmed. I won't tell it. I bought this asteroid long ago as a place for small vacations, and I grew to like it. I kept enlarging the room space, brought furniture and book films from Earth little by little. Eventually I found I had all I needed here. So why not stay here permanently? I asked myself. And I did stay here permanently."

"Sure. Why not? You're smart. Back there it's a mess. Too many people. Too many rut jobs. Next to impossible to get out to the planets, and if you do, it means a job of manual labor. No opportunity for a man any more unless he comes to the asteroids. I'm not old enough to settle down like you. But for a young fellow it's a free life and an exciting one. There's room to be boss."

"The ones who are already boss don't like young fellows with boss notions in their head. Anton, for instance. I've seen him and I know."

"Maybe, but so far he's kept his word," said Lucky.

"He said if I came out winner over this Dingo, I'd have my chance to join the men of the asteroids. It looks as though I'm getting the chance."

"It looks as though you're here, that's all. What if he returns with proof, or what he calls proof, that you're a government man?"

"He won't."

"And if he does? Just to get rid of you?"

Lucky's face darkened and again Hansen looked at him curiously, frowning a bit.

Lucky said, "He wouldn't. He can use a good man and he knows it. Besides, why are you preaching to me? You're out here yourself playing ball with them."

Hansen looked down. "It's true. I shouldn't interfere with you. It's just that being alone here so long, I'm apt to talk too much when a person does come along, just to hear the sound of voices. Look, it's about time for dinner. I would be glad to have you eat with me in silence, if you'd rather. Or else we'll talk about anything you choose."

"Well, thanks, Mr. Hansen. No hard feelings."

"Good."

Lucky followed Hansen through a door into a small pantry lined with canned food and concentrates of all sorts. None of the brand names familiar to Lucky were represented. Instead the contents of each can were described in brightly colored etchings that were themselves integral parts of the metal.

Hansen said, "I used to keep fresh meat in a special freeze room. You can get the temperature down all the way on an asteroid, you know, but it's been two years since I could get that kind of supplies."

He chose half a dozen cans off the shelves, plus a container of milk concentrate. At his suggestion Lucky took up a sealed gallon container of water from a lower shelf.

The hermit set the table quickly. The cans were of the self-heating type that opened up into dishes with enclosed cutlery.

Hansen said, with some amusement, indicating the cans, "I've got a whole valley on the outside brim-filled with these things. Discarded ones, that is. A twenty years' accumulation."

The food was good, but strange. It was yeast-base material, the kind only the Terrestrial Empire produced. Nowhere else in the Galaxy was the pressure of population so great, the billions of people so numerous, that yeast culture had been developed. On Venus, where most of the yeast products were grown, almost any variety of food imitation could be produced: steaks, nuts, butter, candy. It was as nourishing as the real thing too. To Lucky, however, the flavor was not quite Venusian. There was a sharper tang to it.

"Pardon me for being nosy," he said, "but all this takes money, doesn't it?"

"Oh yes, and I have some. I have investments on Earth. Quite good ones. My checks are always honored, or at least they were until not quite two years ago."

"What happened then?"

"The supply ships stopped coming. Too risky on account of the pirates. It was a bad blow. I had a good backlog of supplies in most things, but I can imagine how it must have been for the others."

"The others?"

"The other hermits. There are hundreds of us. They're not all as lucky as I am. Very few can afford to make their worlds quite this comfortable, but they can manage the essentials. It's usually old people like myself, with wives dead, children grown up, the world strange and different, who go off by themselves. If they have a little nest egg, they can get a little asteroid started. The government doesn't charge. Any asteroid you want to settle on, if it's less than five miles in diameter, is yours. Then if they want they can invest in a sub-etheric receiver and keep up with the universe. If not, they can have book films, or can arrange to have news transcripts brought in by the supply ships once a year, or they can just eat, rest, sleep, and wait to die if they'd rather. I wish, sometimes, I'd got to know some of them."

"Why haven't you?"

"Sometimes I've felt willing, but they're not easy people to know. After all, they've come here to be alone, and for that matter, so have I."

"Well, what did you do when the supply ships stopped coming?"

"Nothing at first. I thought surely the government would clean up the situation and I had enough supplies for months. In fact, I could have skimped along for a year, maybe. But then the pirate ships came."

"And you threw in with them?"

The hermit shrugged. His eyebrows drew together in a troubled frown and they finished their meal in silence.

At the end he gathered the can plates and cutlery and placed them in a wall container in the alcove that led to the pantry. Lucky heard a dim grating noise of metal on metal that diminished rapidly.

Hansen said, "The pseudo-grav field doesn't extend to the disposal tube. A puff of air and they sail out to the valley I told you of, even though it's nearly a mile away."

"It seems to me," said Lucky, "that if you'd try a little harder puff, you'd get rid of the cans altogether."

"So I would. I think most hermits do that. Maybe they all do. I don't like the idea, though. It's a waste of air, and of metal too. We might reclaim those cans someday. Who knows? Besides even though most of the cans would scatter here and there, I'm sure that some would circle this asteroid like little moons and it's undignified to think of being accompanied on your orbit by your garbage. Care to smoke? No? Mind if I do?"

He lit a cigar and with a contented sigh went on. "The men of the asteroids can't supply tobacco regularly, so this is becoming a rare treat for me."

Lucky said, "Do they furnish you the rest of your supplies?"

"That's right. Water, machine parts and power-pack renewals. It's an arrangement."

"And what do you do for them?"

The hermit studied his cigar's lighted end. "Not much. They use this world. They land their ships on it and I don't report them. They don't come in here and what they do elsewhere on the rock isn't my business. I don't want to know. It's safer that way. Men are left here sometimes, like yourself, and are picked up later. I have an idea they stop for minor repairs sometimes. They bring me supplies in return."

"Do they supply all the hermits?"

"I wouldn't know. Maybe."

"It would take an awful lot of supplies. Where would they get them from?"

"They capture ships."

"Not enough to supply hundreds of hermits *and* themselves. I mean, it would take an awful lot of ships."

"I wouldn't know."

"Aren't you interested? It's a soft life you have here, but maybe the food we just ate came off a ship whose crew are frozen corpses circling some other asteroid like human garbage. Do you ever think of that?"

The hermit flushed painfully. "You're getting your revenge for my having preached to you earlier. You're right,

but what can I do? I didn't abandon or betray the government. They abandoned and betrayed me. My estate on
Earth pays taxes. Why am I not protected then? I registered this asteroid with the Terrestrial Outer World Bureau in good faith. It's part of the Terrestrial dominion. I
have every right to expect protection against the pirates.
If that's not forthcoming; if my source of supply coolly
says that they can bring me nothing more at any price,
what am I supposed to do?

"You might say I could have returned to Earth, but
how could I abandon all this? I have a world of my own
here. My book films, the great classics that I love. I even
have a copy of Shakespeare; a direct filming of the actual
pages of an ancient printed book. I have food, drink, privacy: I could find nowhere as comfortable as this anywhere else in the Universe.

"Don't think it's been an easy choice, though. I have a
sub-etheric transmitter. I could communicate with Earth.
I've got a little ship that can make the short haul to Ceres.
The men of the asteroids know that, but they trust me.
They know I have no choice. As I told you when we first
met, I'm an accessory after the fact.

"I've helped them. That makes me legally a pirate. It
would be jail, execution, probably, if I return. If not, if
they free me provided I turn state's evidence, the men of
the asteroids won't forget. They would find me no matter
where I went, unless I could be guaranteed complete government protection for life."

"It looks like you're in a bad way," said Lucky.

"Am I?" said the hermit. "I might be able to get that
complete protection with the proper help."

It was Lucky's turn. "I wouldn't know," he said.

"I think you would."

"I don't get you."

"Look, I'll give you a word of warning in return for help."

"There's nothing *I* can do. What's your word?"

"Get off the asteroid before Anton and his men come back."

"Not on your life. I came here to join them, not to go home."

"If you don't leave, you'll stay forever. You'll stay as a dead man. They won't let you on any crew. You won't qualify, mister."

Lucky's face twisted in anger. "What in space are you talking about, old-timer?"

"There it is again. When you get angry, I see it plainly. You're not Bill Williams, son. What's your relationship to Lawrence Starr of the Council of Science? Are you Starr's son?"

7

To Ceres

Lucky's eyes narrowed. He felt the muscles of his right arm tense as though to reach for a hip at which no blaster nestled. He made no actual motion.

His voice remained under strict control. He said, "Whose son? What are you talking about?"

"I'm sure of it." The hermit leaned forward, seizing Lucky's wrist earnestly. "I knew Lawrence Starr well. He was my friend. He helped me once when I needed help. And you're his image. I couldn't be wrong."

Lucky pulled his hand away. "You're not making sense."

"Listen, son, it may be important to you not to give away your identity. Maybe you don't trust me. All right, I'm not telling you to trust me. I've been working with the pirates and I've admitted it. But listen to me anyway. The men of the asteroids have a good organization. It may take them weeks, but if Anton suspects you, they won't stop till you're checked from the ground up. No phony story will fool them. They'll get the truth and they'll learn who you are. Be sure of that! They'll get your true identity. Leave, I tell you. Leave!"

Lucky said, "If I were this guy you say I am, old-timer, aren't you getting yourself into trouble? I take it you want me to use your ship."

"Yes."

"And what would *you* do when the pirates returned?"

"I wouldn't be here. Don't you see? I want to go with you."

"And leave all you have here?"

The old man hesitated. "Yes, it's hard. But I won't have a chance like this again. You're a man of influence; you must be. You're a member of the Council of Science, perhaps. You're here on secret work. They'll believe you. You could protect me, vouch for me. You would prevent prosecution, see that no harm came to me from the pirates. It would pay the Council, young man. I would tell them all I know about the pirates. I would co-operate in every way I could."

Lucky said, "Where do you keep your ship?"

"It's a deal, then?"

The ship was a small one indeed. The two reached it through a narrow corridor, walking single file, their figures grotesque again in space-suits.

Lucky said, "Is Ceres close enough to pick out by ship's telescope?"

"Yes indeed."

"You could recognize it without trouble?"

"Certainly."

"Let's get on board, then."

The fore end of the airless cavern that housed the ship opened outward as soon as the ship's motors were activated.

"Radio control," explained Hansen.

The ship was fueled and provisioned. It worked smoothly, rising out of its berth and into space with the ease and freedom possible only where gravitational forces were virtually lacking. For the first time Lucky saw Hansen's asteroid from space. He caught a glimpse of the valley of the discarded cans, brighter than the surrounding rock, just before it passed into shadow.

Hansen said, "Tell me, now. You are the son of Lawrence Starr, aren't you?"

Lucky had located a well-charged blaster and a holster belt to boot. He was strapping it on as he spoke.

"My name," he said, "is David Starr. Most people call me Lucky."

Ceres is a monster among the asteroids. It is nearly five hundred miles in diameter, and, standing upon it, the average man actually weighs two full pounds. It is quite spherical in shape, and anyone very close to it in space could easily think it was a respectable planet.

Still, if the Earth were hollow, it would be possible to throw into it four thousand bodies the size of Ceres before filling it up.

Bigman stood on the surface of Ceres, his figure bloated in a space-suit which had been loaded to bursting with lead weights and on shoes the soles of which were foot-thick lead clogs. It had been his own idea, but it was quite useless. He still weighed less than four pounds and his every motion threatened to twist him up into space.

He had been on Ceres for days now, since the quick space flight with Conway and Henree from the Moon, waiting for this moment, waiting for Lucky Starr to send in the radio message that he was coming in. Gus Henree and Hector Conway had been nervous about it, fearing Lucky's death, worrying about it. He, Bigman, had known better. Lucky could come through anything. He told them that. When Lucky's message finally came, he told them again.

But just the same, out here on Ceres' frozen soil with nothing between himself and the stars, he admitted a sneaking sensation of relief.

From where he sat he was looking directly at the dome of the Observatory, its lower reaches dipping just a little below the close horizon. It was the largest observatory in the Terrestrial Empire for a very logical reason.

In that part of the Solar System inside the orbit of Jupiter, the planets Venus, Earth, and Mars had atmospheres and were by that very fact poorly suited for astronomic observation. The interfering air, even when it was as thin as that of Mars, blotted out the finer detail. It wavered and flickered star images and spoiled things generally.

The largest airless object inside Jupiter's orbit was Mercury, but that was so close to the Sun that the observatory in its twilight zone specialized in solar observations. Relatively small telescopes sufficed.

The second largest airless object was the Moon. Here again circumstances dictated specialization. Weather forecasts on Earth, for instance, had become an accurate, long-range science, since the appearance of Earth's atmosphere could be viewed as a whole from a distance of a quarter of a million miles.

And the third largest airless object was Ceres, and that was the best of the three. Its almost nonexistent gravity allowed huge lenses and mirrors to be poured without the danger of breakage, without even the question of sag, due to its own weight. The structure of the telescope tube itself needed no particular strength. Ceres was nearly three times as far from the Sun as was the Moon and sunlight was only one eighth as strong. Its rapid revolution kept Ceres' temperature almost constant. In short, Ceres was ideal for observation of the stars and of the outer planets.

Only the day before Bigman had seen Saturn through the thousand-inch reflecting telescope, the grinding of the huge mirror having consumed twenty years of painstaking and continuous labor.

"What do I look through?" he had asked.

They laughed at him. "You don't look through anything," they said.

They worked the controls carefully, three of them, each doing something that co-ordinated with the other two, until all were satisfied. The dim red lights dimmed further and in the pit of black emptiness about which they sat a blob of light sprang into being. A touch at the controls and it focused sharply.

Bigman whistled his astonishment. It was Saturn!

It was Saturn, three feet wide, exactly as he had seen it from space half a dozen times. Its triple rings were bright and he could see three marble-like moons. Behind it was a numerous dusting of stars. Bigman wanted to walk about it to see how it looked with the night shadow cutting it, but the picture didn't change as he moved.

"It's just an image," they told him, "an illusion. You see the same thing no matter where you stand."

Now, from the asteroid's surface, Bigman could spot Saturn with the naked eye. It was just a white dot, but brighter than the other white dots that were the stars. It was twice as bright as it appeared from Earth, since it was two hundred million miles closer here. Earth itself was on the other side of Ceres near the pea-size Sun. Earth wasn't a very impressive sight, since the Sun invariably dwarfed it.

Bigman's helmet suddenly rang with sound as the call flooded his left-open radio receiver.

"Hey, Shortie, get moving. There's a ship coming in."

Bigman jumped at the noise and moved straight upward, limbs flailing. He yelled, "Who're you calling Shortie?"

But the other was laughing. "Hey, how much do you charge for flying lessons, little boy?"

"I'll little boy you," screamed Bigman furiously. He had reached the peak of his parabola and was slowly and hesitatingly beginning to settle downward once more. "What's your name, wise guy? Say your name, and I'll crack your gizzard as soon as I get back and peel the suit."

"Think you can reach my gizzard?" came the mocking rejoinder, and Bigman would have exploded into tiny pieces if he had not caught sight of a ship slanting down from the horizon.

He loped in giant, clumsy strides about the leveled square mile of ground that was the asteroid's space-port, trying to judge the exact spot on which the ship would land.

It dropped down its steaming jets to a feather-touch planetary contact and when the air-locks opened and Lucky's tall, suited figure emerged, Bigman, yelling his joy, made one long leap of it, and they were together.

Conway and Henree were less effusive in their welcome, but no less joyful. Each wrung Lucky's hand as though to confirm, by sheer muscular pressure, the reality of the flesh and blood they beheld.

Lucky laughed. "Whoa, will you? Give me a chance to breathe. What's the matter? Didn't you think I was coming back?"

"Look here," said Conway, "you'd better consult us before you take off on just any old fool notion."

"Well, now, not if it's too much of a fool notion, please, or you won't let me."

"Never mind that. I can ground you for what you've done. I can have you put under detention right now. I can suspend you. I can throw you off the Council," said Conway.

"Which of them are you going to do?"

"None of them, you darned overgrown young fool. But I *may* beat your brains out one of these days."

Lucky turned to Augustus Henree. "You won't let him, will you?"

"Frankly, I'll help him."

"Then I give up in advance. Look, there's a gentleman here I'd like to have you meet."

Until now Hansen had remained in the background, obviously amused by the interchange of nonsense. The two older Councilmen had been too full of Lucky Starr even to be aware of his existence.

"Dr. Conway," said Lucky, "Dr. Henree, this is Mr. Joseph P. Hansen, the man whose ship I used to come back. He has been of considerable assistance to me."

The old hermit shook hands with the two scientists.

"I don't suppose you can possibly know Drs. Conway and Henree," said Lucky. The hermit shook his head.

"Well," he went on, "they're important officials in the Council of Science. After you've eaten and had a chance to rest, they'll talk to you and help you, I'm sure."

An hour later the two Councilmen faced Lucky with somber expressions. Dr. Henree tamped tobacco into his pipe with a little finger, and smoked quietly as he listened to Lucky's accounts of his adventures with the pirates.

"Have you told this to Bigman?" he asked.

"I've just spent some time talking to him," said Lucky.

"And he didn't assault you for not taking him?"

"He wasn't pleased," Lucky admitted.

But Conway's mind was more seriously oriented. "A Sirian-designed ship, eh?" he mused.

"Undoubtedly so," said Lucky. "At least we have that piece of information."

"The information wasn't worth the risk," said Conway, dryly. "I'm much more disturbed over another piece of information we have now. It's obvious that the Sirian organization penetrates into the Council of Science itself."

Henree nodded gravely. "Yes, I saw that too. Very bad."

Lucky said, "How do you make that out?"

"Galaxy, boy, it's obvious," growled Conway. "I'll admit that we had a large construction crew working on the ship and that even with the best intentions careless slips of information can take place. It remains truth, though, that the fact of the booby-trapping and particularly the exact manner of the fusing were known only to Council members and not too many of those. Somewhere in that small group is a spy, yet I could have sworn that all were faithful." He shook his head. "I still can't believe otherwise."

"You don't have to," said Lucky.

"Oh? And why not?"

"Because the Sirian contact was quite temporary. The Sirian Embassy got their information from *me*."

8

Bigman Takes Over

"Indirectly, of course, through one of their known spies," he amplified, as the two older men stared at him in shocked astonishment.

"I don't understand you at all," said Henree in a low voice. Conway was obviously speechless.

"It was necessary. I had to introduce myself to the pirates without suspicion. If they found me on what they thought was a mapping ship, they would have shot me out of hand. On the other hand, if they found me on a booby-trapped ship the secret of which they had stumbled on by what seemed a stroke of fortune, they would have taken me at face value as a stowaway. Don't you see? On a mapping ship I'm only a member of the crew that didn't get away in time. On a booby trap, I'm a poor jerk who didn't realize what he was stowing away on."

"They might have shot you anyway. They might have seen through your double-cross and considered you a spy. In fact, they almost did."

"True! They almost did," admitted Lucky.

Conway finally exploded. "And what about the original plan. Were we or were we not going to explode one of their bases? When I consider the months we spent on the construction of the *Atlas,* the money that went into it—"

"What good would it have done to explode one of their bases? We spoke about a huge hangar of pirate ships, but actually that was only wishful thinking. An organization based upon the asteroids would have to be decentralized. The pirates probably don't have more than three or four ships in any one place. There wouldn't be room for more. Exploding three or four ships would mean very little compared with what would have been accomplished if I had succeeded in penetrating their organization."

"But you didn't succeed," said Conway. "With all your fool risks, you didn't succeed."

"Unfortunately the pirate captain who took the *Atlas* was too suspicious, or perhaps too intelligent for us. I'll try not to underestimate them again. But it's not all loss. We know for a fact that Sirius is behind them. In addition, we have my hermit friend."

"He won't help us," said Conway. "From what you've said about him, it sounds as though he were only interested in having as little to do with the pirates as possible. So what can he know?"

"He may be able to tell us more than he himself thinks is possible," said Lucky coolly. "For instance, there's one piece of information he can give us that will enable me to continue efforts at working against piracy from the inside."

"You're not going out there again," said Conway hastily.

"I don't intend to," said Lucky.

Conway's eyes narrowed. "Where's Bigman?"

"On Ceres. Don't worry. In fact," and a shadow crossed Lucky's face, "he should be here by now. The delay is beginning to bother me a little."

• • •

John Bigman Jones used his special pass card to get past the guard at the door to the Control Tower. He was muttering to himself as he half-ran along the corridors.

The slight flush on his pug-nosed face dimmed his freckles and his reddish hair stood up in tufts like fence pickets. Lucky had frequently told him he cultivated a vertical hair-do to make himself look taller, but he always denied that vigorously.

The final door to the Tower swung open as he broke the photoelectric beam. He stepped inside and looked about.

Three men were on duty. One with earphones sat at the sub-etheric receiver, another was at the calculating machine and the third was at the curved radarized visiplate.

Bigman said, "Which one of you knotbrains called me Shortie?"

The three turned toward him in unison, their faces startled and scowling.

The man with the earphones pulled one away from his left ear. "Who in space are you? How the dickens did you get in here?"

Bigman stood erect and puffed out his small chest. "My name is John Bigman Jones. My friends call me Bigman. Everyone else calls me Mr. Jones. Nobody calls me Shortie and stays in one piece. I want to know which one of you made that mistake."

The man with the earphones said, "My name is Lem Fisk and you can call me anything you blame please as long as you do it somewhere else. Get out of here, or I'll come down, pick you up by one leg, and toss you out."

The fellow at the calculating machine said, "Hey, Lem, that's the crackpot who was haunting the port a while back. There's no point in wasting time on him. Get the guards to throw him out."

"Nuts," said Lem Fisk, "we don't need guards for that guy."

He took off his earphones altogether and set the sub-etherics at AUTOMATIC SIGNAL. He said, "Well, son, you came in here and asked us a nice question in a nice way. I'll give you a nice answer. I called you Shortie, but wait, don't get mad. I have a reason. You see you're such a real tall fellow. You're such a long drink of water. You're such a high-pockets. It makes my friends laugh to hear me call you Shortie."

He reached into his hip pocket and drew out a plastic container of cigarettes. The smile on his face was bland.

"Come down here," yelled Bigman. "Come down here and back up your sense of humor with a couple of fists."

"Temper, temper," said Fisk, clucking his tongue. "Here, boy, have a cigarette. King-size, you know. Almost as long as you are. Liable to create some confusion, though, come to think of it. We won't be able to tell whether you're smoking the cigarette or the cigarette is smoking you."

The other two Tower men laughed vigorously.

Bigman was a passionate red. Words came thickly to his tongue. "You won't fight?"

"I'd rather smoke. Pity you don't join me." Fisk leaned back, chose a cigarette, and held it before his face as though admiring its slim whiteness. "After all, I can't be bothered to fight children."

He grinned, brought his cigarette to his lips, and found them closing on nothingness.

His thumb and first two fingers still held their positions about three eighths of an inch apart, but there was no cigarette between them.

"Watch out, Lem," cried the man at the visiplate. "He has a needle-gun."

"No needle-gun," snarled Bigman. "Just a buzzer."

There was an important difference. A buzzer's projectiles, although needle-like, were fragile and nonexplosive. They were used for target practice and small game. Striking human skin, a buzz needle would do no serious damage, but it would smart like the devil.

Fisk's grin disappeared completely. He yelled, "Watch that, you crazy fool. You can blind a man with that."

Bigman's fist remained clenched at eye level. The thin snout of the buzzer projected between his two middle fingers. He said, "I won't blind you. But I can fix it so you won't sit down for a month. And as you can see, my aim isn't bad. And you," he called over his shoulder to the one at the calculator, "if you move an inch closer to the alarm circuit, you'll have a buzz needle right through your hand."

Fisk said, "What do you want?"

"Come down here and fight."

"Against a buzzer?"

"I'll put it away. Fists. Fair fight. Your buddies can see to that."

"I can't hit a guy smaller than I am."

"Then you shouldn't insult him, either." Bigman brought up the buzzer. "And I'm not smaller than you are. I may look that way on the outside, but inside I'm as big as you. Maybe bigger. I'm counting three." He narrowed one eye as he aimed.

"Galaxy!" swore Fisk. "I'm coming down. Fellas, be my witness that this was forced on me. I'll try not to hurt the crazy idiot too much."

He leaped down from his perch. The man at the calculating machine took his place at the sub-etherics.

Fisk was five feet ten, eight inches taller than Bigman, whose slight figure was more like a boy's than a man's. But Bigman's muscles were steel springs under perfect control. He waited for the other's approach without expression.

Fisk did not bother to put up a guard. He simply extended his right hand as though he were going to lift Bigman by the collar and toss him through the still open door.

Bigman ducked under the arm. His left and right thudded into the larger man's solar plexus in a rapid one-two, and almost in the same instant he danced out of reach.

Fisk turned green and sat down, holding his stomach and groaning.

"Stand up, big boy," said Bigman. "I'll wait for you."

The other two Tower men seemed frozen into immobility by the sudden turn of events.

Slowly Fisk rose to his feet. His face glowed with rage, but he approached more slowly.

Bigman drifted away.

Fisk lunged! Bigman was not there by two inches. Fisk whipped a sharp overhand right. Its thrust ended an inch short of Bigman's jaw.

Bigman bobbed about like a cork on rippling water. His arms lifted occasionally to deflect a blow.

Fisk, yelling incoherently, rushed blindly at his gnat-like opponent. Bigman stepped to one side and his open hand slapped sharply at the other's smooth-shaven cheek. It hit with a sharp report, like a meteor hitting the first layers of dense air above a planet. The marks of four fingers were outlined in red on Fisk's face.

For a moment Fisk stood there, dazed. Like a striking snake, Bigman stepped in again, his fists moving upward to crack against Fisk's jaw. Fisk went down into a half crouch.

Distantly Bigman was suddenly aware of the steady ringing of the alarm.

Without a moment's hesitation he turned on his heel and was out the door. He wove through a startled trio of guards heading up the corridor at a clattering run, and was gone!

"And why," questioned Conway, "are we waiting for Bigman?"

Lucky said, "Here's the way I see the situation. There is nothing we need so badly as more information about the pirates. I mean inside information. I tried to get it and things didn't quite break the way I hoped they would. I'm a marked man now. They know me. But they don't know Bigman. He has no official connection with the Council. Now it's my idea that if we can trump up a criminal charge against him, for realism, you know, he can hightail it out of Ceres in the hermit's ship—"

"Oh, space," groaned Conway.

"Listen, will you! He'll go back to the hermit's asteroid. If the pirates are there, good! If not, he'll leave the ship in plain view and wait for them inside. It's a very comfortable place to wait in."

"And when they come," said Henree, "they'll shoot him."

"They will *not*. That's why he's taking the hermit's ship. They'll have to know where Hansen went, to say nothing of myself, where Bigman came from, how he got hold of the ship. They'll *have* to know. That will give him time to talk."

"And to explain how he picked out Hansen's asteroid out of all the rocks in creation? That would take some tall talking."

"That won't take any talking at all. The hermit's ship was on Ceres, which it is. I've arranged to leave it out there unguarded, so he can take it. He'll find the ship's home asteroid's space-time co-ordinates in the logbook. It would just be an asteroid to him, not too far from Ceres, as good as any other, and he would make a beeline for it in order to wait for the furor on Ceres to die down."

"It's a risk," grumbled Conway.

"Bigman knows it. And I tell you right now, we've *got* to take risks. Earth is underestimating the pirate menace so badly that—"

He interrupted himself as the signal light of the Communi-tube flashed on and off in rapid dots of light.

Conway, with an impatient motion of his hand, cut in the signal analyzer, then sat up straight.

He said, "It's on the Council wave length and, by Ceres, it's one of the Council scramblings."

The small visiplate above the Communi-tube was showing a characteristic rapidly shifting pattern of light and dark.

Conway inserted a sliver of metal, which he took from a group of such in his wallet, into a narrow slot in the Communi-tube. The sliver was a crystallite unscrambler, the active portion of the gadget consisting of a particular pattern of tiny crystals of tungsten embedded in an aluminum matrix. It filtered the sub-etheric signal in a specific way. Slowly Conway adjusted the unscrambler, pushing it in deeper and extracting it again until it matched exactly a scrambler similar in nature but opposite in function, at the other end of the signal.

The moment of complete adjustment was heralded by the sudden sharp focusing of the visiplate.

Lucky half-rose to his feet. "Bigman!" he said. "Where in space are you?"

Bigman's little face was grinning puckishly out at them. "I'm in space all right. A hundred thousand miles off Ceres. I'm in the hermit's ship."

Conway whispered furiously, "Is this another of your tricks? I thought you said he was on Ceres?"

"I thought he was," Lucky said. Then, "What happened, Bigman?"

"You said we had to act quickly, so I fixed things up myself. One of the wise guys in the Control Tower was giving me the business. So I slammed him around a little and took off." He laughed. "Check the guardhouse and see if they're not on the lookout for a guy like me with a complaint of assault and battery against him."

"That wasn't the brightest thing you could have done," said Lucky gravely. "You'll have a hard time convincing the men of the asteroids that you're the type for assault. I don't want to hurt your feelings, but you look a little small for the job."

"I'll knock down a few," Bigman retorted. "They'll believe me. But that's not why I called."

"Well, why did you?"

"How do I get to this guy's asteroid?"

Lucky frowned. "Have you looked in the logbook?"

"Great Galaxy! I've looked everywhere. I've looked under the mattress even. There's no record anywhere of any kind of co-ordinates."

Lucky's look of uneasiness grew. "That's strange. In fact it's worse than strange. Look, Bigman," he spoke rapidly and incisively, "match Ceres' speed. Give me your co-ordinates with respect to Ceres right now and keep them that way, whatever you do, till I call you. You're too close to Ceres now for any pirates to bother you, but if you drift out further, you may be in a bad way. Do you hear me?"

"Check. Got you. Let me calculate my co-ordinates."

Lucky wrote them down and broke connections. He said, "Space, when will I learn *not* to make assumptions."

Henree said, "Hadn't you better have Bigman come back? It's a foolhardy setup at best and as long as you haven't the co-ordinates, give the whole thing up."

"Give it up?" said Lucky. "Give up the one asteroid we know to be a pirates' base? Do you know of any other? One single other? We've got to find the asteroid. It's our only clue to the inside of this knot."

Conway said, "He's got a point there, Gus. It is a base."

Lucky jiggled a switch on the intercom briskly and waited.

Hansen's voice, sleep-filled but startled, said, "Hello! Hello!"

Lucky said briskly, "This is Lucky Starr, Mr. Hansen. Sorry to disturb you, but I would like to have you come down here to Dr. Conway's room as fast as you can."

The hermit's voice answered after a pause, "Certainly, but I don't know the way."

"The guard at your door will take you. I'll contact him. Can you make it in two minutes?"

"Two and a half anyway," he said, good-humoredly. He sounded more awake.

"Good enough!"

Hansen was as good as his word. Lucky was waiting for him.

Lucky paused for a moment, holding the door open. He said to the guard, "Has there been any trouble at the base earlier this evening? An assault, perhaps?"

The guard looked surprised. "Yes, sir. The man who got hurt refused to press charges, though. Claimed it was a fair fight."

Lucky closed the door. He said, "That follows. Any normal man would hate to get up in a guardhouse and admit a fellow the size of Bigman had given him a banging. I'll call the authorities later and have them put the charge on paper anyway. For the record. . . . Mr. Hansen."

"Yes, Mr. Starr?"

"I have a question the answer to which I did not want floating around this intercom system. Tell me, what are the co-ordinates of your home asteroid. Standard and temporal both, of course."

Hansen stared and his china-blue eyes grew round. "Well, you may find this hard to believe, but do you know, I really couldn't tell you."

9

The Asteroid That Wasn't

Lucky met his eye steadily. "That is hard to believe, Mr. Hansen. I should think you would know your coordinates as well as a planet dweller would know his home address."

The hermit looked at his toes and said mildly, "I suppose so. It *is* my home address, really. Yet I don't know it."

Conway said, "If this man is deliberately——"

Lucky broke in. "Now wait. Let's force patience on ourselves if we have to. Mr. Hansen must have some explanation."

They waited for the hermit to speak.

Co-ordinates of the various bodies in the Galaxy were the lifeblood of space travel. They fulfilled the same function that lines of latitude and longitude did on the two-dimensional surface of a planet. However, since space is three dimensional, and since the bodies in it move about in every possible way, the necessary co-ordinates are more complicated.

Basically there is first a standard zero position. In the case of the Solar System, the Sun was the usual standard. Based on that standard, three numbers are necessary. The first number is the distance of an object or a position in space from the Sun. The second and third numbers are two angular measurements indicating the position of the object with reference to an imaginary line connecting the Sun and the center of the Galaxy. If three sets of such co-ordinates are known for three different times, set well apart, the orbit of a moving body could be calculated and its position, relative to the Sun, known for any given time.

Ships could calculate their own co-ordinates with respect to the Sun or, if it were more convenient, with respect to the nearest large body, whatever it was. On the Lunar Lines, for instance, of which vessels traveled from Earth to the Moon and back, Earth was the customary "zero point." The Sun's own co-ordinates could be calculated with respect to the Galactic Center and the Galactic Prime Meridian, but that was only important in traveling between the stars.

Some of all this might have been passing through the hermit's mind as he sat there with the three Councilmen watching him narrowly. It was hard to tell.

Hansen said suddenly, "Yes, I can explain."

"We're waiting," said Lucky.

"I've never had occasion to use the co-ordinates in fifteen years. I haven't left my asteroid at all for two years and before that any trips I made, maybe one or two a year, were short ones to Ceres or Vesta for supplies of one sort or another. When I did that, I used local co-ordinates which I always calculated out for the moment. I never worked out a table because I didn't have to.

"I'd only be gone a day or two, three at the most, and my own rock wouldn't drift far in that time. It travels with the stream, a little slower than Ceres or Vesta when it's further from the Sun and a little faster when it's nearer. When I'd head back for the position I calculated, my rock might have drifted ten thousand or even a hundred thousand miles off its original spot, but it was always close enough to pick up with the ship's telescope. After that, I could always adjust my course by eye. I never used the solar standard co-ordinates because I never had to, and there it is."

"What you're saying," said Lucky, "is that you couldn't get back to your rock now. Or did you calculate its local co-ordinates before you left?"

"I never thought to," said the hermit sadly. "It's been so long since I left it that I never gave the matter a second's attention. Not until the minute you called me in here."

Dr. Henree said, "Wait. Wait." He had lit up a fresh pipeful of tobacco and was puffing strongly. "I may be wrong, Mr. Hansen, but when you first took over ownership of your asteroid, you must have filed a claim with the Terrestrial Outer World Bureau. Is that right?"

"Yes," said Hansen, "but it was only a formality."

"That could be. I'm not arguing that. Still, the co-ordinates of your asteroid would be on record there."

Hansen thought a bit, then shook his head. "I'm afraid not, Dr. Henree. They took only the standard co-ordinate set for January 1 of that year. That was just to identify the asteroid, like a code number, in case of disputed ownership. They weren't interested in anything more than that and you can't compute an orbit from only one set of numbers."

"But you yourself must have had orbital values. Lucky told us that you first used the asteroid as an annual vacation spot. So you must have been able to find it from year to year."

"That was fifteen years ago, Dr. Henree. I *had* the

values, yes. And those values are somewhere in my record books on the rock, but they're not in my memory."

Lucky, his brown eyes clouded, said, "There's nothing else at the moment, Mr. Hansen. The guard will take you back to the room and we'll let you know when we need you again. And, Mr. Hansen," he added as the hermit rose, "if you should happen to think of the co-ordinates, let us know."

"My word on that, Mr. Starr," said Hansen gravely.

The three were alone again. Lucky's hand shot out to the Communi-tube. "Key me in for transmission," he said.

The voice of the man at Central Communications came back. "Was the previous incoming message for you, sir? I couldn't unscramble it so I thought——"

"You did well. Transmission, please."

Lucky adjusted a scrambler and used Bigman's co-ordinates to zero in on the sub-etheric beam.

"Bigman," he said when the other's face appeared, "open the logbook again."

"Do you have the co-ordinates, Lucky?"

"Not yet. Have you got the logbook open?"

"Yes."

"Is there a sheet of scrap paper somewhere in it? Loose, with calculations all over it?"

"Wait. Yes. Here it is."

"Hold it up in front of your transmitter. I want to see it."

Lucky pulled a sheet of paper before him and copied down the figuring. "All right, Bigman, take it away. Now listen, stay put. Get me? Stay put, no matter what, till you hear from me. Signing off."

He turned to the two older men. "I navigated the ship from the hermit's rock to Ceres by eye. I adjusted course three or four times, using his ship's telescope and vernier instruments for observation and measurements. These are my calculations."

Conway nodded. "Now, I suppose, you intend calculating backwards to find out the rock's co-ordinates."

"It can be done easily enough, particularly if we make use of the Ceres Observatory."

Conway rose heavily. "I can't help but think you make too much of all this, but I'll follow your instinct for a while. Let's go to the Observatory."

Corridors and elevators took them close to Ceres' surface, one half mile above the Council of Science offices on the asteroid. It was chilly there, since the Observatory made every attempt to keep the temperature as constant as possible and as near surface temperature as the human body could endure.

Slowly and carefully a young technician was unraveling Lucky's calculations, feeding them into the computer and controlling the operations.

Dr. Henree, in a not too comfortable chair, huddled his thin body together and seemed to be trying to extract warmth from his pipe, for his large-knuckled hands hovered closely about its bowl.

He said, "I hope this comes to something."

Lucky said, "It had better." He sat back, his eyes fixed thoughtfully on the opposite wall. "Look, Uncle Hector, you referred to my 'instinct' a while back. It isn't instinct; not any more. This run of piracy is entirely different from that of a quarter century ago."

"Their ships are harder to catch or stop, if that's what you mean," said Conway.

"Yes, but doesn't that make it all the stranger that their raids are confined to the asteroid belt? It's only here in the asteroids that trade has been disrupted."

"They're being cautious. Twenty-five years ago, when

their ships ranged all the way to Venus, we were forced to mount an offensive and crush them. Now they stick to the asteroids and the government hesitates to take expensive measures."

"So far, so good," said Lucky, "but how do they support themselves? It's always been the assumption that pirates didn't raid for pure joy of it alone, but to pick up ships, food, water, and supplies. You would think that now more than ever that was a necessity. Captain Anton boasted to me of hundreds of ships and thousands of worlds. That may have been a lie to impress me, but he certainly took time for the push-gun duel, drifting openly in space for hours as though he had no fear whatever of government interference. And Hansen said, moreover, that the pirates had appropriated the various hermit worlds as stopping-off places. There are hundreds of hermit worlds. If the pirates dealt with all of them, or even a good part of them, that also means a large organization.

"Now where do they get the food to support a large organization and at the same time mount fewer raids now than pirates did twenty-five years ago? The pirate crewman, Martin Maniu, spoke to me of wives and families. He was a vat-man, he said. Presumably he cultured yeast. Hansen had yeast foods on his asteroid and they weren't Venus yeast. I *know* the taste of Venus yeast.

"Put it all together. They grow their own food in small yeast farms distributed among asteroid caverns. They can get carbon dioxide directly from limestone rocks, and water and extra oxygen from the Jovian satellites. Machinery and power units may be imported from Sirius or obtained by an occasional raid. Raids will also supply them with more recruits, both men and women.

"What it amounts to is that Sirius is building an independent government against us. It's making use of discontented people to build a widespread society that will be difficult or impossible to crush if we wait too long. The leaders, the Captain Antons, are after power in the first place and they're perfectly willing to give half the Terrestrial Empire to Sirius if they themselves can keep the other half."

Conway shook his head. "That's an awfully big structure for the small foundation of fact you have. I doubt if we could convince the government. The Council of Science can act by itself only so far, you know. We don't have a fleet of our own, unfortunately."

"I know. That's exactly why we need more information. If, while it is still early in the game, we can find their major bases, capture their leaders, expose their Sirian connections—"

"Well?"

"Why, it's my opinion the movement would be done with. I'm convinced that the average 'man of the asteroids,' to use their own phrase, has no idea he's being made a Sirian puppet. He probably has a grievance against Earth. He may think he's had a raw deal, resent the fact that he couldn't find a job or advancement, that he wasn't getting along as well as he should have. He may have been attracted to what he thought would be a colorful life. All that, maybe. Still, that's a long way from saying he'd be willing to side with Earth's worst enemy. When he finds out that his leaders have been tricking him into doing just that, the pirate menace will fall apart."

Lucky halted his intense whispering as the technician approached, holding a flexible transparent tape with the computer's code prickings upon it.

"Say," he said, "are you sure these figures you gave me were right?"

Lucky said, "I'm sure. Why?"

The technician shook his head. "There's something wrong. The final co-ordinates put your rock inside of the forbidden zones. That's allowing for proper motion too. I mean it can't be."

Lucky's eyebrows lifted sharply. The man was certainly right about the forbidden zones. No asteroids could possibly be found within them. Those zones represented portions of the asteroid belt in which asteroids, if they had existed, would have had times of revolution about the Sun that were an even fraction of Jupiter's twelve-year period of revolution. That would have meant that the asteroid and Jupiter would have continually approached, every few years, in the same portion of space. Jupiter's repeated pull would slowly move the asteroid out of that zone. In the two billion years since the planets had been formed Jupiter had cleared every asteroid out of the forbidden zones and that was that.

"Are you sure," Lucky said, "that your calculations are right?"

The technician shrugged as though to say, "I know my business." But aloud he only said, "We can check it by telescope. The thousand-incher is busy, but that's no good for close work anyway. We'll get one of the smaller ones. Will you follow me, please?"

The Observatory proper was almost like a shrine, with the various telescopes the altars. Men were absorbed in their work and did not pause to look up when the technician and the three Councilmen entered.

The technician led the way to one of the wings into which the huge, cavernous room was divided.

"Charlie," he said to a prematurely balding young man, "can you swing Bertha into action?"

"What for?" Charlie looked up from a series of photographic prints, star-speckled, over which he had been bending.

"I want to check the spot represented by these coordinates." He held out the computer film.

Charlie glanced at it and frowned. "What for? That's forbidden-zone territory."

"Would you focus the point anyway?" asked the technician. "It's Council of Science business."

"Oh? Yes, *sir*." He was suddenly far more pleasant. "It won't take long."

He closed a switch and a flexible diaphragm sucked inward high above, closing about the shaft of "Bertha," a hundred-twenty-inch telescope used for close work. The diaphragm made an air-tight seal, and above it Lucky could make out the smooth whir of the surface-lock opening. Bertha's large eye lifted upward, the diaphragm clinging, and was exposed to the heavens.

"Mostly," explained Charlie, "we use Bertha for photographic work. Ceres' rotation is too rapid for convenient optical observations. The point you're interested in is over the horizon, which is lucky."

He took his seat near the eyepiece, riding the telescope's shaft as though it were the stiff trunk of a giant elephant. The telescope angled and the young astronomer lifted high. Carefully he adjusted the focus.

He lifted out of his perch then and stepped down the rungs of a wall ladder. At the touch of his finger a partition directly below the telescope moved aside to show a black-lined pit. Into it a series of mirrors and lenses could focus and magnify the telescopic image.

There was only blackness.

Charlie said, "That's it." He used a meter stick as a point. "That little speck is Metis, which is a pretty big rock. It's twenty-five miles across, but it's millions of miles away. Here you have a few specks within a million miles of the point you're interested in, but they're to one side, outside the forbidden zone. We've got the stars blanked out by phase polarization or they'd confuse everything."

"Thank you," said Lucky. He sounded stunned.

"Any time. Glad to help whenever I can."

They were in the elevator, headed downward, before Lucky spoke again. He said distantly, "It can't be."

"Why not?" said Henree. "Your figures were wrong."

"How could they be? I got to Ceres."

"You may have intended one figure and put down another by mistake, then made a correction by eye and forgot to correct the paper."

Lucky shook his head. "I couldn't have done that. I just don't— Wait. *Great Galaxy!*" He stared at them wildly.

"What's the matter, Lucky?"

"It works out! Space, it fits in! Look, I was wrong. It's not early in the game at all; it's darned late in the game. It may be too late. I've underestimated them again."

The elevator had reached the proper level. The door opened and Lucky was out with a rapid stride.

Conway ran after, seized his elbow, swung him about. "What are you talking about?"

"I'm going out there. Don't even think of stopping me. And if I don't come back, for Earth's sake, *force* the government to begin major preparations. Otherwise the pirates may be in control of the entire System within a year. Perhaps sooner."

"Why?" demanded Conway violently. "Because you couldn't find an asteroid?"

"Exactly," said Lucky.

10

The Asteroid That Was

Bigman had brought Conway and Henree to Ceres on Lucky's own ship, the *Shooting Starr,* and for that Lucky was grateful. It meant he could go out into space with it, feel its deck beneath his feet, hold its controls in his hands.

The *Shooting Starr* was a two-man cruiser, built this last year after Lucky's exploits among the farmboys of Mars. Its appearance was as deceptive as modern science could make it. It had almost the appearance of a space-yacht in its graceful lines, and its extreme length was not more than twice that of Hansen's little rowboat. No traveler in space, meeting the *Shooting Starr,* would have estimated it to be anything more than a rich man's plaything, speedy perhaps but thin-skinned and unequal to hard knocks. Certainly it would not have seemed the type of vessel to trust in the dangerous reaches of the asteroid belt.

An investigation of the interior of the vessel might have changed some of those notions, however. The gleaming hyperatomic motors were the equal of those on armored space-cruisers ten times the *Shooting Starr's* weight. Its energy reserve was tremendous and the capacity of its hysteretic shield was sufficient to stop the largest projectile that could be put out against it by anything short of a dreadnought. Offensively its limited mass prevented it from being first-class, but weight for weight it could outfight any ship.

It was no wonder that Bigman capered with delight once he had entered the air-lock and thrown off his space-suit.

"Space," Bigman said, "I'm glad to get off that other tub. What do we do with it?"

"I'll have them send up a ship from Ceres to scoop it in."

Ceres was behind them, a hundred thousand miles away. In appearance it was about half the diameter of the Moon as seen from Earth.

Bigman said curiously, "How about letting me in on all this, Lucky? Why the sudden change of plans? I was heading out all by myself, the last I heard."

"There aren't any co-ordinates for you to head to," said Lucky. Grimly he told him the events of the last several hours.

Bigman whistled. "Then where are we going?"

"I'm not sure," said Lucky, "but we begin by aiming at the place where the hermit's rock ought to be now."

He studied the dials, and added, "And we leave here fast too."

He *meant* fast. Acceleration on the *Shooting Starr* went high as velocity built up. Bigman and Lucky were pinned back to their diamagnetically cushioned chairs and the growing pressure spread evenly over their entire body surfaces. The oxygen concentration in the cabin was built up by the acceleration-sensitive air-purifier controls and allowed shallower breathing without oxygen starvation. The g-harness (g being the usual scientific symbol for acceleration) they both wore was light and did not hamper their movements, but under the stress of increasing velocity it stiffened and protected the bones, particularly the spine, from breaking. A nylotexmesh girdle kept the abdominal viscera from undue harm.

In every respect the cabin accessories had been designed by experts at the Council of Science to allow of twenty to thirty per cent greater acceleration on the *Shooting Starr* than on even the most advanced vessels of the fleet.

Even on this occasion the acceleration, though high, was less than half of that of which the ship was capable.

When velocity leveled off, the *Shooting Starr* was five million miles from Ceres, and, if Lucky or Bigman had been interested in looking for it, they would have found it to have become, in appearance, merely a speck of light, dimmer than many of the stars.

Bigman said, "Say, Lucky, I've been wanting to ask you. Do you have your glimmer shield?"

Lucky nodded and Bigman looked grieved.

"Well, you big dumb ox," the little fellow said, "why in space didn't you take it with you when you went out pirate-hunting then?"

"I did have it with me," said Lucky calmly. "I've had it with me since the day the Martians gave it to me."

As Lucky and Bigman (but no one else in the Galaxy) knew, the Martians to whom Lucky referred were not the farmboys and ranchers of Mars. They were rather a race of immaterial creatures who were the direct descendants of the ancient intelligences that once inhabited the surface of Mars in the ages before it had lost its oxygen and water. Excavating huge caverns below Mars' surface by destroying cubic miles of rock, converting the matter so destroyed into energy and storing that energy for future use, they now lived in comfortable isolation. Abandoning their material bodies and living as pure energy, their existence remained unsuspected by Mankind. Only Lucky Starr had penetrated their fastnesses and as the one souvenir of that eerie trip he had obtained what Bigman called the "glimmer shield."

Bigman's annoyance increased. "Well, if you had it, why didn't you use it? What's wrong with you?"

"You have the wrong idea of the shield, Bigman. It won't do everything. It won't feed me and wipe my lips when I'm through."

"I've seen what it can do. It can do plenty."

"It can, in certain ways. It can soak up all types of energy."

"Like the energy of a blaster bolt. You're not going to kick about that, are you?"

"No, I admit I'd be immune to blasters. The shield would soak up potential energy too, if the mass of a body weren't too great or too small. For instance, a knife or an ordinary bullet couldn't penetrate, though the bullet might knock me down. A good sledge hammer would swing right through the shield, though, and even if it didn't its momentum would crush me. And what's more, molecules of air can go through the shield as if it weren't there because they're too small to be handled. I'm telling you this so that you'll understand that if I were wearing the shield and Dingo had broken my face-plate when we were both tangled up in space, I would have died anyway. The shield wouldn't have prevented the air in my suit from scattering away in a split second."

"If you had used it in the first place, Lucky, you wouldn't have had any trouble. Don't I remember when you used it on Mars?" Bigman chuckled at the reminiscence. "It glimmered all over you, smoky-like, only luminous, so you could just be seen in a haze. All except your face anyway. That was just a sheet of white light."

"Yes," said Lucky dryly, "I would have scared them. They would have hit at me with blasters and I wouldn't have been hurt. So they would have all high-tailed it off the *Atlas*, gone off about ten miles, and blasted the ship. I would have been stone dead. Don't forget that the shield is only a shield. It doesn't give me any offensive powers whatever."

"Aren't you ever going to use it again?" asked Bigman.

"When it's necessary. Not till then. If I use it too much, the effect would be lost. Its weaknesses would be found out and I would be just a target for anyone I came up against."

Lucky studied the instruments. Calmly he said, "Ready for acceleration again."

Bigman said, "Hey——"

Then, as he was pushed back into his seat, he found himself fighting for breath and could say nothing more. The redness was rising to his eyes and he could feel the skin drawing backward as though it were trying to peel off his bones.

This time the *Shooting Starr's* acceleration was on full.

It lasted fifteen minutes. Toward the end Bigman was scarcely conscious. Then it relaxed and life crept back.

Lucky was shaking his head and panting for breath.

Bigman said, "Hey, that wasn't funny."

"I know," said Lucky.

"What's the idea? Weren't we going fast enough?"

"Not quite. But it's all right now. We've shaken them."

"Shaken whom?"

"Whoever was following us. We were being followed, Bigman, from the minute you stepped foot on the deck of the old Shooter. Look at the Ergometer."

Bigman did so. The Ergometer resembled the one on the *Atlas* in name only. The one on the *Atlas* had been a primitive model designed to pick up motor radiation for the purpose of releasing the lifeboats. That had been its only purpose. The Ergometer on the *Shooting Starr* could pick up the radiation pattern of a hyperatomic motor on ships no larger than an ordinary lifeboat and do it at a distance of better than two million miles.

Even now the inked line on the graphed paper jiggled very faintly, but periodically.

"That isn't anything," said Bigman.

"It was, a while ago. Look for yourself." Lucky unreeled the cylinder of paper that had already passed the needle. The jigglings grew deeper, more characteristic. "See that, Bigman?"

"It could be any ship. It could be a Ceres freighter."

"No. For one thing, it tried to follow us and did a good job of it too, which means it had a pretty good Ergometer of its own. Besides that, did you ever see an energy pattern like this?"

"Not exactly like this, Lucky."

"I did, you see, in the case of the ship that boarded the *Atlas*. This Ergometer does a much better job of pattern analysis, but the resemblance is definite. The motor of the ship that's following us is of Sirian design."

"You mean it's Anton's ship."

"That or a similar one. It doesn't matter. We've lost them."

"At the moment," said Lucky, "we're right where the hermit's rock should be, plus or minus, say, a hundred thousand miles."

"Nothing's here," said Bigman.

"That's right. The gravitics register no asteroidal mass

anywhere near us. We're in what the astronomers call a forbidden zone."

"Uh-huh," said Bigman wisely, "I see."

Lucky smiled. There was nothing to see. A forbidden zone in the asteroid belt looked no different from a portion of the belt that was thickly strewn with rocks, at least not to the naked eye. Unless an asteroid happened to be within a hundred miles or so, the view was the same. Stars or things that looked like stars filled the heavens. If some of them were asteroids and not stars, there was no way of telling the difference short of watching intently for several hours to see which "stars" changed relative position, or using a telescope to begin with.

Bigman said, "Well, what do we do?"

"Look around the neighborhood. It may take us a few days."

The path of the *Shooting Starr* grew erratic. It headed outward from the Sun, away from the forbidden zone and into the nearest constellation of asteroids. The gravitics jumped their needles at the pull of distant mass.

Tiny world after tiny world slid into the field of the visiplate, was allowed to remain there while it rotated, and was then permitted to slip out. The *Shooting Starr's* velocity had decelerated to a relative crawl, but the miles still passed by the hundreds of thousands and into the millions. The hours passed. A dozen asteroids came and went.

"You better eat," said Bigman.

But Lucky contented himself with sandwiches and catnaps while he and Bigman watched visiplate, gravitics and Ergometer in turn.

Then, with an asteroid in view, Lucky said in a strained voice, "I'm going down."

Bigman was caught by surprise. "Is that the asteroid?" He looked at its angularity. "Do you recognize it?"

"I think I do, Bigman. In any case, it's going to be investigated."

It took half an hour to manipulate the ship into the asteroid's shadow.

"Keep it here," Lucky said. "Someone's got to stay with the ship and you're the one. Don't forget it. It can be detected, but if it's in the shadow, with the lights out and the motors at minimum, it will make it as hard as possible for them. According to the Ergometer, there's no ship in space near us now. Right?"

"Right!"

"The most important thing to remember is this: Don't come down after me for any reason. When I'm through, I'll come up to you. If I'm not back in twelve hours and haven't called, either, back you go to Ceres with a report, after taking photographs of this asteroid at every angle."

Bigman's face grew sullenly stubborn. "No."

"This is the report," said Lucky calmly. He withdrew a personal capsule from an inner pocket. "This capsule is keyed to Dr. Conway. He's the only one who can open it. He's got to get the information, regardless of me. Do you understand?"

"What's in it?" asked Bigman, making no move to take it.

"Just theories, I'm afraid. I've told no one of them, because I've come out here to try to get facts to back them up. If I can't make it, the theories, at least, must get through. Conway may believe them and he may get the government to act upon them."

"I won't do it," said Bigman. "I won't leave you."

"Bigman, if I can't trust you to do what's right regardless of yourself and myself, you won't be much use to me after this if I come through safely."

Bigman held out his hand. The personal capsule was dropped into it.

"All right," he said.

Lucky dropped through vacuum to the asteroid's surface, hastening the drop by use of the suit's push-gun. He knew the asteroid to be about the right size. It was roughly the shape he remembered it to be. It was jagged enough and the sunlit portion looked the right color. All that, however, might have held true for any asteroid.

But there was the other item. That was not likely to be duplicated very often.

From his waist pouch he took out a small instrument that looked like a compass. Actually it was a pocket radar unit. Its enclosed emission source could put out radio short waves of almost any range. Certain octaves could be partially reflected by rock and partially transmitted through reasonable distances.

In the presence of a thick layer of rock the reflection of radiation activated a needle on the dial. In the presence of a thin layer of rock, as, for instance, on a surface under which lay a cave or hollow, some radiation was reflected, but some penetrated into the hollow and was reflected from the further wall. In this way a double reflection occurred, one component of which was much weaker than the second. In response to such a double reflection the needle responded with a characteristic double quiver.

Lucky watched the instrument as he leaped easily over the stony peaks. The needle's smooth pulsing gained a quiver, and then a distinct subsidiary movement. Lucky's heart bounded. The asteroid was hollow. Find where the subsidiary movements were strongest and there the hollow would be nearest the surface. There would be the air-lock.

For a few moments all of Lucky's faculties were concentrated on the needle. He was unaware of the magnetic cable snaking its way toward him from the near horizon.

He was unaware of it until it snapped about him in coil after coil, clinging close, its momentum tossing his nearly weightless body first clear of the asteroid and then down to the rock, where he lay helpless.

11

At Close Quarters

Three lights came over the horizon and toward the prostrate Lucky. In the darkness of the asteroid's night he could not see the figures that accompanied the lights.

Then there was a voice in his ear and the voice was the well-known hoarseness of the pirate, Dingo. It said, "Don't call your pal upstairs. I've got a jigger here that can pick up your carrier wave. If you try to, I'll blast you out of your suit right now, nark!"

He spat out the final word; the contemptuous term of all lawbreakers for those they considered to be spies of the law-enforcement agencies.

Lucky kept silent. From the moment he had first felt the tremor of his suit under the lash of the magnetic cable he knew that he had fallen into a trap. To call Bigman before he knew more about the nature of the trap would have been putting the *Shooting Starr* into danger, and that without helping himself.

Dingo stood over him, a foot on either side. In the light of one of the flashes Lucky caught a quick glimpse of Dingo's face-plate and of the stubby goggles that covered his eyes. Lucky knew those to be infrared translators, capable of converting ordinary heat radiation into visible light. Even without flashes and in the asteroid's dark night they had been able to watch him by the energy of his own heaters.

Dingo said, "What's the matter, nark? Scared?"

He lifted a bulky leg with its bulkier metal swathing and brought his heel down sharply in the direction of Lucky's face-plate. Lucky turned his head swiftly away to let the blow fall on the sturdier metal of the helmet, but Dingo's heel stopped midway. He laughed whoopingly.

"You won't get it that easy, nark," he said.

His voice changed as he spoke to the other two pirates. "Hop over the jag and get the air-lock open."

For a moment they hesitated. One of them said, "But, Dingo, the captain said you were too——"

Dingo said, "Get going, or maybe I'll start with him and finish with you."

In the face of the threat the two hopped away. Dingo said to Lucky, "Now suppose we get you to the airlock."

He was still holding the butt end of the magnetic cable. With a flick at the switch he turned off its current and momentarily demagnetized it. He stepped away and pulled it sharply toward himself. Lucky dragged along the rocky floor of the asteroid, bounced upward, and rolled partly out of the cable. Dingo touched the switch again and the remaining coils suddenly clung and held.

Dingo flicked the whip upward. Lucky traveled with it, while Dingo maneuvered skillfully to maintain his own balance. Lucky hovered in space and Dingo walked with him as though he were a child's balloon at the end of a string.

The lights of the other two were visible again after five minutes. They were shining into a patch of darkness of which regular boundaries were proof enough that it was an open air-lock.

Dingo called, "Watch out! I've got a package to deliver."

He demagnetized the cable again, and flicked it downward, rising six inches into the air as he did so. Lucky rotated rapidly, spinning completely out of the cable.

Dingo leaped upward and caught him. With the skill of a man long used to weightlessness, he avoided Lucky's attempts to break his hold, and hurled him in the direction of the air-lock. He broke his own backward tumble by a quick double spurt of his suit's push-gun and righted himself in time to see Lucky enter the air-lock cleanly.

What followed was clearly visible in the light of the pirates' flashes. Caught in the pseudo-grav field that existed within the air-lock, Lucky was hurled suddenly downward, hitting the rocky floor with a clatter and force that knocked the breath out of him. Dingo's braying laughter filled his helmet.

The outer door closed, the inner opened. Lucky got to his feet, actually thankful for the normality of gravity.

"Get in, nark." Dingo was holding a blaster.

Lucky paused as he entered the asteroid's interior. His eyes shifted quickly from side to side while the frost gathered at the rims of his face-plate. What he saw was not the soft-lit library of the hermit, Hansen, but a tremendously long hallway, the roof of which was supported by a series of pillars. He could not see to the other end. Openings to rooms pierced the wall of the corridors regularly. Men hurried to and fro and there was the smell of ozone and machine oil in the air. In the distance he could hear the characteristic drum-drum of what must have been gigantic hyperatomic motors.

It was quite obvious that this was no hermit's cell, but a large industrial plant, *inside an asteroid.*

Lucky bit his lower lip thoughtfully and wondered despondently if all this information would die with him now.

Dingo said, "In there, nark. Get in there."

It was a storeroom he indicated, its shelves and bins well filled, but empty of human beings other than themselves.

"Say, Dingo," said one of the pirates nervously, "why are we showing him all this? I don't think—"

"Then don't talk," said Dingo, and laughed. "Don't worry, he won't tell anyone about anything he sees. I guarantee that. Meanwhile I have a little something to finish with him. Get that suit off him."

He was removing his own suit as he spoke. He stepped out, monstrously bulky. One hand rubbed slowly over the hairy back of the other. He was savoring the moment.

Lucky said firmly, "Captain Anton never gave you orders to kill me. You're trying to finish a private feud and it will only get you into trouble. I'm a valuable man to the captain and he knows it."

Dingo sat down on the edge of a bin of small metal objects, with a grin on his face. "To listen to you, nark, you'd think you had a case. But you didn't fool us, not for one minute. When we left you on the rock with the hermit, what do you think we did? We *watched.* Captain Anton's no fool. He sent me back. He said, 'Watch that rock and report back.' I saw the hermit's dinghy leave. I could have blasted you out of space then, but the order was to follow.

"I stayed off Ceres for a day and a half and spotted the hermit's dinghy hitting out for space again. I waited some more. Then I caught this other ship coming out to meet it. The man off the dinghy got on to the other ship and I followed you when you took off."

Lucky could not help smiling. "Tried to follow, you mean."

Dingo's face turned a blotchy red. He spat out, "All

right. You were faster. Your kind is good at running. What of it? I didn't have to chase you. I just came here and waited. I knew where you were heading. I've got you, haven't I?"

Lucky said, "All right, but what have you got? I was unarmed on the hermit's rock. I didn't have any weapons, while the hermit had a blaster. I had to do what he said. He wanted to get back to Ceres and he forced me along so he could claim he was being kidnapped if the men of the asteroids stopped him. You admit yourself that I got off Ceres as fast as I could and tried to get back here."

"In a nice, shiny government ship?"

"I stole it. So? It just means that you've got another ship for your fleet. And a good one."

Dingo looked at the other pirates. "Doesn't he throw the comet-dust, though?"

Lucky said, "I warn you again. The captain will take anything that happens to me out on you."

"No he won't," snarled Dingo, "because he knows who you are and so do I, Mr. David Lucky Starr. Come on, move out into the middle of the room."

Dingo rose. He said to his two companions, "Get those bins out of the way. Pull them over to one side."

They looked at his staring, blood-congested face once and did as he said. Dingo's bulbously thickset body was slightly stooped, his head sank down into his bulging shoulders, and his thick, somewhat bandy legs planted themselves firmly. The scar on his upper lip was a vivid white.

He said, "There are easy ways of finishing you and there are nice ways. I don't like a nark and I especially don't like a nark who fouls me in a push-gun fight. So before I finish you, I'm breaking you into little pieces."

Lucky, looking tall and spindly in comparison with the

other, said, "Are you man enough to take care of me alone, Dingo, or will your two friends help you?"

"I don't need help, pretty boy." He laughed nastily. "But if you try to run, they'll stop you, and if you keep on trying to run, they've got neuronic whips that will *really* stop you." He raised his voice. "And use them, you two, if you have to."

Lucky waited for the other to make his move. He knew that the one most nearly fatal tactic would be to try to mix it up at close quarters. Let the pirate enclose his chest in the hug of those enormous arms and broken ribs would be the nearly certain result.

Dingo, right fist drawn back, ran forward. Lucky stood his ground as long as he dared, then stepped quickly to his right, seized his opponent's extended left arm, pulled backward, taking advantage of the other's forward momentum, and caught the other's ankle against his foot.

Dingo went sprawling forward and down heavily. He was up immediately, however, one cheek scraped and little lights of madness dancing in his eyes.

He thundered toward Lucky, who retired nimbly toward one of the bins lining the wall.

Lucky seized the ends of the bin and swung his legs up and out. Dingo caught them in his chest, halted momentarily. Lucky whirled out of the way and was free in the center of the room again.

One of the pirates called out, "Hey, Dingo, let's stop fooling around."

Dingo panted, "I'll kill him, I'll kill him."

But he was more cautious now. His little eyes were nearly buried in the fat and gristle that surrounded his eyeballs. He crept forward, watching Lucky, waiting for the moment he might strike.

Lucky said, "What's the matter, Dingo? Afraid of me? You get afraid very quick for such a big talker."

As Lucky expected, Dingo roared incoherently and dashed heavily and directly at him. Lucky had no trouble in evading the bull rush. The side of his hand came sharply and swiftly down on the back of Dingo's neck.

Lucky had seen any number of men knocked unconscious by that particular blow; he had seen more than one killed. But Dingo merely staggered. He shook it off and turned, snarling.

He walked flat-footedly toward the dancing Lucky. Lucky lashed out with his fist, which landed sharply on Dingo's scraped cheek bone. Blood flowed, but Dingo did not so much as attempt to block the blow, nor did he blink when it landed.

Lucky squirmed away and struck sharply twice more at the pirate. Dingo paid no attention. He came forward, always forward.

Suddenly, unexpectedly, he went down, apparently as a man who had stumbled. But his arms shot out as he fell and one hand closed about Lucky's right ankle. Lucky went down too.

"I've got you now," whispered Dingo.

He reached up to catch Lucky's waist and in a moment, fast-locked, they were rolling across the floor.

Lucky felt the growing, enclosing pressure and pain wash inward like an advancing flame. Dingo's fetid panting was in his ear.

Lucky's right arm was free, but his left was enclosed in the numbing vise of the other's grip about his chest. With the last of his fading strength, Lucky brought his right fist up. The blow traveled no more than four inches, catching the point where Dingo's chin met his neck with a force that sent stabs of pain the length of Lucky's arm.

Dingo's grip loosened for a moment and Lucky, writhing, flung himself out of the deadly embrace and onto his feet.

Dingo got up more slowly. His eyes were glassy, and fresh blood was trickling out the corner of his mouth.

He muttered thickly, "The whip! The whip!"

Unexpectedly he turned upon one of the pirates who had been standing there, a frozen onlooker. He wrested the weapon from the other's hand and sent him sprawling.

Lucky tried to duck, but the neuronic whip was up and flashing. It caught his right side and stimulated the nerves of the area it struck into a bath of pain. Lucky's body stiffened and went down again.

For a moment his senses recorded only confusion, and with what consciousness he possessed he expected death to be a second off. Dimly he heard a pirate's voice.

"Look, Dingo, the captain said to make it look like an accident. He's a Council of Science man and . . ."

It was all Lucky heard.

When he swam back to consciousness with an excruciating tingle of pins and needles down the length of his side, he found himself in a space-suit again. They were just about to put on his helmet. Dingo, lips puffed, cheek and jaw bruised, watched malignantly.

There was a voice in the doorway. A man was entering hurriedly, full of talk.

Lucky heard him say, "—for Post 247. It's getting so *I* can't keep track of all the requisitions. I can't even keep our own orbit straight enough to keep up the coordinate corrections of——"

The voice flickered out. Lucky twisted his head and caught sight of a small man with spectacles and gray hair. He was just inside the doorway, looking with mingled astonishment and disbelief at the disorder that met his eyes.

"Get out," roared Dingo.

"But I've got to have a requisition—"

"Later!"

The little man left and the helmet was fitted over Lucky's head.

They took him out again, through the air-lock, to a surface which was now in the feeble blaze of the distant Sun. A catapult waited on a relatively flat table of rock. Its function was no mystery to Lucky. An automatic winch was drawing back a large metal lever which bent more and more slowly till its original slant had strained back into a complete horizontal at the tip. Light straps were attached to the bent lever and then buckled about Lucky's waist.

"Lie still," said Dingo. His voice was dim and scratchy in Lucky's ear. There was something wrong with the helmet receiver, Lucky realized. "You're just wasting your oxygen. Just to make you feel better, we're sending ships up to blast your friend down before he can pick up speed, if he feels like running."

An instant after that Lucky felt the sharp tingling vibration of the lever as it was released. It sprang elastically back into its original position with terrific force. The buckles about him parted smoothly and he was cast off at a speed of a mile a minute or better, with no gravitational field to slow him. There was one glimpse of the asteroid with the pirates looking up at him. The whole was shrinking rapidly even as he watched.

He inspected his suit. He already knew that his helmet radio had been maltreated. Sure enough, the sensitivity knob hung loose. It meant his voice could penetrate no more than a few miles of space. They had left him his space-suit's push-gun. He tried it but nothing happened. Its gas stores had been drained.

He was quite helpless. There were only the contents of one oxygen cylinder between himself and a slow, unpleasant death.

12

Ship versus Ship

With a clammy constriction of his chest Lucky surveyed the situation. He thought he could guess the pirates' plans. On the one hand, they wished to get rid of him, since he obviously knew far too much. On the other hand, they must want him to be found dead in such a way that the Council of Science would be unable to prove conclusively that his death was by pirate violence.

Once before, pirates had made the mistake of killing an agent of the Council and the resultant fury had been crushing. They would be more cautious this time.

He thought, They'll rush the *Shooting Starr*, blanket it with interference to keep Bigman from sending out a call for help. Then they can use a cannon blast on its hull. It would make a good imitation of a meteorite collision. They can make that look better by sending their own engineers on board to hocus the shield activators. It would look as though a defect in the mechanism had prevented the shield from going up as the meteorite approached.

They would know his own course through space, Lucky knew. There would be nothing to deflect him from whatever his original angles of flight had been. Later, with him safely dead, they would pick him up and send him whirling in an orbit about the broken *Shooting Starr.* The discoverers (and perhaps one of their own ships would send in an anonymous report of the find) would reach an obvious conclusion. Bigman at the controls, maneuvering to the last, killed at his post. Lucky, on the other hand, scrambling into a suit, damaging the external sensitivity knob of the suit's radio in the excitement. He would have been unable to call for help. He would have expended his push-gun's gas in a desperate and futile attempt to find a place of safety. And he would have died.

It would not work. Neither Conway nor Henree could possibly believe that Lucky would be concerned only with his own safety while Bigman stuck loyally at the controls. But then, the failure of the scheme would be small satisfaction to a dead Lucky Starr. Worse yet, it would not only be Lucky Starr who would die, but all the information now locked in Lucky Starr's head.

For a moment he was sick with outrage at himself that he had not forced all his suspicions on Conway and Henree before leaving, that he had waited till he boarded the *Shooting Starr* before preparing the personal capsule. Then he gained control of himself. No one would have believed him without facts.

For that very reason he would have to get back.

Have to!

But how? What good was "have to" when one was alone and helpless in space with a few hours' worth of oxygen and nothing else?

Oxygen!

Lucky thought, There's my oxygen. Anyone but Dingo would have drained his cylinder of all but dregs, to let death come quickly. But if Lucky knew Dingo, the pirate had sent him on his way with a loaded cylinder simply to prolong the agony.

Good! Then he would reverse that. He would use the oxygen otherwise. And if he failed, death would come the sooner, despite Dingo.

Only he must not fail.

The asteroid had been crossing his line of vision periodically as he spun in space. First, it was a shrinking rock, its sunlit highlights slanting jaggedly across the blackness of space. Then it had been a bright star and a single line of light. The brightness was fading quickly now. Once the asteroid became dim enough to be simply one more in the myriad of stars, it was all over. Not many minutes were left before that would be the case.

His clumsy, metal-covered fingers were already fumbling with the flexible tube that led from the air inlet just under the face-plate to the oxygen cylinder in back. He twisted strenuously at the bolt that held the air tube tightly fixed to the cylinder.

It gave. He paused to fill his helmet and suit with oxygen. Ordinarily oxygen leaked slowly in from the cylinders at about the rate it was used up by human lungs. The carbon dioxide and water formed as the result of respiration were mostly absorbed by the chemicals contained in the valved canisters affixed to the inner surface of the suit's chest plates. The result was the oxygen was kept at a pressure one fifth that of Earth's atmosphere. This was exactly right, since four fifths of Earth's atmosphere is nitrogen anyway, which is useless for breathing.

However, this left room for higher concentrations, up to somewhat more than normal atmospheric pressure, before there was danger of toxic effects. Lucky let the oxygen pour into his suit.

Then, having done so, he closed the valve under his face-plate entirely and removed the cylinder.

The cylinder was itself a sort of push-gun. It was an unusual push-gun, to be sure. For a person marooned in space to use the precious oxygen that stood between himself and death as motive power, to blow it into space, meant desperation. Or else, a firm resolution.

Lucky cracked the reducing valve and let a blast of oxygen issue out. There was no line of crystals this time. Oxygen, unlike carbon dioxide, froze at very low temperatures indeed and before it could lose sufficient heat to freeze, it had diffused out into space. Gas or solid, however, Newton's third law of motion still held. As the gas pushed out one way, Lucky was pushed in the opposite direction by a natural counterpush.

His spinning slowed. Carefully he allowed the asteroid to come into full view before stopping the spin completely.

He was still receding from the rock. It was no longer particularly brighter than the neighboring stars. Conceivably he had already mistaken his target, but he closed his mind against that uncertainty.

He fixed his eyes firmly on the spot of light he assumed to be the asteroid and let the cylinder blast in the opposite direction. He wondered if he would have enough to reverse the direction of his travel. There was no way of telling at the moment.

In any case, he would have to save some gas. He would need it to maneuver about the asteroid, get on its night side, find Bigman and the ship, unless . . .

Unless the ship had already been driven away, or destroyed, by the pirates.

It seemed to Lucky that the vibration of his hands, due to the escaping oxygen, was lessening. Either the cylinder was running low, or its temperature was dropping. He was holding it away from his suit so it was no longer absorbing heat from it. It was from the suit that oxygen cylinders gained enough heat to be breathable, and the carbon dioxide cylinders of the push-guns gained enough heat to keep their contents gaseous. In the vacuum of space heat could be lost only by radiation, a slow process, but, even so, the oxygen cylinder had had time to drop in temperature.

He encircled the cylinder in his arms, hugged it to his chest, and waited.

It seemed hours, but only fifteen minutes passed before it seemed to him that the asteroid was growing brighter. Was he approaching the rock again? Or was it imagination? Another fifteen minutes passed and it was distinctly brighter. Lucky felt a deep gratitude to the chance that had shot him out on the sunlit side of the rock so that he could see it plainly as a target.

It was getting harder to breathe. There was no question of carbon dioxide asphyxiation. That gas was removed as it was formed. Still, each breath also removed a small fraction of his precious oxygen. He tried to breathe shallowly, close his eyes, rest. After all, he could do nothing more until he had reached and passed the asteroid. There on the night side, Bigman might still be waiting.

Then, if he could get close enough to Bigman, if he could call him on his limping radio before he passed out, there might yet be a chance.

The hours had passed slowly and torturously for Bigman. He longed to descend, but dared not. He reasoned with himself that, if the enemy existed, he would have shown himself by now. Then he argued it out bitterly and came to the conclusion that the very silence and motionlessness of space meant a trap, and that Lucky was caught.

He put Lucky's personal capsule before him and wondered about its contents. If only there were some way of bursting it, of reading the thin roll of microfilm within. If he could do that, he could radio it to Ceres, get if off his hands, and be free to go slamming down to the rock. He would blast them all, drag Lucky out of whatever mess he was in.

No! In the first place he dared not use the sub-etherics. True, the pirates could not break the code, but they would detect the carrier wave and he had been instructed not to give away the location of the ship.

Besides, what was the use of thinking of breaking into a personal capsule. A solar furnace could melt and destroy it, an atom blast could disintegrate it, but nothing could open it and leave its message intact except the living touch of the person for whom it had been "personalized." That was that.

More than half of the twelve-hour period had passed when the gravitics gave their entirely distinctive warning.

Bigman roused himself out of his frustrated reverie and stared with shocked surprise at the Ergometer. The pulsations of several ships were blending themselves into complicated curves that melted snakelike from one configuration to another.

The *Shooting Starr's* shield, which had been glimmering routinely at a strength sufficient to ward off casual "debris" (the usual space term for wandering meteorites an inch or less in diameter) stiffened to maximum. Bigman heard the soft purr of the power output grow strident. One by one, he let the short-range visiplates glow into life, bank on bank of them.

His mind churned. The ships were rising from the asteroid, since none could be detected further away. Lucky must be caught, then; dead, probably. He didn't care now how many ships came at him. He would get them all, every single one of them.

He sobered. The first Sun glint had caught in one of the visiplates. He maneuvered the cross hairs and centered them. He then depressed something that looked like a piano key and, caught in an invisible burst of energy, the pirate ship glowed.

The glow was not due to any action upon its hull, but was rather the result of the energy absorption of the enemy screen. It glowed brightly and more brightly still. Then it dimmed as the enemy turned tail and put distance between them.

A second ship and a third were in view. A projectile was making its way toward the *Shooting Starr*. In the vacuum of space there was no flash, no sound, but the Sun caught it and it was a little sparking spot of light. It became a little circle in the visiplate, then a larger one, until finally it moved out of the plate's field.

Bigman might have dodged, flashed the Shooter out of the way, but he thought, Let it hit. He wanted them to see what they were playing with. The Shooter might look like a rich man's toy, but they weren't going to put it out of action with a few slingshooters.

The projectile struck and slogged to a halt against the *Shooting Starr's* hysteretic shields, which, Bigman knew, must have flashed momentarily into brilliance. The ship itself moved smoothly, absorbing the momentum that had leaked past the shield.

"Let's return that," Bigman muttered. The *Shooting Starr* carried no projectiles, explosive or otherwise, but its store of energy projectors was varied and powerful.

His hand was hovering over the blaster controls when he saw in one of the visiplates something that brought a scowl to his small, determined face, something that looked like a man in a space-suit.

It was strange that the space-ship was more vulnerable to a man in a space-suit than to the best weapons of another ship. An enemy ship could be easily detected by gravitics at a distance of miles and by Ergometers at a distance of thousands of miles. A single man in a space-suit could only be detected by a gravitic at a hundred yards and by an Ergometer not at all.

Again, a hysteretic shield worked more effectively the greater the velocity of the projectile. Huge lumps of metal tearing at miles per second could be stopped cold. One man, however, drifting along at ten miles an hour was not even aware of the existence of the shield except for a tiny warming of his suit.

Let a dozen men creep toward a ship at once and only great skill could bring them all down. If two or three penetrated and succeeded in blasting open the air-lock with hand weapons, the ship they attacked was seriously crippled.

And now Bigman caught the little speck that could only mean the advance guard of such a suicide squadron. He brought one of the secondaries to bear. The single figure was centered and Bigman was ready to fire when his radio receiver sounded.

For a moment he was startled. The pirates had attacked without warning and had not tried to communicate, to call for surrender, to offer terms, anything. What now?

He hesitated and the sounding became a word, repeated three times, "Bigman . . . Bigman . . . Bigman . . ."

Bigman jumped from his seat, ignoring the suited man, the battle, everything. "Lucky! Is that you?"

"I'm near the ship . . . Space-suit . . . Air . . . nearly gone."

"Great Galaxy!" Bigman, white-faced, maneuvered the *Shooting Starr* nearer the figure in space, the figure whom he had nearly destroyed.

Bigman watched over Lucky, who, helmet off, was still gulping air. "You'd better get some rest, Lucky."

"Later," said Lucky. He climbed out of his suit. "Have they attacked yet?"

Bigman nodded. "It doesn't matter. They're just breaking their teeth on the old Shooter."

"They've got stronger teeth than any they've shown," said Lucky. "We've got to get away and fast. They'll be bringing out their heavy craft, and even *our* energy stores won't last forever."

"Where are they going to get heavy craft from?"

"That's a major pirate base down there! *The* major base, perhaps."

"You mean it *isn't* the hermit's rock?"

"I mean we've got to get away."

He took the controls, face still pale from his ordeal. For the first time the rock below them moved from its position on the screens. Even during the attack Bigman had heeded Lucky's parting order to stay put for twelve hours.

The rock grew larger.

Bigman protested. "If we've got to get away, why are we landing?"

"We're not landing." Lucky watched the screen intently, while one hand set the controls of the ship's heavy blaster. Deliberately he widened and softened the focus of the blaster till it could cover a broad area indeed, but at an energy intensity reduced to little more than that of an ordinary heat ray.

He waited, for reasons that the wondering Bigman could not divine, and then fired. There was a startling blazing brightness on the asteroid's surface which subsided almost instantly into a glowing redness that in a further minute or so blackened out.

"Now let's go," said Lucky, and, as new ships spiraled up from the pirate base, acceleration took hold.

Half an hour later, with asteroid gone and any pursuing ships safely lost, he said, "Get Ceres, I want to speak to Conway."

"Okay, Lucky. And listen, I've got the co-ordinates of that asteroid. Shall I send them along? We can send a fleet back and—"

"It won't do any good," said Lucky, "and it isn't necessary."

Bigman's eyes widened. "You don't mean you destroyed the rock with that blaster bolt?"

"Of course not. I hardly touched it," said Lucky. "Have you got Ceres?"

"I'm having trouble," said Bigman pettishly. He knew Lucky was in one of his tight-mouthed moods and would give no information. "Wait, here it is, but, hey—They're broadcasting a general alarm!"

There was no need to explain that. The call was strident and uncoded. "General call to all fleet units outside Mars. Ceres under attack by enemy force, presumed pirates. . . . General call to all fleet units . . ."

Bigman said, "Great Galaxy!"

Lucky said tightly, "They stay one step ahead of us, no matter what we do. We've got to get back! Quickly!"

13

Raid!

The ships came swarming out of space in perfect coordination. An entire wing struck directly at the Observatory. In response to this, almost inevitably, the defending forces on Ceres concentrated their power at that point.

The attack was not pressed full-force. Ship after ship dived downward to launch energy beams at an obviously impregnable shield. None took the risky step of trying to blast the underground power plants, the location of which they must have known. Government ships took to space and ground batteries opened up. In the end two pirate ships were destroyed when their shields broke down and they flared into glowing vapor. Another one, its energy reserves down to a trickle, was almost captured in the eventual pursuit. It was blown up at the last moment, probably by its own crew.

Even during the attack some of the defenders suspected it to be a feint. Later, of course, they knew that for a fact. While the Observatory was engaged, three ships landed on the asteroid a hundred miles away. Pirates disembarked and with hand weapons and portable blasting cannon attacked the residential air-locks from flitting "space-sleds."

The locks were blasted open and space-suited pirates swarmed down the corridors from which air emptied. The upper reaches of the corridors were factories and offices, the occupants of which had evacuated at the first alarm. Their place was taken by space-suited members of the local militia who fought bravely, but were no match for the professionals of the pirate fleet.

In the lower depths, in the peaceful apartments of Ceres, the noise of blasting battle sounded. Calls for help were sent out. Then, almost as suddenly as they came, the pirates retreated.

When they left, the men of Ceres counted their casualties. Fifteen Cereans were dead and many more hurt in one way or another, as against the bodies of five pirates. Damage to property was very high.

"And one man," Conway explained furiously to Lucky when the latter arrived, "is missing. Only he's not on the list of inhabitants and we've been able to keep his name out of the news reports."

Lucky found Ceres the focus of almost hysterical excitement now that the raid was over. It had been the first attack on an important Terrestrial center by any enemy in a generation. He had had to pass three inspections before being allowed to land.

He sat in the Council office with Conway and Henree and said bitterly, "So Hansen is gone! That's what it boils down to."

"I'll say this for the old hermit," said Henree. "He had guts. When the pirates penetrated, he insisted on getting into a suit, grabbing up a blaster, and going up there with the militia."

"We weren't short on militia," said Lucky. "If he had stayed down here, he would have done us a much greater service. How is it you didn't stop him? Under the circum-

stances was he a person to be allowed to do such a thing?"
Lucky Starr's usually even voice contained a repressed
anger.

Conway said patiently, "We weren't with him. The
guard we left in charge had to report for militia duty.
Hansen insisted on joining him and the guard decided he
could do both duties at once that way; fight the pirates
and guard the hermit."

"But he didn't guard the hermit."

"Under the circumstances he can scarcely be blamed.
The guard saw Hansen last charging a pirate. Next thing
he knew there was no one in sight and the pirates were
retreating. Hansen's body hasn't been recovered. The pirates must have him alive or dead."

"So they must," said Lucky. "Now let me tell you
something. Let me tell you exactly what a bad mistake
this was. I'm certain that the whole attack on Ceres was
arranged simply to capture Hansen."

Henree reached for his pipe. "You know, Hector," he
said to Conway, "I'm almost tempted to go along with
Lucky on that. The attack on the Observatory was a mis-
erable one, an obvious false alarm to draw off our defenses. Getting Hansen was the only thing they did
accomplish."

Conway snorted. "One possible information leak like
the hermit isn't worth risking thirty ships."

"That's the whole point," said Lucky vehemently.
"Right now, it may be. I told you about the asteroid I was
on, the kind of industrial plant it must have been. Suppose they're almost at the point where they're ready to
make the big push? Suppose Hansen knows the exact date
for when the push is scheduled? Suppose he knows the
exact method?"

"Then why hasn't he told us?" demanded Conway.

"Maybe," said Henree, "he's waiting to use it as material with which to buy his own immunity. We never did have a chance really to discuss that question with him. You've got to admit, Hector, that if he had that kind of key information, any number of ships would have been worth the risk. And you've got to admit Lucky is probably right about their being ready for the big push."

Lucky looked sharply from one to the other. "Why do you say that, Uncle Gus? What happened?"

"Tell him, Hector," said Henree.

"Why tell him anything," growled Conway. "I'm tired of his one-man trips. He'll be wanting to go to Ganymede."

"What's on Ganymede?" asked Lucky coldly. As far as he knew, there was little or nothing on Ganymede to interest anyone. It was Jupiter's largest moon, but the very nearness of Jupiter made it difficult to maneuver spaceships, so that space travel in its vicinity was unprofitable.

"Tell him," said Henree.

"Look," said Conway. "Here it is. We knew Hansen was important. The reason we didn't have him under tighter observation, the reason Gus and I weren't there ourselves, was that two hours before the pirate attack a report came in from the Council to the effect that there was evidence that Sirian forces had landed on Ganymede."

"What kind of evidence?"

"Tight-beam sub-etheric signals had been penetrated. It's a long story, but the nub of it was that, more by accident than by anything else, a few scraps of code were picked up. The experts say it's a Sirian code and certainly there isn't anything Terrestrial on Ganymede that's capable of putting out signals in a beam *that* tight. Gus and I were going to take Hansen and return to Earth when the pirates attacked, and that's it. Right now we've still got to return to Earth. With Sirius on the scene there may be war at any time."

Lucky said, "I see. Well, before we go to Earth, there's one thing I would like to check on. Do we have motion pictures of the pirate attack? I'm supposing the defenses of Ceres weren't so disorganized that pictures weren't taken?"

"They've been taken. How do you expect them to help?"

"I'll tell you after I've seen them."

Men in the uniform of the fleet, and wearing high-rank insignia, projected the top-secret motion pictures of what later became known in history as the "Ceres Raid."

"Twenty-seven ships attacked the Observatory. Is that right?" asked Lucky.

"Right," said a commander. "No more than that."

"Good. Now let's see if I have the rest of the facts straight. Two of the ships were accounted for during the fight and a third during the pursuit. The remaining twenty-four got away, but you have one or more shots of each of them in retreat."

The commander smiled. "If you're implying that any of them landed on Ceres and are still hidden here, you're quite wrong."

"As far as those twenty-seven ships are concerned, perhaps. But three more ships *did* land on Ceres and their crew attacked the Massey Air-lock. Where are the pictures of those?"

"Unfortunately we didn't get many of those," admitted the commander uncomfortably. "It was a case of complete surprise. But we have pictures of them in retreat too, and we showed you those."

"Yes, you did, and there were only two ships in those pictures. Eyewitnesses reported three as having landed."

The commander said stiffly, "And three took off and retreated. There's eyewitness evidence of that also."

"But you have pictures of only two?"

"Well . . . yes."

"Thank you."

Back in the office Conway said, "Now what was that all about, Lucky?"

"I thought Captain Anton's ship might be in an interesting place. The motion pictures proved it was."

"Where was it?"

"Nowhere. That was what was interesting. His ship is the one pirate ship I would recognize, yet no ship faintly similar took part in the raid. This is strange because Anton must be one of their very best men or they wouldn't have sent him out after the *Atlas*. Or it would be strange if the truth wasn't that thirty ships attacked Ceres and we had pictures of only twenty-nine. The missing thirtieth was Anton!"

"I could figure that out too," said Conway. "What of it?"

Lucky said, "The attack on the Observatory was a feint. That's admitted even by the defending ships, now. It was the three ships that attacked the air-lock that were important and they were under Anton's command. Two of those ships joined the rest of the squadron in their retreat, a feint within a feint. The third ship, Anton's own, the only one we didn't see, continued on with the main business of the day. It left on an entirely different trajectory. People saw it lift into space but it veered off so radically that our own ships, chasing the main body of enemy with all its might, never even caught it on film."

Conway said unhappily, "You're going to say that it's going to Ganymede."

"Doesn't it follow? The pirates, however well organized, can't attack Earth and its dependencies on their own. But they *can* put up an excellent diversionary fight. They can keep enough Terrestrial ships patrolling the endless asteroid belt to allow Sirian fleets to defeat the remainder. On the other hand, Sirius can't safely conduct a war eight light years away from their own planet unless they can count on major help from the asteroids. After all, eight light years amounts to forty-five trillion miles. Anton's ship is speeding to Ganymede to assure them of that help and to give the word to begin the war. Without warning, of course."

"If only," muttered Conway, "we could have stumbled on their Ganymede base sooner."

"Even with the knowledge of Ganymede," said Henree, "we would not have known the seriousness of the situation without Lucky's two trips into asteroid territory."

"I know. My apologies, Lucky. Meanwhile we have very little time to do anything. We'll have to strike at the heart instantly. A squadron of ships sent to the key asteroid Lucky has told us of—"

"No," said Lucky. "No good."

"Why do you say that?"

"We don't want to start a war, even if it's with a victory. That's what *they* want to do. Look here, Uncle Hector, the pirate, Dingo, might have burned me down right there on the asteroid. Instead, he had orders to set me adrift in space. For a while I thought that was to make my death look like an accident. Now I feel it was intended to anger the Council. They were going to broadcast the fact they had killed a Councilman, not hide it, goading us into a premature attack. One of the reasons for the Ceres Raid might have been to insure an added provocation."

"And if we do start the war with a victory?"

"Here on this side of the Sun? And leave Earth on the

other side stripped of important units of the fleet? With Sirian ships waiting at Ganymede, also on the other side of the Sun? I predict that it would be a very costly victory. Our best bet is not to start a war, but to prevent one."

"How?"

"Nothing will happen until Anton's ship reaches Ganymede. Suppose we intercept him and prevent the meeting."

"Interception is a long chance," said Conway doubtfully.

"Not if *I* go. The *Shooting Starr* is faster and has better Ergometrics than any ship in the fleet."

"*You* go?" cried Conway.

"It would be unsafe to send fleet units. The Sirians on Ganymede would have no way of being certain an attack wasn't heading their way. They'd have to take counteraction and that would mean the very war we're trying to avoid. The *Shooting Starr* would look harmless to them. It would be one ship. They'd stay put."

Henree said, "You're overeager, Lucky. Anton has a twelve-hour head start. Even the *Shooting Starr* can't make that up."

"You're wrong. It can. And once I catch them, Uncle Gus, I think I can force the asteroids into surrender. Without them Sirius won't attack and there'll be no war."

They stared at him.

Lucky said earnestly, "I've come back twice now."

"Each time by half a miracle," grumbled Conway.

"The other times I didn't know what I was tackling. I had to feel my way. This time I do know. I know exactly. Look, I'll warm up the *Shooting Starr* and make the necessary arrangements with the Ceres Observatory while that's taking place. You two can get on the sub-ether to Earth. Get the Co-ordinator to——"

Conway said, "I can take care of that, son. I've been

dealing with government affairs since before you were born. And Lucky, *will* you take care of yourself?"

"Don't I always, Uncle Hector? Uncle Gus?"

He shook hands warmly and whirled away.

Bigman scuffed the dust of Ceres disconsolately. He said, "I've got my suit on. Everything."

"You can't go, Bigman," said Lucky. "I'm sorry."

"Why not?"

"Because I'm taking a short cut to get to Ganymede."

"So what? What kind of a short cut?"

Lucky smiled tightly. "I'm cutting through the Sun!"

He walked out on to the field toward the *Shooting Starr*, leaving Bigman standing there, mouth open.

14

To Ganymede via the Sun

A three-dimensional map of the Solar System would have the appearance of a rather flat plate. In the center would be the Sun, the dominant member of the System. It is *really* dominant, since it contains 99.8% of all the matter in the Solar System. In other words, it weighs five hundred times as much as everything else in the Solar System put together.

Around the Sun circle the planets. All of them revolve in nearly the same plane, and this plane is called the Ecliptic.

In traveling from planet to planet space-ships usually follow the Ecliptic. In doing so they are within the main sub-etheric beams of planetary communication and can most conveniently make intermediate stops on the way to their destination. Sometimes, when a ship is interested in speed or in escaping detection, it veers away from the Ecliptic, particularly when it must travel to the other side of the Sun.

This, Lucky thought, might be what Anton's ship was

intending to do. It would lift up from the "plate" that was the Solar System, make a huge arc or bridge above the Sun, and come down to the "plate" on the other side, in the neighborhood of Ganymede. Certainly Anton must have started in that direction, or the defending forces on Ceres wouldn't have missed filming him. It was almost second nature for men to make all spationautical observations along the Ecliptic first of all. By the time they thought of turning away from the Ecliptic, Anton would have been too far away for observation.

But, thought Lucky, the chances were that Anton would *not* leave the Ecliptic permanently. He might have started out as though that would be the case, but he would return. The advantages in a return would be many. The asteroid belt extended completely about the Sun, in the sense that asteroids were evenly distributed all the way around. By keeping within the belt Anton could remain among the asteroids all the way to within a hundred million miles or so of Ganymede. This would mean security for him. The Terrestrial government had virtually abdicated its power over the asteroids and, except for the routes to the four large rocks, government ships did not penetrate the area. Moreover, if one did, Anton would always be in the position of being able to call for reinforcements from some nearby asteroidal base.

Yes, thought Lucky, Anton would remain in the belt. Partly because he thought this, and partly because he had his own plans, Lucky lifted the *Shooting Starr* out of the Ecliptic in a shallow arc.

The Sun was the key. It was the key to the entire System. It was a roadblock and a detour to every ship man could build. To travel from one side of the System to another, a ship had to make a wide curve to avoid the Sun. No passenger ship approached closer than sixty million miles, the distance of Venus from the Sun. Even there, cooling systems were imperative for the comfort of the passengers.

Technical ships could be designed to make the trip to Mercury, the distance of which from the Sun varied from forty-three million miles in some parts of its orbit to twenty-eight million in others. Ships had to hit it at the furthest region of its retirement from the Sun. At closer than thirty million miles various metals melted.

Still more specialized ships were sometimes built for close-by solar observation. Their hulls were permeated by a strong electric field of peculiar nature which induced a phenomenon known as "pseudo-liquefaction" in the outermost molecular skin. Heat reflection from such a skin was almost total, so that only a tiny fraction penetrated into the ship. From outside such ships would appear perfect mirrors. Even so, enough heat penetrated to raise the temperature within the ship above the boiling point of water at distances of five million miles from the Sun, the closest recorded approach. Even if human beings could survive such a temperature, they couldn't survive the short-wave radiation that flooded out of the Sun and into the ship at such distances. It could kill anything living in seconds.

The disadvantage of the Sun's position with respect to space travel was obvious in the present instance, in which Ceres was on one side of the Sun while Earth and Jupiter were almost diametrically opposed on the other side. If one was in the asteroid belt, the distance from Ceres to Ganymede was about one billion miles. If the Sun could be ignored and a ship could cut straight across space through it, the distance would be only six hundred million miles, a saving of about forty per cent.

This, as far as was possible, Lucky intended to do.

He drove the *Shooting Starr* hard, virtually living in his g-harness, eating and sleeping there, feeling the pressure of acceleration continuously. He gave himself only fifteen minutes respite out of each hour.

He passed high above the orbits of Mars and Earth but there was nothing to see there, not even with the ship's telescope. Earth was on the other side of the Sun, and Mars was at a position nearly at right angles to his own.

Already the Sun was at its normal size as seen from Earth and he could view it only through the most strongly polarized visiplates. A little more and he would have to use the stroboscopic attachments.

The radioactivity indicators began to chuckle occasionally. Within Earth's orbit the density of short-wave radiation started to reach respectable values. Inside Venus's orbit special precautions would have to be taken, such as the wearing of lead-impregnated semi-space-suits.

I, myself, thought Lucky, would have to do better than lead. At the approach to the Sun that he would have to make, lead would not do. Nothing material would do.

For the first time since his adventure on Mars the previous year Lucky drew out of a special pouch glued to his waist the flimsy, semitransparent object obtained from the Martian energy beings.

He had long since abandoned any effort at speculation as to the method by which the object worked. It was the development of a science that had continued for a million years longer than the science known to Mankind and along alien paths. It was as incomprehensible to him as a space-ship would be to a cave man, and as impossible to duplicate. But it worked! That was what counted!

He slipped it on over his head. It molded itself to his skull as though it carried a strange life of its own, and as it did so, light gleamed out all over him. Over his body it was a glimmer like a billion fireflies, and it was for that reason that Bigman referred to it as a "glimmer shield."

Over his face and head it was a solid sheet of brilliance that covered his features entirely, without, on the other hand, preventing light from reaching his eyes.

It was an energy shield, designed by the alien Martians for Lucky's needs. That is, it was impervious to all forms of energy other than that required by his body, such as a certain intensity of visible light and a certain amount of heat. Gases penetrated freely, so that Lucky could breathe, and heated gases, in passing, were robbed of their heat and came through cool.

When the *Shooting Starr* passed the orbit of Venus, still heading in toward the Sun, Lucky put on his energy shield permanently. While he wore it, he would not be able to eat or drink, but the enforced fast would not last for more than a day, at the outside.

He was now traveling at a terrific speed, far greater than any he had previously experienced. In addition to the slugging pull of the hyperatomics of the *Shooting Starr*, there was the unimaginable attraction of the Sun's giant gravitational field. He was traveling at millions of miles an hour now.

He activated the electric field that rendered the outer skin of the ship pseudo-liquid and was grateful, as he did so, for the foresight that had made him insist on that accessory during the building of the *Shooting Starr*. The thermocouple which had been registering temperatures above one hundred degrees began to show a drop. The visiplates went dark as metal shields passed over the thick glassite to keep them from damage and from softening in the heat of the Sun.

By the time Mercury's orbit was reached the radiation counters had gone completely mad. Their chatter was continuous. Lucky placed a glimmering hand over their windows and their noise stopped. Down to the hardest gamma rays the radiation penetrating and filling the ship was stopped by the resistance of the insubstantial aura that surrounded his body.

The temperature, which had reached a low of eighty, was climbing again, despite the mirror skin of the *Shooting Starr*. It passed one hundred fifty and still went up. The gravimetrics indicated the Sun to be only ten million miles away.

A shallow dish of water, which Lucky had placed upon the table, and which had been steaming for an hour past, was now bubbling outright. The thermocouple reached the boiling point of water, two hundred and twelve degrees.

The *Shooting Starr*, whipping about the Sun, was now five million miles away. It would approach no closer. Actually it was inside the outermost wisps of the most rarefied portion of the Sun's atmosphere, its corona. Since the Sun was gaseous through and through (though most of it was a gas the like of which could not exist even under the most extreme laboratory conditions on Earth), it had no surface, and its "atmosphere" was part of the very body of the Sun. By going through the corona, then, Lucky was, in a way, going through the Sun, as he had told Bigman he would.

Curiosity tugged at him. No man had ever been this close to the Sun. No man, perhaps, ever would again. Certainly, any man who did, could not look at the Sun with his unaided eyes. The shortest possible glimpse of the Sun's tremendous radiation at that distance would mean instant death.

But he was wearing the Martian energy shield. Could it handle solar radiation at five million miles? He felt he ought not take the chance and yet the impulse tugged desperately at him. The ship's chief visiplate was outfitted with a stroboscopic outlet-series, one which would expose, one by one, each of a series of sixty-four outlets to the Sun, each for a millionth of a second every four seconds. To the eye (or to the camera), it would seem a continuous exposure, but actually any given piece of glass would only get one four millionth of the radiation the Sun was emitting. Even that required specially designed, nearly opaque lenses.

Lucky's fingers moved remorselessly, almost without conscious volition, to the controls. He could not bear the thought of losing the chance. He adjusted the plate direction toward the Sun, using the gravimetrics as indicators.

Then he turned his head away and plunged the contact home. A second passed, then two seconds. He imagined an increase in heat on the back of his neck; he half-waited for radiation death. Nothing happened.

Slowly he turned.

What he saw was to stay with him the rest of his life. A bright surface, puckered and wrinkled, filled the visiplate. It was a portion of the Sun. He could not see the whole, he knew, in the visiplate, for at his distance, the Sun was twenty times as wide as it seemed from Earth and covered four hundred times as much of the sky.

Caught in the visiplate were a pair of sunspots, black against the brightness. Threads of glowing white curled into it and were lost. They were heaving areas of activity that moved across the plate visibly as he watched. This was not due to the Sun's own motion of rotation, which, even at its equator, was not more than fourteen hundred miles an hour, but rather to the tremendous velocity of the *Shooting Starr*.

As he watched, gouts of red, flaming gas shot up toward him, dim against the blazing background, and turning a smoky black as it receded from the Sun and cooled.

Lucky shifted the plate, catching a portion of the rim of the Sun, and now the flaming gas (which were the so-called "prominences," consisting of gigantic puffs of hy-

drogen gas) stood out sharply crimson against the black of
the sky. They spread outward in slow motion, thinning
and taking on fantastic shapes. Lucky knew that each one
of them could engulf a dozen planets the size of Earth,
and that the Earth could be dropped into the sunspot he
saw without even making a respectable splash.

He closed the stroboscopics with a sudden movement.
Even though physically safe, no man could stare at the
Sun from that distance without becoming oppressed by
the insignificance of Earth and all things Earthly.

The *Shooting Starr* had whipped half around the Sun and
was now receding rapidly past the orbits of Mercury and
Venus. It was decelerating now. The ship's prow opposed
the direction of its flight and its powerful main engines
were acting as brakes.

Once past Venus's orbit, Lucky removed his shield
and stowed it away. The ship's cooling system strained to
get rid of the excess heat. Drinking water was still uncomfortably hot and the canned foods bulged where liquid
within had bubbled into gas.

The Sun was shrinking. Lucky looked at it. It was an
even, glowing sphere. Its irregularities, its churning spots,
and heaving prominences could no longer be seen. Only
its corona, always visible in space, though visible on Earth
only during eclipses, thrust out in every direction for millions of miles. Lucky shuddered involuntarily to think that
he had passed through it.

He passed within fifteen million miles of Earth, and
through his telescope he spied the familiar outlines of the
continents peeping through the ragged white masses of
cloud banks. He felt a twinge of homesickness and then a
new resolve to keep war away from the teeming, busy
billions of human beings that inhabited that planet, which

was the origin of all the men that now occupied the far-flung star systems of the Galaxy.

Then the Earth, too, receded.

Past Mars and back into the asteroid belt, Lucky still aimed at the Jovian system, that miniature solar system within the greater one. At its center was Jupiter, larger than all the other planets combined. About it swung four giant moons, three of them, Io, Europa, and Callisto, about the size of the Earth's Moon, and the fourth, Ganymede, much larger. Ganymede, in fact, was larger than Mercury, and almost as large as Mars. In addition there were dozens of moonlets, ranging from some hundreds of miles in diameter down to insignificant rocks.

In the ship's telescope Jupiter was a growing yellow globe, marked with faintly orange stripes, one of which bellied out into what was once known as the "Great Red Spot." Three of the main moons, including Ganymede, were on one side, the fourth was on the other.

Lucky had been in guarded communication with the Council's main offices on the Moon for the better part of a day now. His Ergometrics probed space with widely stretching fingers. It detected many ships, but Lucky watched only for the one with the Sirian motor pattern which he would recognize with certainty the instant it appeared.

Nor did he fail. At a distance of twenty million miles, the first quiverings roused his suspicions. He veered in the proper direction, and the characteristic curves grew more pronounced.

At one hundred thousand miles, his telescope showed it as a faint dot. At ten thousand, it had form and shape and was Anton's ship.

At a thousand miles (with Ganymede still fifty million miles away from both ships), Lucky sent out his first message, a demand that Anton turn his ship back toward Earth.

At one hundred miles Lucky received his answer—a blast of energy that made his generators whine and shook the *Shooting Starr* as though it had collided with another ship.

Lucky's tired face took on a drawn look.

Anton's ship was better-armed than he had expected.

15

Part of the Answer

For an hour the maneuvers of both ships were indecisive. Lucky had the faster ship and the better, but Captain Anton had a crew. Each of Anton's men could specialize. One could focus and one could release, while a third could control the reactor banks and Anton himself could direct operations.

Lucky, trying to do everything at once and by himself, had to rely heavily on words.

"You can't get to Ganymede, Anton, and your friends won't dare tip their hand by coming out now before they know what's up. . . . You're all through, Anton; we know all your plans. . . . There's no use trying to get a message through to Ganymede, Anton; we're blanketing the sub-ether from you to Jupiter. Nothing can get through. . . . Government ships are coming, Anton. Count your minutes. You don't have many, unless you surrender. . . . Give up, Anton. Give up."

And all this while the *Shooting Starr* dodged through as concentrated a fire as Lucky had ever seen. Nor were all the blasts successfully dodged. The Shooter's energy stores began to show the strain. Lucky would have liked to believe that Anton's ship was suffering equally, but he himself was aiming few blasts at Anton and landing virtually none.

He dared not take his eyes off the screen. Terrestrial ships, speeding to the scene, would not be there for hours. In those hours, if Anton beat down his energy banks, broke away, and made good head toward Ganymede, while a limping *Shooting Starr* could only pursue, without catching . . . Or if a pirate fleet suddenly sparkled on-screen . . .

Lucky dared not follow those lines of thought further. Perhaps he had been wrong in not entrusting the interception to government ships in the first place. No, he told himself, only the *Shooting Starr* could have caught Anton still fifty million miles from Ganymede; only the Shooter's speed; more important still, only the Shooter's Ergometers. At this distance from Ganymede it was safe to call in units of the fleet for the kill. Closer to Ganymede and fleet action would have been unsafe.

Lucky's receiver, open all this time, was suddenly activated. Anton's face filled it, smiling and carefree.

"You got away from Dingo again, I see."

Lucky said, "Again? You're admitting he was working under orders in the push duel!"

An energy feeler toward Lucky's ship suddenly hardened into a beam of disruptive force. Lucky moved aside with an acceleration that wrenched him.

Anton laughed. "Don't watch me too closely. We almost caught you then with a lulu. Certainly Dingo was working under orders. We knew what we were doing. Dingo didn't know who you really were, but I did. Nearly from the first."

"Too bad the knowledge didn't help you," said Lucky.

"It's Dingo that it hasn't helped. It may amuse you to know that he has been, shall we say, executed. It's bad to

PART OF THE ANSWER

make mistakes. But this kind of talk is out of place here. I'm only plating you to say that this has been fun, but I'll be going now."

"You have nowhere to go," said Lucky.

"I'll try Ganymede."

"You'll be stopped."

"By government ships? I don't see them yet. And there's not one that can catch me in time."

"I can catch you."

"You have caught me. But what can you do with me? From the way you're fighting, you must be the only man on board. If I had known that from the beginning, I wouldn't have bothered with you as long as this. You can't fight a whole crew."

Lucky said in a low, intense voice, "I can ram you. I can smash you completely."

"And yourself. Remember that."

"That wouldn't matter."

"Please. You sound like a space-scout. You'll be reciting the junior scout-patrol oath next."

Lucky raised his voice. "You men aboard the ship, listen! If your captain tries to break away in the direction of Ganymede, I will ram the ship. It is certain death for all of you, unless you surrender. I promise you all a fair trial. I promise all of you the utmost consideration possible if you co-operate with us. Don't let Anton throw your lives away for the sake of his Sirian friends."

"Talk on, government boy, talk on," said Anton. "I'm letting them listen. They know what kind of a trial they can expect and they know what kind of consideration too. An injection of enzymic poison." His fingers made the quick movements of someone inserting a needle into another's skin. "That's what they'll get. They're not afraid of you. Good-by, government boy."

The needles on Lucky's gravimetrics wavered downward as Anton's ship picked up speed and moved away. Lucky watched his visiplates. Where were the government ships? Blast all space, where were the government ships?

He let acceleration take hold. Gravimetric needles moved upward again.

The miles between the ships were sliced away. Anton's ship put on more speed; so did the *Shooting Starr.* But the accelerative possibilities of the Shooter were higher.

The smile on Anton's face did not alter. "Fifty miles away," he said. Then, "Forty-five." Another pause. "Forty. Have you said your prayers, government boy?"

Lucky did not answer. For him there was no way out. He would have to ram. Sooner than let Anton get through, sooner than allow war to come to Earth, he would have to stop the pirates by suicide, if there were no other way. The ships were curving toward one another in a long, slow tangent.

"Thirty," said Anton lazily. "You're not frightening anyone. You'll look a fool in the end. Veer off and go home, Starr."

"Twenty-five," retorted Lucky firmly. "You have fifteen minutes to surrender or die." He himself, he reflected, had the same fifteen minutes to win or die.

A face appeared behind Anton's in the visiplate. It held a finger to pale, tight lips. Lucky's eyes might have flickered. He tried to conceal that by looking away, then coming back.

Both ships were at maximum acceleration.

"What's the matter, Starr?" asked Anton. "Scared? Heart beating fast?" His eyes were dancing and his lips were parted.

Lucky had the sudden, sure knowledge that Anton was enjoying this, that he considered it an exciting game, that it was only a device whereby he might demonstrate his power. Lucky knew at that moment that Anton would never surrender, that he would allow himself to be rammed rather than back away. And Lucky knew that there was no escape from death.

"Fifteen miles," Lucky said.

It was Hansen's face behind Anton. The hermit's! And there was something in his hand.

"Ten miles," said Lucky. Then, "Six minutes. I'll ram you. By space, I'll ram you."

It was a blaster! Hansen held a blaster.

Lucky's breath came tightly. If Anton turned . . .

But Anton was not going to miss a second of Lucky's face if he could help it. He was waiting to see the fright come and grow. To Lucky, that was plain as could be in the pirate's expression. Anton would not have turned for a much noisier event than the careful lifting of a blaster.

Anton caught it in the back. Death came too suddenly for the eager smile to disappear from his face, and though life left it, the look of cruel joy did not. Anton fell forward across the visiplate and for a moment his face remained pressed there, larger than life-size, leering at Lucky out of dead eyes.

Lucky heard Hansen's shout, "Back, all of you. Do you want to die? We're giving up. Come and get us, Starr!"

Lucky veered the direction of acceleration by two degrees. Enough to miss.

His Ergometers were registering the motors of approaching government ships strongly now. They were coming at last.

The screens on Anton's ship were glowing white as a sign of surrender.

It was almost an axiom that the fleet was never entirely pleased when the Council of Science interfered too much in what they considered to be the province of the military. Especially so when the interference was spectacularly successful. Lucky Starr knew that well. He was quite prepared for the admiral's poorly hidden disapproval.

The admiral said, "Dr. Conway has explained the situation adequately, Starr, and we commend you for your actions. However, you must realize that the fleet has been aware of the Sirian danger for some time now and had a careful program of its own. These independent actions on the part of the Council can be harmful. You might mention that to Dr. Conway. Now I have been requested by the Co-ordinator to co-operate with the Council in the next stages of the fight against the pirates, but," he looked stubborn, "I cannot agree to your suggestion that we delay an attack on Ganymede. I think the fleet is capable of making its own decisions where battle and victory are concerned."

The admiral was in his fifties and unused to consulting on equal terms with anyone, let alone a youngster of half his age. His square-cut face with its bristly gray mustache showed it.

Lucky was tired. The reaction, now that Anton's ship had been taken in tow and its crew in custody, had set in. He managed, however, to be very respectful. He said, "I think that if we mop up the asteroids first, the Sirians on Ganymede will automatically cease being a problem."

"Good Galaxy, man, how do you mean 'mop up.' We've been trying to do that for twenty-five years without success. Mopping up the asteroids is like chasing feathers. As for the Sirian base, we know where it is, and we have a good notion as to its strength." He smiled briefly. "Oh, it may be hard for the Council to realize this, but the fleet is on its toes as well as they are. Perhaps even more so. For instance, I know that the power at my command is enough to break their strength on Ganymede. We are ready for the battle."

"I have no doubt that you are and that you can defeat the Sirians. But the ones on Ganymede are not all the Sirians there are. You may be ready for a battle, but are you ready for a long and costly war?"

The admiral reddened. "I have been asked to cooperate, but I cannot do so at the risk of Earth's safety. I can under no conditions lend my voice to a plan which involves dispersing our fleet among the asteroids, while a Sirian expedition is in being in the Solar System."

"May I have an hour?" interrupted Lucky. "One hour to speak with Hansen, the Cerean captive I had brought aboard this ship just before you boarded, sir?"

"How will that help?"

"May I have an hour to show you?"

The admiral's lips pressed together. "An hour may be valuable. It may be priceless. . . . Well, begin, but quickly. Let's see how it goes."

"Hansen!" called Lucky without taking his calm eyes from the admiral.

The hermit entered from the bunk room. He looked tired, but managed a smile for Lucky. His stay on the pirate ship had apparently left his spirits unmarked.

He said, "I've been admiring your ship, Mr. Starr. It's quite a piece of metal."

"Look here," said the admiral, "none of that. Get on with it, Starr! Never mind your ship."

Lucky said, "This is the situation, Mr. Hansen. We've stopped Anton, with your invaluable help, for which I thank you. That means we've delayed the start of hostilities with Sirius. However, we need more than delay. We must remove the danger completely, and as the admiral will tell you, our time is very short."

"How can I help?" asked Hansen.

"By answering my questions."

"Gladly, but I've told you all I know. I'm sorry that it turned out to be worth so little."

"Yet the pirates believed you to be a dangerous man. They risked a great deal to get you out of our hands."

"I can't explain that."

"Is it possible that you have a piece of knowledge without being aware of it? Something that could be deadly for them?"

"I don't see how."

"Well, they trusted you. By the information you yourself gave me, you were rich; a man with good investments on Earth. Certainly you were much better off than the average hermit. Yet the pirates treated you well. Or at least they didn't mistreat you. They didn't rifle your belongings. In fact, they left your very luxurious home completely in peace."

"Remember, Mr. Starr, I helped them in return."

"Not very much. You said that you allowed them to land on your rock, to leave people there sometimes and that's about all. If they had simply shot you down, they could have had that and your quarters as well. In addition, they would not have had to worry about your becoming an informer. You eventually did become one, you know."

Hansen's eyes shifted. "That's the way it was, though. I told you the truth."

"Yes, what you told me was true. It wasn't the whole truth, however. I say that there must have been a good reason for the pirates to trust you so completely. They must have known that it meant your life to go to the government."

"I told you that," said Hansen mildly.

"You said that you had incriminated yourself by helping the pirates, but they trusted you when they first arrived, *before* you had begun helping them. Otherwise they would have blasted you to begin with. Now, let me guess. I'd say that once, before you became a hermit, you were a pirate yourself, Hansen, and that Anton and men like him knew about it. What do you say?"

Hansen's face went white.

Lucky said, "What do you say, Hansen?"

Hansen's voice was very soft. "You are right, Mr. Starr. I was once a member of the crew of a pirate ship. That was a long time ago. I have tried to live it down. I retired to the asteroids and did my best to be dead as far as Earth was concerned. When a new group of pirates arose in the Solar System and entangled me, I had no choice but to play along with them.

"When you landed, I found my first chance to leave; my first chance to take the risk of facing the law. Twenty-five years had passed, after all. And I would have in my favor the fact that I had risked my life to save the life of a Councilman. That was why I was so anxious to fight the pirate raiders on Ceres. I wanted to make another point in my favor. Finally, I killed Anton, saving your life a second time, and giving Earth a breathing space, you tell me, in which a war may be prevented. I was a pirate, Mr. Starr, but that's gone, and I think I've evened the score."

"Good," said Lucky, "as far as it goes. Now do you have any information for us that you didn't mention before?"

Hansen shook his head.

Lucky said, "You didn't tell us you were a pirate."

"That was irrelevant, really. And you found out for yourself. I didn't try to deny it."

"Well, then let's see if we can find anything else which you won't deny. You see, you still haven't told the whole truth."

Hansen looked surprised. "What remains?"

"The fact that you've never stopped being a pirate.

The fact that you are a person who was only mentioned once in my hearing, and that by one of Anton's crewmen shortly after my push-gun duel with Dingo. The fact that you are the so-called Boss. You, Mr. Hansen, are the mastermind of the asteroid pirates."

16

All of the Answer

Hansen jumped out of his seat, and remained standing. His breath whistled harshly through parted lips.

The admiral, scarcely less astonished, cried, "Great Galaxy, man! What is this? Are you serious?"

Lucky said, "Sit down, Hansen, and let's try it on for size. Let's see how it sounds. If I'm wrong, there'll be a contradiction somewhere. It begins with Captain Anton, landing on the *Atlas*. Anton was an intelligent and capable man, even if his mind was twisted. He mistrusted me and my story. He took a trimensional photograph of me (that wouldn't be hard, even without my noticing) and sent it to the Boss for instructions. The Boss thought he recognized me. Certainly, Hansen, if you were the Boss, that would follow, because as a matter of fact, when you saw me face to face later, you *did* recognize me.

"The Boss sent back a message to the effect that I was to be killed. It amused Anton to do that by sending me out in a push-gun duel with Dingo. Dingo was given definite instructions to kill me. Anton admitted that in our last conversation. Then, when I returned, with Anton's word that I was to be given a chance to join the organization if I survived, you had to take over yourself. I was sent to your rock."

Hansen burst out, "But this is mad. I did you no harm. I saved you. I brought you back to Ceres."

"So you did, and came along with me too. Now it had been my idea to get into the pirate organization, learn the facts from within. You got the same idea in reverse and were more successful. You brought me to Ceres and came yourself. You learned how unprepared we were and how we underestimated the pirate organization. It meant you could go ahead at full speed.

"The Ceres Raid makes sense now. I imagine you got word to Anton somehow. Pocket sub-etherics are not unheard of and clever codes can be worked out. You went up the corridors *not* to fight the pirates but to join them. They didn't kill you, they 'captured' you. That was very queer. If your story were true, you would have been a dangerous informer to them. They should have blasted you the moment you came within range. Instead they did not harm you. Instead, they put you on Anton's flagship and took you with them to Ganymede. You weren't even bound or under surveillance. It was perfectly possible for you to move quietly behind Anton and shoot him down."

Hansen cried, "But I did shoot him. Why in the name of Earth would I have shot him if I were who you say I am?"

"Because he was a maniac. He was ready to let me ram him rather than back down or lose face. You had greater plans and had no intention of dying to soothe his vanity. You knew that even if we stopped Anton from contacting Ganymede, it would mean only a delay. By attacking Ganymede afterward, we would provoke the war anyway. Then by continuing your role as hermit, you would eventually find a chance to escape and take on your real identity. What was Anton's life and the loss of one ship compared with all that?"

Hansen said, "What proof is there to all this? It's guesswork, that's all! Where's the proof?"

The admiral, who had been looking from one to the other through all of this, bestirred himself. "Look here, Starr, this man's mine. We'll get whatever truth is in him."

"No hurry, Admiral. My hour isn't up. . . . Guesswork, Hansen? Let's go on. I tried to get back to your rock, Hansen, but you didn't have the co-ordinates, which was strange, despite your painstaking explanations. I calculated out a set of co-ordinates from the trajectory we had taken going from your rock to Ceres, and those turned out to be in a forbidden zone, where no asteroids could be in the ordinary course of nature. Since I was certain that my calculations were correct, I knew that your rock had been where it was *against* the ordinary course of nature."

"Eh? What?" said the admiral.

"I mean that a rock need not travel in its orbit if it's small enough. It can be fitted with hyperatomic motors and can *move out of its orbit like a space-ship*. How else can you explain an asteroid being in a forbidden zone."

Hansen said wildly, "Saying so doesn't make it so. I don't know why you're doing this to me, Starr. Are you testing me? Is it a trick?"

"No trick, Mr. Hansen," said Lucky. "I went back for your rock. I didn't think you'd move it far. An asteroid that can move has certain advantages. No matter how often it is detected, its co-ordinates noted and its orbit calculated, observers or pursuers can always be thrown off by movement out of the orbit. Still, a moving asteroid runs certain risks. An astronomer at a telescope, happening to observe it at the time, might wonder why an asteroid should be moving out of the Ecliptic or into a forbidden zone. Or, if he were close enough, he would wonder why an asteroid should have reactor exhaust glow at one end.

"You had already moved once, I imagine, to meet Anton's ship part way so that I could be landed on your rock. I was certain you would not move very far so soon after. Perhaps just far enough to get into the nearest cluster of asteroids for camouflage purposes. So I returned and searched among the asteroids nearest at hand for one that was the right size and shape. I found it. I found an asteroid that was actually a base, factory, and storehouse all at once, and on it I heard the sound of giant hyperatomics perfectly capable of moving it through space. A Sirian importation, I think."

Hansen said, "But that wasn't *my* rock."

"No? I found Dingo waiting on it. He boasted that he had had no need to follow me; that he knew where I was heading. The only place to which he knew I was heading was your rock. From that I conclude that one and the same rock had your living quarters at one end and the pirate base at the other."

"No. No," shouted Hansen. "I leave it to the admiral. There are a thousand asteroids the size and shape of mine, and I'm not responsible for some casual remark made by a pirate."

"There's another piece of evidence that may sound better to you," said Lucky. "On the pirate base was a valley between two outcroppings of rock; a valley full of used cans."

"Used cans!" shouted the admiral. "What in the Galaxy has that to do with anything, Starr?"

"Hansen discarded his used cans into a valley on his own rock. He said he didn't like his rock to be accompanied by its own garbage. Actually he probably didn't want it surrounding his rock and advertising it. I saw the valley

of the cans when we were leaving his rock. I saw them
again when I approached the pirate base. It was the reason I chose that asteroid to reconnoiter and no other.
Look at this man, Admiral, and tell me whether you can
doubt that I have the truth."

Hansen's face was contorted with fury. He was not the
same man. All trace of benevolence was gone. "All right.
What of it? What do you want?"

"I want you to call Ganymede. I'm sure you con-
ducted previous negotiations with them. They'll know
you. Tell them that the asteroids are surrendering to Earth
and will join us against Sirius if necessary."

Hansen laughed. "Why should I? You've got me, but
you haven't got the asteroids. You can't clean them out."

"We can, if we capture your rock. It has all necessary
records on it, hasn't it?"

"Try and find it," said Hansen, hoarsely. "Try to locate
it in a forest of rocks. You say yourself it can move."

"It will be easy to find," said Lucky. "Your valley of
cans, you know."

"Go ahead. Look at every rock till you find the valley.
It will take you a million years."

"No. Only a day or so. When I left the pirate base, I
paused just long enough to burn the valley of cans with a
heat beam. I melted them and let them freeze back into a
bumpy, angled sheet of fresh, gleaming metal. There was
no atmosphere to rust or corrode them, so its surface remains just like the metal-foil goal posts used in a push-
gun duel. It catches the Sun and sends reflections glittering back in tight beams. All Ceres Observatory has to
do is quarter the heavens, looking for an asteroid about
ten times as bright as it should be for its size. I had them
begin the search even before I left to intercept Anton."

"It's a lie."

"Is it? Long before I reached the Sun, I received a

sub-etheric message that included a photograph. Here it is." Lucky drew it out from under the blotter on the desk. "The bright dot with the arrow pointing to it is your rock."

"Do you think you're frightening me?"

"I should be. Council ships landed on it."

"What?" roared the admiral.

"There was no time to waste, sir," said Lucky. "We found Hansen's living quarters at the other end and we found the connecting tunnels between it and the pirate base. I have here some sub-etherized documents containing the co-ordinates of your main subsidiary bases, Hansen, and some photographs of the bases themselves. The real thing, Hansen?"

Hansen collapsed. His mouth opened and hopeless sobbing sounds came out.

Lucky said, "I've gone through all this, Hansen, to convince you that you've lost. You've lost completely and finally. You have nothing left but your life. I make no promises, but if you do as I say, you may end up by at least saving that. Call Ganymede."

Hansen stared helplessly at his fingers.

The admiral said with stunned anguish, "The Council cleaned out the asteroids? They've done the job? They haven't consulted the Admiralty?"

Lucky said, "How about it, Hansen?"

Hansen said, "What's the difference now? I'll do it."

Conway, Henree, and Bigman were at the space-port to greet Lucky when he returned to Earth. They had dinner together in the Glass Room on the highest level of Planet Restaurant. With the room's walls made of curving, clear one-way glass, they could look out over the warm lights of the city, fading off into the level plains beyond.

Henree said, "It's fortunate the Council was able to

penetrate the pirate bases before it became a job for the fleet. Military action wouldn't have solved the matter."

Conway nodded. "You're right. It would have left the asteroids vacant for the next pirate gang. Most of those people there had no real knowledge that they were fighting alongside Sirius. They were rather ordinary people looking for a better life than they had been experiencing. I think we can persuade the government to offer amnesty to all but those who had actually participated in raids, and they weren't many."

"As a matter of fact," said Lucky, "by helping them continue the development of the asteroids, by financing the expansion of their yeast farms, and supplying water, air, and power, we're building a defense for the future. The best protection against asteroid criminals is a peaceful and prosperous asteroid community. That way lies peace."

Bigman said belligerently, "Don't kid yourself. It's peace only till Sirius decides to try again."

Lucky put a hand to the little man's frowning face and shoved it playfully. "Bigman, I think you're sorry we're short one nice war. What's the matter with you? Can't you enjoy a little rest?"

Conway said, "You know, Lucky, you might have told us more at the time."

"I would have liked to," said Lucky, "but it was necessary for me to deal with Hansen alone. There were important personal reasons involved."

"But when did you first suspect him, Lucky? What gave him away?" Conway wanted to know. "The fact that his rock had blundered into a forbidden zone?"

"That was the final straw," admitted Lucky, "but I knew he was no mere hermit within an hour after meeting him. I knew from that time on that he was more important to me than anyone else in the Galaxy."

"How about explaining that?" Conway sank his fork into the last of the steak and munched away contentedly.

Lucky said, "Hansen recognized me as the son of Lawrence Starr. He said he had met Father once, and he must have. After all, Councilmen get no publicity and a personal greeting is necessary to explain the fact that he could see the resemblance in my face.

"But there were two queer angles to the recognition. He saw the resemblance most clearly when I grew angry. He said that. Yet from what you tell me, Uncle Hector, and you, Uncle Gus, Father hardly ever got angry. 'Laughing' is the adjective you usually use when you talk about Father. Then, too, when Hansen arrived on Ceres, he recognized neither of you. Even hearing your names meant nothing."

"What's wrong with that?" asked Henree.

"Father and you two were always together, weren't you? How could Hansen have met Father and not you two. Met my father, moreover, at a time when he was angry and under circumstances which fixed his face so firmly in Hansen's mind that he could recognize me from the resemblance twenty-five years later.

"There's only one explanation. My father was separated from you two only on his last flight to Venus, and Hansen had been in at the kill. Nor was he there as an ordinary crewman. Ordinary crewmen don't become rich enough to be able to build a luxurious asteroid and spend twenty-five years after the government's raids on the asteroids building a new and bigger organization from scratch. He must have been the captain of the attacking pirate ship. He would have been thirty years old then; quite old enough to be captain."

"Great space!" said Conway blankly.

Bigman yelled indignantly, "And you never shot him down?"

"How could I? I had bigger affairs at hand than squaring a personal grudge. He killed my father and mother, yes, but I had to be polite to him just the same. At least for a while."

Lucky lifted a cup of coffee to his lips and paused to look down at the city again.

He said, "Hansen will be in the Mercury Prison for the rest of his life, which is better punishment really than a quick, easy death. And the Sirians have left Ganymede, so there'll be peace. That's a better reward for me than his death ten times over; and a better offering to the memory of my parents."

ABOUT THE AUTHOR

ISAAC ASIMOV was America's most prolific author, with more than 440 published books to his credit. His Foundation Trilogy was given a special Hugo Award as Best All-Time Science Fiction Series. *Foundation's Edge* won a Hugo Award as Best Science Fiction Novel of 1982, and Dr. Asimov was presented the Science Fiction Writers of America Grand Master Award in 1988. Dr. Asimov died in 1992.

ROBOTS FREE

ROBOTS FROM ASIMOV'S

By subscribing to Isaac **Asimov's Science Fiction Magazine** you'll receive a FREE copy of **Robots From Asimov's** with your paid subscription. Asimov's contains Nebula-award-winning stories, editorials by Isaac Asimov himself, and much more. Each issue is filled with provocative stories on the cutting edge of today's science fiction and fantasy... from worlds of myth to futures of imagination.